I0671057

# On Standby

## D. D. Riessen

# ddr
## books

San Diego, CA 92119

On Standby - adult fiction

Library of Congress Control Number:  2014904778

ISBN - 10: 0991663004
ISBN - 13: 978-0-9916630-0-2

Here's to the working class!

For those of you who don't actually "*do*" the work, this is a story about how it gets done.

What can go wrong? Everything. Get over it. Pick up the pieces and move on.

## Call-out

Monday morning, five-o'clock, four forty-two actually, not the time of day for this guy to be walking up the middle of the street wearing what looked like Speedos. At least that's what Darin hoped it was and not some drunk who had somehow lost his pants.

He was still about a hundred feet away, wearing a black dinner jacket and tie but somehow had lost the shirt. He was a stocky man, big barreled chest and, with his shoulder length blonde hair and artificial tan, the guy reminded Darin of a wrestler he had seen on TV.

Wobbling erratically, the man stumbled forward, straight toward Darin, who was standing at the corner, pushing the button, hoping the light would turn.

*Damn! Bastard's coming right at me.*

The office across the street, a five-story building, was his responsibility. Keep the power turned on. The call had come in at two forty-five, that much he remembered. He had looked at the clock, knew he had to be up at four anyway, but somehow another hour passed before getting up. Surely the Center had already called the guard, Willy, and inquired whether or not he had arrived.

Approaching from Darin's right, Speedos quickened his pace and, oddly, the man had a smile on his face like Darin was someone he knew.

"Hey!" he yelled, waving. "Dude!"

Darin usually waited for the light, having seen his co-worker get a jaywalking ticket at mid-night leaving the building. He'd just waved good-bye, still laughing at the joke they had just shared, got half-

1

way across the street when this cop came out of nowhere and gave him a forty dollar ticket.

Against the light, Darin started for the front door, cutting left to shorten the distance. He pulled the security card out of his wallet in case Willy, the guard stationed behind the blind tint, bulletproof glass, was not there to let him in.

Speedos broke into a run. "Hey! I'm talking to *you*!"

Darin got to the alcove first. Sliding up to the door, he ran the card through the reader. The door's lock did not click. He pounded on the glass. "Willy? You in there?"

Fighting a desire to rip the door off of its hinges, Darin slid the card through the reader again, slowly, hoping that it would read. Nothing. Speedos stumbled into the alcove, bounced off of the corner of the wall, a backward leaning regrouping of balance, and then staggered forward. As Darin turned to face him, the front door opened, a hand reached out, pulled him in backwards and slammed shut.

Speedos lunged for the door handle. "Hey! Open up!"

"Shoulda' seen your face!" Willy howled, now nearly doubled over.

"Willy? What the...,?"

"Better....," Willy burst into laughter again. "Better check your shorts!"

Now using the butts of both hands, Speedos pummeled the bulletproof glass.

"Not funny," said Darin. "I coulda been robbed!"

"Naw," said Willy, wiping the tears out of his eyes, stumbling back to the other side of his desk. "Raped, more like. God, that was good!" He reached for the phone. "I'm gonna call the cops now. I just wanted you to meet him. Got that high camera

2

up at the loading dock. Saw him...," he burst into laughter again. "Saw him pissin' on cars all the way up the street. And then I saw you drive up."

"You *knew*?"

"Hey, gotta stay awake somehow."

"I'm not buying you donuts anymore."

"Worth it," said Willy. "I didn't know you could run so fast."

"You have a sick sense of humor."

Willy picked up a note from his desk and handed it to Darin. "Norm says to call him soon as you get in. Says he can't do nothin' until you fix your stuff."

"I'm gonna have to buy him breakfast. Generators running on both sides of the building?"

"Ask Norm. Fire alarms went out same time. I been dying to take a leak ever since. Two fire trucks rolled up and five firemen stormed the door carryin' axes. I had to get there first and tell 'em it was a false alarm."

"What'd they say?"

"Said next time they was gonna fine us five G's if it's not for real."

"Where's Norm?"

"Somewhere downstairs," said Willy, grinning. "Waitin' for you, now that you're all warmed up."

"Bastard."

"Willy laughed. "Anytime."

Circling the Place

Norm was one of those perpetually happy people. His round face, boyish looks, and easy laugh belied the fact that his job was dangerous, continuous, and unforgiving. The basic needs of, not only this building but several others in the area, were on his shoulders twenty-four-seven and it didn't seem to bother him a bit.

Norm had an insatiable appetite for knowing how things worked. If it lifted, pushed or pulled, rotated, made too much noise, not enough noise or had a weird sound, Norm was there, investigating.

His true love was speed. If it went fast, he wanted to know how to make it go faster. Two weeks out of every year he was off to Bonneville as an official timekeeper. Watching competing team's attempts to set land speed records, he noticed how little things make a big difference and began to design his own car. Within two years he owned the world land speed record for any vehicle powered by a 1000 cc, or under engine.

But on this morning he had other concerns. "The problem," he said walking briskly down the long, dimly lit basement hallway toward the equipment room on the other side of the building, "is that I have only one pump running."

"How many do you need?" Darin asked, nearly running alongside to keep up.

"Two," said Norm. "Or we go into a tailspin."

"What does that mean?"

"The building starts heating up."

"Isn't that good? People pay a lot of money for heat."

They paused at the first of three security doors,

4

inserted the code, waited for the lock to click, and then passed through.

"Not when everything starts shutting down on over-temp."

"Oh."

The location of the chiller pumps, located in the southwest part of the building, was a special memory for Darin. His office was located in the northeast, a city block away. And although he frequently traveled between the two rooms, taking the southern route through the basement, he had never tried to find the pumps by taking the darker, far less traveled, northern route, if there was one.

"Aren't there three pumps in that room?"

"Third one's down, parts on order," said Norm. "Due in next week."

"Can't get here any faster?"

"Already called the guy this morning. Said he could tape it to the front of the plane."

"Wise ass, huh?"

"He's the only one in the U.S. that has the parts, back in Kansas City. We've got a job to replace all three, but that doesn't start until the weather cools down, supposedly in the next few months."

"So..., for now, you only need power for one?"

"Exactly."

"What happens if we can't fix it?"

"We make the front page."

"How long do we have?"

"We had four hours. Since you were slow getting here, we're down to two."

Darin smiled. "I ran all the way to the front door."

Norm laughed. "I heard. Willy called, told me what happened."

They passed by the door leading out to the loading dock and, looking up, Darin spotted the camera that was trained on them.

There were cameras everywhere and Willy used them. If anyone wanted a guard that snooped into everything and knew everyone's business, Willy was the man. He knew who went to the bathroom and when, who took too long of breaks, who arrived late or left early. He knew who was seeing whom on the side and who was meeting whom behind closed doors.

Darin smiled up at the camera and flipped Willie the bird. "Two hours, huh?"

This was precisely the thing Darin didn't like about power. Being a cautious person, he liked to make sure everything was in place, thought out, and planned.

*Don't like sparks, explosions or any kind of electrical surprise.*

*Didn't like Speedos this morning either.*

*Nope.*

Soon after he'd been assigned to this building, Darin, exploring on his own, ventured further and further into the dimly lit, deserted northern parts of the building, going counter-clockwise out of his office, following the wall until it led to a dark area behind the old "retired in place" power room, beyond the dilapidated wooden stalls where the toilets probably hadn't been used for ten years, past the row of stained wash basins and yellowed mirrors, an entirely dreary room lit by a single incandescent bulb. Beyond all of that was a door, locked.

"Building temp's already gone up four degrees," said Norm, stepping into the equipment room. He opened a large gray metal cabinet and pointed to three contacts. "Supposed to have power there."

Darin unfolded a schematic located inside and

studied it for nearly a full minute. "This thing's hand drawn! Is this what came from the factory?"

"I said the equipment's old. That's why we're replacing it."

"Is this your only copy?"

"Actually, it is."

"Man. I'd make copies. Someone could walk away with it, spill coffee on it...,"

"I don't drink coffee."

"Whatever. It's your only copy."

"We only need it for another month. If it lasted forty years, it'll last another four or five weeks."

"I'd make two copies today."

Take your time and plan ahead. Nothing worse than being stuck in the bottom of a huge building when the lights go out, unless it's being stuck in the bottom of a huge building when the lights go out and you're the one responsible to get them back on.

Darin began carrying a canvas tool bag full of essential tools, meter, insulated screwdrivers and pliers and extra batteries for the flashlight clipped to his belt.

The locked door in the back of the old power room worried him and he felt compelled to explore. Someday there might be a fire or an earthquake. Spending eight or more hours a day in the basement of this huge complex upped his chances significantly of being trapped if the front exit was somehow blocked. You have to know what's on the other side of that door.

Searching through the drawers of the many old cabinets and desks, Darin found several keys, collected them onto a ring and eventually found one that fit the lock. Opening the door with a creak, he discovered a second windowless steel door, unlocked, Opening that, he found a dark, narrow staircase, going up.

The light switch was just out of reach and the bulb blew out when he flipped it on, a flash that left him with a glowing negative image of the stairway. In the process of breaking out his flashlight, the steel door closed behind him. Shining his light back on the door, Darin noticed the key code lock.

He turned the handle, hoping. But the door did not open. He shined his light up the stairs, about twelve steps to the top, saw that it had no lock, but decided that before he tried to open it, he'd like to know how to get back, just in case something worse was lingering up there.

None of the codes that he knew worked. A moment of panic, not long, just the casual wondering about, if the door at the top of the stairs would not open, just how long it would be until the next person came through? Years from now, would they finally discover the mystery of the missing power maintenance man, a skeleton identified by dental records, still holding his precious flashlight?

A last ditch effort, one-three at the same time, and then a five all by itself, caused the lock to click and the door to open. Knowing that, Darin continued up the stairs.

Leaving the damp, musty smell of the basement behind, the door at the top opened into a brightly lit hallway, recessed lighting, well-polished floors and freshly painted white walls.

Darin wandered left, what he thought was west, (no windows), and twice heard voices, always somewhere out of view, and of doors opening and closing. All doors had coded locks and, other than designated room numbers, had no title to suggest what was going on inside or who was in there.

8

Continuing down the hallway, he discovered a break room, freshly snuffed out cigarette, still smoking in an ashtray, half drunk cup of coffee sitting on the drain side of a stainless steel counter top, and an old black and white version of, " I Love Lucy," playing on the TV mounted up in a corner of the wall. The room was empty. Darin felt like he'd just entered the Twilight Zone...,

No one returned for their coffee. Darin butted the smoking cigarette, watched Lucy fall into the vat of grapes and then continued down the hallway.

He went through a set of double doors and discovered, going down twelve steps, a much larger break room containing several Formica-topped tables, a whole wall dedicated to telephones, each with their own little desktop, a wall of vending machines, a nearly solid glass wall that looked out onto a garden patio, doors locked, alarmed, and a lush outside courtyard surrounded by a ten foot concrete wall. And still, not one soul to be seen.

Continuing through the break room he entered a long hallway, lined with closed and locked doors on either side, and at the other end of that hallway, Darin discovered the pumps that Norm was now working on. From there, he knew how to get back to his office taking the southern route.

"So what do you think?" Norm asked.

"No power," said Darin, pulling the probes away and wrapping them around the voltmeter. "The breaker probably didn't transfer. That's in the room across the hall."

"Shouldn't that be automatic?"

"Should be. Let's go look."

The breaker had not transferred. Darin pushed the manual transfer button, a motor whirred inside the cabinet, followed by a loud BAM. The Standby Power indicator lights blinked on.

"I'll go check," said Norm, hurrying back to his equipment. "Don't go anywhere."

Darin made a note to check out the operation of this breaker later in the day, an item for the upcoming meeting.

"Good news and bad news," said Norm, returning from his equipment. "Pump has power now and I got it running. We'll see if I can keep it on-line. It keeps wanting to shut down. But, at least it has power."

"Is that the good news, or the bad news?"

"That's the good news. Bad news is that when the contactor closed, it must've thrown out some sparks." Norm held up a small corner of paper. "Your warning gave it the kiss of death."

"The schematic?"

"I can't believe it. Forty years! Ten minutes after your warning, this."

"That's all that's left?"

Norm nodded. "Had to turn on the exhaust fan to get the smoke out of the room. That would've set off the fire alarm again and the fire department would pay us another visit. If Merry had to pay five grand to the fire department for a false alarm, she'd go through the roof. At least this corner has the drawing number on it. Guess I'd better order a copy. Breakfast after this?"

"It's on me. I got here late and burned up your schematic."

"I'll buy. You got power to the pump. Uh, oh. I just heard it shut down. Talk to you later."

Darin followed Norm out the door and headed back to his office. About half way down the long corridor, heading east, Merry came around the cor-

ner, heading west. She waved. Darin smiled, knowing he was trapped.

*Damn!*

Normally, Darin would have ducked into one of the many doors between Merry and himself. He would have waved and found a sudden need to go left or right and then accelerate once out of her view.

But in this section of the hallway there were no other doors except for the one leading out to the loading dock and, even if he hustled, he would still only get to there about the same time as her. There was no way of faking it, no way to convey through a rolling of the eyes and a snap of the fingers that there was something that he had forgotten to do back in the opposite direction.

Talking to Merry was like talking to glue. Somehow, her words stuck and, parting, Darin always had new, unwanted responsibilities within the building. Merry was everywhere and into everything, taking notes, putting her touch on this hazard or that, like..., molasses with a note pad.

"Hey, Darin," she said, smiling. "How's it going?"

"Great. You're in early."

"I'm going out to the antenna site today. It's a long drive so I've got to start early. The standby generators are running?"

"Yeah."

"No commercial power?"

"Yea. Don't know why yet. I'll call the electric company when I get to my office."

Merry pulled a pen out from her clipboard and scribbled something down. "What time did it happen?"

"Don't know. I got the call around three, so sometime before that."

"Can you leave me a message when you find out?"

"Sure."

"And the cause."

"Right."

"Thanks," said Merry, smiling and continuing on, much to Darin's relief. And then, stopping, she turned back. "And the name of the person you talked to if you don't mind."

"Right," said Darin.

"Oh," she flipped a page on her clipboard. "I noticed that the rubber insulation blanket in the power room on the third floor is out of date."

"It is? OK. I'll exchange it," said Darin, slowing, but not stopping, making a mental note to carry a note pad and write down problems that he could give to her the next time they crossed paths.

*Responsibility swapping!*

*A new game for the corporations.*

"Thanks, Merry."

"And I noticed that one of the battery stands up on the forth floor doesn't have any eye wash."

"I'll look into it. Thanks, Merry."

Darin hurried away.

*Jesus! Damn, she's good!*

*Got to get some distance between us.*

The eyewash requirement was especially irksome. It used to be as long as the eyewash container had never been opened, the contents were safe to use. The same bottles sat in the same places for years because nobody ever used them anyway.

Not seeing an expiration date, Merry called the company wondering why they didn't have one. Their explanation was that as long as the bottle was not opened the contents were still sealed and safe to use.

That was not good enough. Merry pushed for dated water bottles and the manufacturer happily complied, putting a two year date on all of their bottles. Not quite happy with that, Merry decided that if someone got battery acid in their eyes, they would need a water bottle close by, one at each end of a battery stand for example, about twenty feet long, another one in the middle, if longer.

Convincing upper level management was easy because they had never worked in that field either and it only made sense to be *more-safe*. And it sounded good on the resume.

*worked hard to improve working conditions,*

*a corporate leader with the worker's safety in mind.*

Soon, this was the requirement and, whereas before there were only two or three bottles in each power room for years at a time, now twenty or thirty sat in handy places around the room, all having to be phased out every two years.

It was such a good idea that it went state-wide and eventually nation-wide. Merry was given an Excellence in Workmanship award for her insight into worker safety problems, fame, and recognition.

Therefore, it was common consensus, but never proven, that Merry Dick Tracy had bought stock in the eyewash bottle company before she came up with all of the new requirements.

# Airwaves

Although there was almost never anybody at the antenna site, today there was no place to park. The three available spots were already taken, a big company truck parked on the pad out back beneath the antenna tower, and two non-company trucks taking the two spaces in the front.

Jerome put his truck into reverse and backed down the single lane, winding road, about a hundred feet, to a dirt cutout in the side of the road. He locked his truck, thinking that he really didn't even need to do that, and started walking up to the site.

The structure located at the bottom of the tower was made of concrete block, windowless, completely white except for the gray metal doors at opposite ends of the building, a single heavy duty steel door at the front, and a steel double door at the back, used for bringing in equipment, and an outhouse on the east side, overlooking the valley below.

The tower, located at the back of the building, was about sixty feet high and was loaded with antennas that pointed toward the other mountain peaks. Line of sight, that's what they called it, point to point, micro-wave.

Jerome had not gone to the last crew meeting and had somehow been volunteered for this project, an action typical of the crew. Those who missed the meetings are volunteered. The instructions had come in this morning's e-mail:

Jerome,

Drop everything. The antenna crew is a man short and they have to get the antenna up today. Any other appointments you have, let me know and I'll get someone to cover. Everybody else is too booked up to lose a day.

Good luck, Martin

PS Better take a lunch. You'll be out there most of the day.

Jerome groaned when he read the message. *This was supposed to be an easy day!* *Lunch with Pamela..,* The phone rang.

"Power maintenance. Jerome here."

"Hey, Jerome. Sorry to do that to you."

"No, you're not."

"Everybody else had their days scheduled."

"Everybody else says they had their day scheduled. How come the antenna crew's a man short?"

"Guy's mother is dying. He's going to be off for at least two weeks, taking vacation time. He may be off longer than that, depending."

"Can't they just bring in someone else? There are all kinds of surplus technicians around."

Jerome immediately regretted saying that. Pamela was a surplus technician out of L.A. That would put her out on a mountaintop with a bunch of horny guys.

"They want somebody who knows power in case something goes wrong. Besides, you're going to have to fuse up the equipment when it's ready to go."

"What ever happened to the meetings we're supposed to have to make sure we're all on the same page?"

"Discussed at the crew meeting but you weren't there. Remember? They have to get the antenna up today. They start at five. Smitty, the guy in charge, says they have about three hours of work to do before you got there, so you'd better hurry. It's an

16

hour's drive. Thanks for your help. Gotta go. My other line's ringing."

"But,...,"

Click.

"It's gonna be a shitty day," thought Jerome. "I have no idea what I'm supposed to do. Gotta get hold of Pamela. And no..., I didn't bring a lunch."

The front door to the site was wide open, a security violation. Jerome followed the sound of voices to another smaller room in the back, checking out the power equipment on the way in.

Two men were standing around the antenna, a six foot wide dish lying on its' back, about two feet high around the circumference. A tall, skinny man wearing a white hard hat with a lightning bolt on one side and the name Smitty on the other, nodded.

"You Jerome?"

"Yea."

"We was expecting you 'bout an hour ago."

"I just got the message."

"You shoulda been here sooner."

"It's an hour's drive."

"They didn't tell you to get here early?"

"I didn't know until I got to work. What's the rush?"

"Gotta get this up before the winds hit."

Jerome examined the dish a little more carefully. "How much that thing weigh?"

"About six hundred pounds," said Smitty. "But it's not the weight. It's the wind. Can't hang an antenna if the wind's blowin'."

"Why's that?"

"Bangs against the tower. That's why you're here, keep it from banging."

"It's not windy. I just came in."

"Will be in about thirty minutes, soon as the sun

heats up the east side of the mountains. So we ain't got time to talk."

"I'm Hal," said the second man, walking around the antenna to shake Jerome's hand. "And that low-life piece-a-shit drunk with his head between his legs over there in the corner is Billy. Found himself a whore last night and didn't get in until four-thirty. He's gonna have a hard day. Didn't bring himself any water, either."

"Worth it," said Billy, head still between his legs. "I ain't never been fucked like that before."

"Says that every time," said Hal, grinning. "You wouldn't think he'd have Alzheimer's yet, being so young. Come on, Billy boy. We got work to do."

Smitty motioned for Jerome to follow as he headed out through the double doors to the base of the tower. Billy got up with a groan, his uncombed blonde hair matching his bleary red eyes, and started to follow. He ran into the wall and bounced back into the room. Jerome caught him before he fell into the antenna dish and helped him through the doorway.

"Don't baby him, none," said Hal. "He needs to learn."

"Jerome," said Smitty. "Listen up. The four of us," he paused, studying Billy's condition and, seeing that Billy's eyes were closed and that he was swaying, standing up, "the three of us, and maybe dip-shit there for a little bit, are gonna carry the antenna out and set it down here. Got it?"

Jerome nodded.

"Can't be droppin' it, neither," said Smitty, walking back to the door. "If you can't hold on, let us know so's we can all set it down."

"Right," said Jerome, following. "You're going to winch it up?"

"Yep, fifty feet. Hal, get dip-shit and bring him in here. You checked all the nuts and bolts, right?"

"Right. Everything's tight."

Jerome found a place to grip the antenna. "How am I going to keep this thing from banging? Do I have to climb the tower?"

"I'm gonna give you about two hundred feet a rope," said Smitty, positioning himself opposite Jerome. "One end's gonna be attached to the dish and you'll be on the other, on the ground keepin' it from hittin'. Dip-shit over there is gonna be on the other side doin' the same thing. You still with us, dip-shit?"

Billy nodded, smiled, staggered forward and positioned himself between Smitty and Jerome. Hal grabbed the opposite side. Together, they lifted the antenna and walked it outside. Jerome noticed a small breeze when they had finally moved the dish beneath the tower, just a whisper passing through.

"Feel that?" said Smitty. "Startin' already."

The cable from the winch on the truck had already been threaded through a pulley up on the tower. Hal was quick to get the dish hooked up and within five minutes the antenna was standing vertically.

Smitty attached two ropes to the dish, one at the four o'clock and one at the eight o'clock position, handed Jerome one of the coils and threw the other at Billy, who wobbled under the new imbalance.

"If you start to lose control," he said, glaring at Billy, "tie it around your balls." Looking at Jerome, he said, "Think you can handle it?"

"Don't know," said Jerome, shrugging.

"Go as far back as you can," said Hal, now starting up the tower. "The longer the rope, the easier it

19

gets."

Billy beamed. "That's what she said."

Backing away from the tower, uncoiling the rope as he went, Jerome noticed that it was going to be difficult to go anywhere except back down the road toward his truck.

If the wind decided to come over the bluff, he was going to have to climb up the bank, about six feet above the road, and then back through the brush up onto several large rocks that formed the top of the ridge, rattlesnake haven, possibly. Billy's direction, he noticed, the down-wind side, was a gentle slope downward that was mostly flat rock.

It didn't seem like there was much wind, but Jerome noticed a slight tug as the antenna was being raised. The dish began to sway, as if finding some kind of rhythm with the wind.

"Resonant frequency," Jerome thought, now beginning to understand the futility of his task, a six hundred pound dish being steadied by his meager one hundred and sixty pounds. And his hands were getting not only tired, but red as well. He had left two pairs of leather gloves in the truck.

Smitty waved for Jerome to move toward the eye of the breeze, up into the brush, difficult with six hundred pounds pulling him backward. Turning, looking for the best way up, he saw Merry Dick Tracy arriving.

She smiled. "Hi Jerome. Sure is a pretty day, huh?"

"Hey, Merry. Getting a little windy. How's it going?"

"I can see you're busy, so I'll make it quick. In Building Fourteen, someone has stored some equipment in front of the one of the breaker cabinets. There's going to be an inspection in that building next Friday, so it has to be moved out of the way."

"OK, Merry. Thanks."

"And I saw a can of solvent in your office that doesn't have a MSDS sheet listed in the building."

"Oh, yeah. I was trying to clean a stain off of the floor."

"Call Norm, in Building Maintenance. He's got all of the approved stuff. He'll come out and do it for you."

"I was trying to save him the trouble. Hey, Merry, I've got to get back to this. The antenna's banging and Smitty's getting pissed."

"Thanks Jerome. Oh, you do know it's a security violation for that door to remain open, right?"

"Right," said Jerome, thinking that other than this woman, they were the only ones on top of this mountain and that if anyone tried to get inside they would surely be observed by one of them, except maybe Billy, and that the double doors in the back were open anyway.

"Have a nice day," said Merry, heading toward the building.

The higher the antenna, the more the wind affected the operation. Jerome struggled to get a foothold, wrapped the rope around his hands two or three times to keep it from slipping and it still pulled him across loose rock and through an occasional bush. Looking down, he noticed that Billy was not having a hard time at all.

*And why should he? Wind's blowing toward him.*

*That's the trick, isn't it? Grab the rope on the downwind side.*

*No work over there. Ground is flatter, too. And the bastard's got gloves!*

"Hey! Billy!" Jerome yelled. "Pick up the fuckin'

21

slack, will ya?"

Tonight would be a night for blisters. Tonight would be a double martini night, just for starters.

Due to high winds, it took an extra hour to finally secure the antenna.

Prevailing Winds

It was already in the high eighties by seven in the morning. Riding shotgun, Roberta absentmindedly watched as they dropped down into the valley, as the terrain slowly changed from rocks, millions of boulders, probably billions and not much of anything else, to vast fields of alfalfa, soybeans, beets, whatever else they grew in the El Centro area.

Beyond that, further along the road, sand dunes replaced crops while cactus replaced the scrub brush, all of it part of the fading footprint of civilization.

"I brought sunscreen in case you need it," said Tony, adjusting his sunglasses back up on his nose. "And extra water."

"We're going to be inside, right?"

"That's the plan. But out here, never can tell. I got a flat tire one time, thought I could change it out in fifteen, twenty minutes. It was a hundred and ten that day, no shade. Turns out, the spare was flat. I had to start the generator to get the compressor going so I could fill the spare. Somebody in the company had borrowed my truck when I was on vacation and used up all the gas in the generator."

"Don't you hate people like that?"

"Yea. Still, my fault. I should've checked, knowing I was coming out here. I siphoned some gas out of the tank, put it in the generator, got the air compressor going and filled the spare only to find that I couldn't get one of the lug nuts off of the flat."

"Why didn't you just fill the flat with air?"

"Blew a tread. It had to come off."

"Oh."

"So, I put all the other lug nuts back on, sprayed WD40 on everything and tightened the lug nuts tighter than the one that wouldn't come off. Then, I could break it. I was stuck on that road for two hours. Not one other car came by. Thought I was gonna die of heat stroke. It doesn't take long to get in big trouble out here."

"How often you make this trip?"

"Once a month, takes a whole day. And if I've got more than two or three hours of work, I'll be late getting back."

"Don't know why you like this loop. It's so desolate."

"I couldn't stand a loop like yours. Too much traffic along the beach, no parking. It'd drive me nuts."

"At least there're people. I'd shoot myself if I had to work out here."

"You get used to it. Folks are friendly. Nobody's in a hurry."

"What folks?"

Tony laughed. "Well, when you come across one."

Roberta removed the cap from her water bottle, took a long sip and swished it around before swallowing, watching an old, deserted building pass by, about a hundred yards off of the road, front window boarded up, door kicked open, hanging by the upper hinge. Looked like it used to be a house or maybe a store, something more than some storage shed anyway, big as it was.

*Why build something way out here, guaranteed to fail? Owner had a heart attack and died? Too far away to get help? Got shot in a robbery? Divorced when their dreams didn't pan out?*

*That's it. What dreams ever come true out here? Wouldn't take much to leave. Life's too slow. Drive a person crazy.*

*Make the transaction and move on. Slow talk only gets you into trouble. People always want to know too much.*

Wasn't much to say, anyway. Daryl had moved out unexpectedly, finding not only a new, better paying job up the coast, but also moving in with a beautiful, single and very much in heat, young bitch who was looking for a roommate.

Daryl was ecstatic, big apartment, good view of the ocean from the balcony and rent was cheap. "How can it be wrong," he asked, "when everything feels so right?"

*Well, Mr. Daryl. You know where you can put that. You say you'll come visit on the weekends? Hardly. Think you're going to get it coming and going? Screw you.*

*Better to know now than later. Make the adjustments and move on. For now, don't want any time to think. Don't want to go for long walks or stop and smell the roses. Got tons of books to read soon as the walls don't close in.*

Vanessa, her best friend, had seen the dangers and had insisted on hanging out, going to movies, to plays, getting drunk together.

*Seems like Vanessa's always around. Getting a little too friendly? Hmm.*

Replacing the cap to her water bottle, Roberta looked over at Tony. "When's the turn-off?"

"Coming up." Tony let go of the steering wheel to screw the lid on his thermos. "Couple more miles."

"Pretty desolate."

"Why did you volunteer to ride along?"

"We're supposed to know each other's loops, right?"

"I guess I'll have to visit yours one day. I know a

few of your buildings."

"It's pretty easy."

"Can I ask a question?"

"Maybe."

"What made you want to join our crew?"

Roberta smiled. "Money."

"You had a pretty good inside job though, right?"

"Yea. But this pays more and I was getting fat sitting and watching a screen all day. And it was a chance to get outside."

"So, it wasn't just the money."

"I can see the ocean all day long and get paid for it."

"We've got to check in before we go through the gate," said Tony, easing the truck into third, turning on his signal even though there was no one else around. He turned left onto a dirt road, heading north.

"Why? It's our building."

"This is a Navy bombing area. Jets shoot up remote controlled targets. We want to make sure they know we're not one of them."

"We're getting back on time, right?"

"We should be back around four."

They approached a small weathered, faded green stucco building with several antennas mounted on the roof. Tony parked next to an old Chevy van sitting in the shade of the building.

"You've gotta come in," said Tony, stepping out into the blazing sun.

"Why?"

"They have to know who we are, what we're doing, and how many."

"Jesus, it's hot," said Roberta, getting out.

"Still morning." Tony led the way up the wooden steps and held the door open for Roberta. "Wait until one or two. You'll think you're in an oven."

"I already do."

"Hey, Tony," said Helen, a gray haired, heavy-set woman from behind the counter. She moved her coffee cup out of the way and slid the sign-in sheet toward him. "I see you got company today."

"Hi Helen. This is Roberta. She works the beach route."

"Quite a change, huh?" said Helen. "The only waves around here are sand."

"So I've noticed. Don't know how anything lives out here."

"Best place on Earth," said Helen. "Quiet. No smog. You just have to take it easy and that's just fine with me."

"Me too," said Tony. "Heard it was windy out here last night."

"Haven't seen it blow like that since, golly, was it eighty-two?"

"Before my time," said Tony. "I didn't pay any attention to this place until I had to start coming out here."

"Hope your building's OK."

"Should be. It's brand new."

"Flash flood warnings," said Helen. "In case you're goin' further north."

"Not today. Gotta check the engine."

"It ran last night?" said Roberta, signing the log.

"About two hours, according to the Center," said Tony.

Helen grabbed her cup and headed for the coffee pot. "You guys want coffee? I just made a pot."

"No, thanks. I've got to get her back on time. They don't want two of us collecting overtime."

Helen stopped halfway to the coffee pot. "Hey! What makes that engine run?"

27

"Power failure," said Tony. "Starts up automatically. At least it's supposed to."

"That's why my oven clock was flashing. If it happened after nine, I wouldn't know."

"Bye, Helen." Roberta followed Tony out the door. "Nice meeting you."

"Stay cool," said Helen.

The inside of the truck was already suffocating when they got in.

"It's always this hot down here?"

"Usually," said Tony, using his mirrors to back up. He put the truck into first and eased forward, heading for the gate. "For this time of the year anyway. It's great during the spring."

"And that's when you get the flash floods, right?"

"Those are fun to watch as long as you're not in it."

"I'll take your word for it. What key to open the gate?"

"ER4. You've got one?"

"Yea. How come the fence only goes out twenty feet from the road?"

"Pure sand. Only a fool would try to go around. They won't make it."

"Dune buggies?"

"I guess, if you're stupid enough to break into a bombing range."

Driving up to the building, Tony moaned.

"What's the matter?"

"See all that sand on the east side?"

"Yea."

"The air intake for the engine is over there."

"So? It's filtered, right?"

"I told them they had to put a wall up outside, something to stop the drifts. But no. That was going to put it over budget."

"How bad can it get? It's just a little sand. Right?" said Roberta, getting out.

The room was small compared to the engine rooms Roberta was used to. This one was barely ten by twelve. And the engine seemed more like a lawn mower compared to the high-powered, heavy duty ones that she maintained. Another difference was that this room was not air-conditioned, probably a hundred inside already.

The sand had found a way around the wall air filters in two different locations and had drifted into the room, varying in depth from one to two feet across the floor. Judging by the shadow on the other side of the filters, it was three feet high outside.

"Well," said Tony, with a groan. "I've got buckets, shovels, and a couple of brooms in the back of the truck. Looks like we'll be here for a while. I hope you're up for some exercise."

"No cleaning crew, huh?"

"We're it. And if the winds come back tonight, I could have the same problem again tomorrow."

# Building Twelve

Sergio was taking a shortcut through the engine room on the way to his office when he noticed that the fuel gage on the day tanks was indicating empty. He tapped the glass, hoping that the needle was stuck, but it didn't move.

He turned a switch, located beneath the meter, from Auto to Manual, and the pump started pumping fuel from the main tank up into the above ground tank.

*Hundred-gallon tank. Gonna take a while. Got time to get myself a cup of coffee and check mail.*

*Wonder why the auto didn't kick in. I guess I'll have to...,*

The phone rang.

"Power Maintenance, Sergio, here."

"Ricardo's missing."

"Ricardo? He was in bed when I left, about five."

Her voice sounded frantic. "I was up at six. Back door's unlocked. Should I call the police?"

"No," said Sergio, not wanting to get the police involved. "Maybe he just went up to the store to get some donuts."

"His bike is still here."

"Maybe he walked or took his skateboard, or...,"

"That's just it. We don't know, Sergio! I'm calling the police."

"Wait. Don't call yet. Let's...,"

Click.

Sergio headed for the exit, reaching into his pocket for his car keys at the same time.

*Dammed woman, getting crazier all the time. Ricardo's twelve. He knows how to take care of himself.*

30

Turned out, Ricardo had left a note reminding them that he was going fishing with Joey and his dad. The  police found the note between the night stand and the wall, probably knocked over by the cat.

Sergio, now remembering that he'd turned on the pump, raced back to work.

*Everything should be OK. The day  tank does have a return line. Should go in one side and out the other. It's just a big loop once the tank is full. What can go wrong with that?*

## Breakfast

It took a long time for Robby to open his eyes. Not that he needed to. He knew where he was already, the refrigerator's hum from the kitchen, the constant yapping of the tiny dog, Spiffy, in the apartment next door, footsteps from the family living in the apartment upstairs, showers on and off, the sounds of people going out for the day.

What he didn't remember was when he got home. Sometime after two because he remembered closing time at Lucky's, downtown. And then there was an hour at the coffee shop trying to sober up, one grilled cheese, one slice of apple pie and endless cups of coffee.

*Must've been around four. Right? Tanya had kicked the blankets off and looked too good to pass up. How long did that take? Half hour? Must've got to sleep around four-thirty. Probably eight now. What day is this?*

Robby groaned.

*Monday.*

It was all coming back now. He had dropped Tanya off at seven and was going to a friend's place to watch the game. Sunday night football.

Today was not going to be a hard day at work. Report in, check messages, get into the truck and drive through his loop. No big deal.

Going in late didn't matter either. Martin was forgiving. He didn't mind tardy as long as the work was getting done and that he wasn't getting any calls complaining of anything in the loop.

"Just stay late and make up the time," he'd say.

*Part of the plan, work late, not get home in time to eat, take a shower and go to church.*

This was not Tanya's view. "Robby," she'd say, using that tone of voice that said, pay attention. "There are a lot of good people at church and I know it'll do you a lot of good to be around them. There are lawyers and writers and doctors...,"

"And scum bags and thieves and perverts and child molesters and people on the take in the name of the Lord," Robby would be thinking while she was still talking. Hardly a one of them was walking with both feet on the ground, the way they keep talking about how the Lord changed their lives.

One orange, three scrambled eggs, two pieces of jelly toast and two cups of coffee later, carrying a travel cup of coffee, Robby called Martin to say he'd overslept.

"You forgot about the meeting, Robby?"

"What meeting?"

"I sent you an e-mail. Of course, if you didn't check it Friday night before you left, and if you haven't gotten to work yet today, you wouldn't have read it yet either."

"Sorry, Boss."

"Come straight over, soon as you get your truck."

"OK."

# Jelly Roll

Bart was the first one in the conference room. He seated himself at the middle of the long mahogany table so that anyone entering from the hallway would have to pass by him, and busied himself with stirring out the chunks of Cremora in his coffee.

At his old job he would've used half and half fresh out of the fridge. And the coffee would have been fresh ground, brewed a cup at a time. This was definitely a downgrade in that regard.

*That's OK. Drinking bad coffee in San Diego is better than drinking good coffee in LA. Air's cleaner, traffic's better, and pay's the same.*

You think you're doing a good job, think you're making a difference and then, Wham!

Sorry pal, the numbers show that we don't need you anymore. We will give you a severance package. Not much for all of your loyalty and great work, but it'll help keep you on your feet until you find another job. And you'll still have medical until the end of the year.

Sorry. Can't fight upper management. Or, if you choose to stay with our fine company, we do have an opening in another town.

Yes, this might seem like an inconvenience, but we hear that San Diego is not so bad. And if you decide that this is the best option, the opening will be in power maintenance.

Yes. We know that you don't have any experience in that field.

All jobs have some dangerous aspects.

You will be trained. We can assure you.

No. The opening is for the midnight shift only.

Probably until someone with less seniority comes into your group.

No, last guy died of a heart attack. Don't know if it happened on the job.

What are you going to do? Move, that's what. You've got all these years of seniority built up and any other job you go to outside the company, you'll be bossed around by someone half your age and making more money.

*Screw you, LA. Never should have built there in the first place. Smog stays trapped in the valley...,*

"Hi," said a tall, thin dishwater blonde as she seated herself across the table from Bart. "I'm Carly."

Bart stood, reached across the table and shook her hand. "Hi. Bart, out of LA."

"Are you our new nights person?"

"That's what I'm told."

"Well, good luck."

"Will I need it?"

"What'd you do before?"

"Parts warehouse."

"Well, you will be lugging a lot of stuff around."

"How many of us on the night crew?"

"One."

"What..., me?"

Carly laughed. "You're it."

"I'll get training, right?"

"Yea. You'll get Basic Electricity and you'll tag along with each of us for a while and we'll show you what not to do, and then when you're utterly confused, about two months from now, Martin will put you on nights."

Bart, feeling a growing uneasiness in his stomach, glanced toward the coffee pot.

"Those donuts for everyone?"

"Yea. They always buy donuts now, ever since they figured out that we don't complain so much and we're not in as big a hurry to leave. Nobody here likes meetings."

"Nobody likes them up there, either." Bart headed for the donuts. "Oh, great, jelly filled."

"Your favorite?"

"Actually, it brings back a bad memory."

"How can you have bad memories about a jelly-filled?"

"Did they have those town hall meetings down here?"

"Last year's mandatory meetings? Yea. Everyone had to go."

"They set up our meeting in the warehouse," said Bart, reaching for a maple bar. "About fifty chairs in a big circle. The place was just about empty when I sat down. Fifteen minutes later it was full, standing room only. Someone went around the room with a tray of donuts. When they got to me, there was only a jelly filled left, so I took it. First bite, jelly squirts out the other end, a big glob into my hand."

"Bummer," said Carly, smiling."

"No napkins that I can see. So I'm thinking I've got time to go wash it off. But before I get up, this guy on my right starts talking to the crowd, telling everyone to listen up. The place gets quiet. Turns out, he's the VP."

"I wouldn't have taken the donut."

"It's not really jelly either, more like a jam."

"Still, red and sticky. What'd you do?"

"The guy sitting on my left was President of the Union. As soon as the VP stopped talking, he started. You know, union's response? Somehow I wound up sitting in between. What are the odds? The jelly warmed up and started oozing out from between my fingers and down my wrist. Everyone was staring at me. The VP and union guy thought they had everyone's attention, but they didn't. Everyone was wondering what I was going to do next."

"Why didn't you excuse yourself."

"Mandatory meeting."

"You had a good reason."

"Do you want fifty people waiting for you to return from the potty?"

"Right."

"I started thinking I'd been set up. Maybe I was on candid camera or something."

"What did you do?"

"Licked it off."

Carly laughed. "I couldn't have done that."

"Worst part was they were talking about my job. I didn't hear a word."

Martin entered the room with an armful of papers. "Hey, Bart. Hi Carly. I see you two have already met. Bart, you'll be riding with Carly for the next week. After that you'll be with Darin until your school starts."

Carly opened her note pad, and searched through her purse for a pen. "Where is everybody?"

"Darin's got a power failure at Building One. Robby is going to be late. Roberta's riding with Tony out to the desert site. Heard they had a storm out there last night. Serge should be here any minute. Floyd just called and said he was in the parking lot. And I had to send Jerome out to the antenna site to cover for one of their guys. So, it should be a short meeting today. Probably should have just cancelled it."

## The Shortest Meeting

Floyd parked his company car between the two portable generators and pulled on the emergency brake with a sigh. He remembered to grab the keys this time, having locked himself out of his car last Tuesday when he was visiting a remote site and wound up having to get someone drive the fifty miles to bring a spare set.

He struggled to get out, discovering as always that the distance between the bottom of his seat and the frame of the doorway was shorter than the length of his foot, which he had to turn sideways to get it past the opening. The same held true for his head and the top of the door frame, which he always hit while getting both in and out of the car, two of many irritants about this company vehicle.

Floyd was a big man with an overly large head, thick neck, and his appearance, at least down through his broad sloping shoulders to his enormous hands, was of a bear standing on his hind legs. Back in the day nobody ever sold him bad dope or in any way pissed him off. That was just not smart.

His hair had thinned through the years, transitioning from blonde and curly in his youth when he was playing football, to an Afro during his college days in the sixties, to gray and thin around the sides of his head, today's look.

In spite of his large size, Floyd was a gentle man. He wrote poetry in his quiet times, never submitted anything for publication or even for someone else to scrutinize, except Darla, his wife, for whom all of his poetry was written. And occasionally he picked up the guitar and wrote ballads, for himself mostly.

But his favorite pastime was to launch his canoe, birch, painstakingly hand built over a whole year, that he took along when camping, wanting not so much to fish as to glide over silent waters, early morning and late at night, and explore the shoreline, pushing the brush aside with his paddle, wanting to know how far back the inlets would go.

For the last few years, the canoe sat in the garage gathering dust. The company had cancelled all engineer's vacations, company needs is what they said, and were reluctant to hire or train more engineers because, when the growth spurt had been addressed, they didn't want to have a surplus of engineers.

As a result, the workday had gotten longer. What used to be seven to three-thirty ratcheted up to six to six, with homework in the evenings.

Darla was not happy. "We only go around once, Floyd. The kids are grown and gone. It's time for you and me. Remember our dreams?"

Tell that to the boss. Insist on that vacation and you may not have a job when you come back.

Floyd tried to explain. Darla remained unconvinced. "Our time is passing," she would say, quietly.

Taking the outside stairs up from the parking lot, Floyd paused at the platform halfway up, set down his brief case and wiped his brow.

*Didn't seem this hot when I got out of the car. Take the stairs. That's what the doc said. Get more exercise. Blood pressure's up and cholesterol's through the roof.*

*No eggs, no dairy, no fatty foods and no red meat. What kind of life is that? Jesus! Only one half flight and I'm winded.*

Floyd entered the building, turned right, and

headed down the long hallway toward the conference room, following the smell of fresh brewed coffee.

Inside the room, Martin was pouring himself a cup. "Hey, Floyd. How's it going?"

"Surviving."

"Coffee?"

"I'd kill for a cup, cream, two sugars. No, wait. Just black. Thanks."

"Diet?"

"I guess."

"So, you won't like the next question."

"What's that?"

"Donut?"

"Screw you."

"What willpower," said Carly, pushing the rest of the glazed into her mouth.

Martin set the coffee on the table next to Floyd. "It'll be a small group today."

"Oh?"

"Tony called. Said he's got an engine room full of sand."

Floyd groaned. "Out in the desert?"

"Yea."

"The job at the bombing range, right?"

"Yea. They were supposed to build a wall?"

Pulling out his note pad, Floyd sighed. "I tried to push that through. But it was going to go over budget. I told them that had nothing to do with it."

"Well, it does. They're going to be out there all day. I'll have to pay overtime."

"I told them that, too. They don't care. Maintenance dollars aren't their responsibility."

"Wrong thing to say," said Carly, shaking her head.

"Wait until I bill them," Martin replied. "We have

to...,"

Martin's cell rang. "Power Maintenance, Martin here."

"Hey, Boss. We've got a problem."

"Sergio. Where are you? The meeting's about to start."

"Building twelve."

"You're supposed to be here. What's the problem?"

"Fuel spill. You'd better get up here."

"Fuel? How much?"

"Um, hard to say."

"Are we talking more than a few gallons?"

"Um..., yea."

"I'm on my way." Martin pulled his papers back together, gulped down his coffee and headed for the door. "Sorry, Floyd. Got a problem at Twelve. I'll call later to reschedule."

"What's going on?"

"Fuel spill. Carly? Take Bart with you and meet me up there. Afterward, if you have time, take him over to Motor Pool and see if you can find him a good truck, at least a three-quarter ton van."

"It's going to take your signature," said Carly, wiping her hands on a napkin.

"I know. Just pick a good one and give me the ID number. Bart, I'm working on getting you your own set of keys."

Floyd blew the steam off of his coffee. "Wouldn't you know it? I finally get a chance to get out of the office, get nothing done, get bad news, and then have to go back even before lunch. That's cruel, Martin, cruel."

"Sorry Floyd. I owe you lunch next time. Don't know if I can make it good news, or not."

"Oh, well," said Carly, "Pays the same."

Lights. Action!

$M$artin pulled into the parking lot and picked the spot closest to the engine room even though the curb was painted red. He hurried down the outside steps, put his key in the lock and stepped into the room.

The light switch was on the other wall, where people normally came in. There had been discussion about putting a light switch on this side as well, to be included on the next upgrade for the building, one of the items for discussion with Floyd this morning.

Stepping into the room, Martin felt something odd around his feet as he groped along the wall. One or two more steps and he realized that he was standing in fuel. Across the room, Sergio slid to a halt at the doorway, staying behind the dam built into the threshold, and shined his flashlight down at Martin's feet.

"Tried to get here first and warn you."

Martin didn't know whether to go toward Sergio, ten feet away, or back to the door, five feet away. "Jesus!"

"Been a slight accident, I...,"

"My shoes!"

"Uh, probably your pants, too," said Sergio. "Diesel smells never come out."

"Sergio, what the hell?"

"I can explain. The day tank was almost empty, so I...,"

"Crimenently, Sergio!"

"I'll get you a towel," said Sergio, turning. "Come this way."

"I can't believe it! Tell me the drain is blocked.

42

Otherwise, it's the Fish and Game Dept., the Health Dept., the six o'clock news. My God! Tell me the fricking drain is blocked!"

"Yea," said Sergio. "It's blocked."

Martin waded toward the door. "Thank you. Thank you. Thank you."

"Saw you pull into the parking lot. Thought you'd come to the front door."

"The tank's underground, Sergio! For crying out loud! How'd fuel get up here?"

"There's a simple explanation...,"

"Brand new, and they're melting! My Hush puppies! Look at that! Soles are coming right off! Damn!"

# Meeting

"OK, everybody," said Martin, his voice rising above the din of the crew while they seated themselves around the table. "Listen up. We've got a lot to cover today and I know you guys have got a lot to do, so let's get going."

"I've got this vendor problem," said Carly.

Martin held up his hand. "Save it for the roundtable. Everybody here met Bart? Make friends with him. He's going to be the guy that covers for you while you're sleeping. It's going to take him a while to come up to speed. He'll be riding with each of you over the next couple of months. Let him know your problems so he knows what to expect."

"Hey Bart," said Darin, turning to shake his hand. "I'm Darin. I've got this list of problems I've been working on and...,"

"He's riding with me," said Carly, coolly. "If anyone's going to give him a list, it'll be after me. Right, Bart?"

"I guess," said Bart, shaking Darin's hand. "I'm the new guy here. I don't know the rules."

"The rules are," said Martin, looking up from his agenda, "that we keep this meeting moving forward."

"Anyone having problems with Spark Electric?" Jerome asked.

"Yea," said Roberta. "They got wire clippings in the ringing machine."

"What's with that?" said Jerome. "These guys are supposed to be...,"

"Wait," said Martin. "Save it for the roundtable, so we can all hear it."

"Hey, Serge," said Carly. "Do you have to buy

Martin new shoes? Or does the company?"

"Don't know," said Sergio, laughing. "He may think he can walk on water but we know he can't walk on diesel fuel."

"I heard that," said Martin, fumbling with his papers. "I'll expense it and it'll come out of your bonus."

"I'm just gonna glue the soles back on," said Sergio.

"Can't do it," said Martin. "The soles are gooey."

"Isn't that how they sell them?" Jerome asked. "I mean, Hush puppies. Come on."

"I know what they used to feel like," said Martin. "And if it's slimy, I'm not wearing it."

"Hey, Roberta," said Darin, talking from across the table. "I heard you and Tony wore out your shovels at the bombing range."

"We're getting to that," said Martin.

"Never do a ride along with Tony," said Roberta. "He knew it was windy the night before and he knew what was going to happen. He just wanted help."

"And a witness," said Tony. "I needed someone else to help convey my pain."

"Rode all the way out there with him," said Roberta. "Two hours! He never said a word about shoveling. But he had extra shovels, buckets and brooms in his truck."

"Since we're on that subject," said Martin. "Let's go with that. Floyd here has got some news for us. Floyd?"

"Got them to re-open the job," said Floyd, talking to Tony. "A crew's going out next Monday to pour the foundation for the wall. They'll finish up on Tuesday."

"I can do Monday, but not Tuesday," said Tony.

"Who's got Tuesday open?" Martin asked.

By the sudden silence, it was evident that every-one definitely had something more important going on than driving out to a bombing range on Tuesday.

"OK. Who's not here," said Carly, always the one to volunteer someone else.

"How about Bart?" Darin suggested. "He'll eventually have to know where it is."

"Not qualified," Bart replied.

"How qualified you have to be?" Darin asked. "It's just a matter of opening up the building for the vendor and making sure everything's locked up when they go."

"I don't know how to get there."

"Anybody else knows how to get there?" Martin asked.

"Roberta," Jerome replied, knowing that he would be the next one volunteered.

"Paid my dues," Roberta replied, smiling at Jerome. "But you know where it is."

"I'm behind in my loop," Jerome replied. "Ever since I lost a day to the antenna crew. Thanks a lot, you guys. Not to mention the...,"

"Save it for the roundtable," said Martin. "Who's it gonna be on Tuesday?"

"Darin," said Carly, smiling. "You know where it is, don't you?"

"I'm swamped. There's so much work going on in my building right now. I should be over there, not at this meeting."

"That's why we're trying to make this meeting short," said Martin. "Way I see it, we don't need someone out there to watch these guys put up a wall. If they have to take a leak, they don't need to go inside. Who's there to see?"

"Bathroom's on the outside anyway," said Tony. "That's not the problem."

46

"It's not a bathroom," said Roberta. "More like a hole in the ground with four walls around part of it, full of spiders, possibly snakes, and it is a problem."

"The inside bathroom will be done in about another week," said Tony. "The problem is that they have to sign in at the gate and they're not authorized unless one of us is there to sign them in."

"That's a problem," said Martin.

"How about Wednesday?" said Floyd. "We could have them build the wall on Wednesday."

"Where's Robby?" Carly asked.

"Don't know," said Martin. "He's not getting back to me."

"He's been out there," said Carly. "I think he should go. And let's just keep Tuesday as the day. That gives Martin four days to let him know. What do you say, guys?"

This was a self-managed crew. Martin was the boss, the man in charge, but he was supposed to let the crew make the decisions. The crew gave their approval. Robby was voted the Tuesday Man.

"Jerome," said Martin. "I have some good news for you. Smitty really liked the way you hung in there on that antenna job. He's going to write a letter to put in your file."

Jerome nodded in agreement. "That's cool."

"Suck up," said Darin.

"Hey, it was hard work out there. You wouldn't believe how much the wind can blow that antenna around. It was swinging...,"

Carly made a clucking sound into her cupped hand, using it like a microphone. "Kiss ass."

"I want a letter in my file for shoveling all that sand," said Roberta, above the rising din of the crew.

"I do that all the time out there," said Tony. "No

one ever writes a letter for me."

"The reason I said this," said Martin, loudly, "is because they need another volunteer for Friday, starting early."

"Way I see it," said Darin, into the sudden silence. "Jerome's the man."

"Wait a...,"

"Yep," said Carly, nodding in agreement. "You're the new expert."

"Can't do it." Jerome held up his hands. "Look at these blisters. Someone else has gotta go."

"It's not for raising an antenna," said Martin. "You'll be rolling out wave-guide."

"Isn't that just hollow tubing, aluminum or something?" Tony asked.

"Yea," Darin nodded. "Comes on a big reel. Hell, Jerome. How hard can that be? Just tie one end to the antenna base, kick the rock out from under the reel, and watch it roll down the hill."

"I'll even loan you my gloves," said Sergio.

"We voted," said Carly. "Jerome's the man."

"Fuck you, guys! I paid my dues."

"You got da letter. You da man!" said Darin, gleefully.

"It's not like I get any more money. Take that letter out of my file!"

"This is a merciless crew," said Bart, glancing over at Martin.

Sitting against the wall, quietly taking notes, Merry was in hog heaven. All it took was one little e-mail to Martin, cc'd to his boss, and his boss's boss, requesting that she be invited to all crew meetings. So much more could be accomplished, she argued, if she could meet with them when they were all in one place.

Collectively, the crew groaned when they learned

48

of this.

What a gold mine, Merry thought. Sit here for an hour and get the inside scoop on everything.

*Praise the Lord for disgruntled people.*

Roundtable finally finished, the meeting was about to adjourn. It was time for lunch and everyone had their spot they wanted to get to before the crowds hit.

"One little question," said Merry, as the crew was getting up.

"Yes, Merry," said Martin, motioning for everyone to remain seated.

"Can everyone test their day tank return lines so we don't have something like Sergio's fuel spill happen again?"

A groan drifted through the crowd.

"Good idea," said Martin. "Everybody test the return lines and report back to me within a week."

"I have a list of all your buildings," said Merry, beaming. "If you can tell me which ones have day tanks, that would be so helpful. Thank you, everybody."

## Out in Traffic

Robby took the turn-off going south and headed up out of the valley, up the long, steep four-lane road leading into the residential section. It was five-thirty and traffic was heavy.

At the top of the hill he turned east, across traffic, and entered into the parking lot of a long row of stores that had been built parallel to the road, found a spot facing west, away from the store fronts, set his emergency brake and rolled down his window.

*Getting dark already. Man! Look at those clouds. Even smells like rain. Any minute now..., it's gonna hit.*

Tired of listening to all of his CD's, Robby tuned in various stations on the radio, stopping only briefly on talk shows, teeny bop, rap, country, sports, afternoon sermons, politics, and then turned it off.

*Don't know why San Diego doesn't have a good blues station. What's with that?*

*Man, look at that traffic. Stoplight's still broke, two months now. You're pissin' off the voters, man. Two lanes into one, traffic backed up. Dug up for over a month. Ought to be a law.*

*Back home, it'd be quiet, everybody waitin', sittin' on the porch knowin' it's gonna come. Out here, nobody cares. Everybody just wantin' to get home.*

*Where is Jose? We agreed to six. Dude's always late. His life that out of control?*

*You'd think this'd be a good corner for a business. Nope. These cars are just passing through. Out in the morning, back at night. People wantin' to go home, get that buzz, wantin' to feel like the last few hours of the day are theirs.*

*Everybody's got somewhere to go, somethin' to do. Everybody's got a reason.*

*Honda's got clean lines this year. Wonder why domestics can't get it. But if I had the money, Beemer.*

*Come on, Jose. Fashionably late don't make it. People are gonna start noticing that I'm hanging around. Let's get this over with. It's a business deal. You're supposed to be on time.*

*Whoa. Look at that! Mercedes. Bet that thing flies.*

*Gonna pour any minute. Comin' up from the south, makin' it warm, like that time in Florida, seventy-two hours of rain, foot of water everywhere, walking barefoot, hoping I don't run into a snake.*

*Here it comes. Big drops. Man. Now I gotta keep the wipers goin'. Hope Jose still drives his van. Don't know what else to look for.*

Jerome stepped out of the shower smiling, thinking about his earlier conversation with Pamela.

*Sorry, couldn't make it. Had to go help hang an antenna up in the mountains. How about if I cook dinner for the two of us? Of course, I can cook. No. I don't burn the salad. Depends. What do you like? No. I don't do snails. Oh. Good. We agree on that anyway.*

*About six? You bringing the wine? You don't have to. I have a pretty good..., You insist? That's what I like, a woman who knows what she wants. I'm looking forward to it, too.*

*You bet! Gotta love those eyes, dark and sassy. Keeps up with the conversation too. Gotta love that. What a body! Can't wait to slide my hands up beneath her blouse. I think I am in love! Damn blisters.*

Pamela arrived at six-fifteen carrying a chilled bottle of chardonnay, a jar of olives, a small bottle of gin, a bag of ice, a bottle of vermouth and two martini glasses.

"I hope you're up for a party," she said, setting the stuff down on the kitchen counter. "It's been a hard day."

"Can't argue with that."

"I have half my stuff in this town and the other half up in L.A. Seems like whatever I'm looking for is always at the other place."

"I hope that doesn't apply here."

Pamela smiled. "Who knows? The night's early."

"How do you like our town?"

"Not bad. But my friends are up there."

"You'll make new ones," said Jerome. "This place

is friendly."

Pamela took the two glasses to the sink for a rinse.

"You drink martinis?"

"Been known to. Not notorious, though."

"What are you notorious for?"

Jerome opened the bag of ice and filled the shaker. Pamela dried the glasses.

"Cooking."

Jerome couldn't believe his luck. Thank God for her being surplused. She'd still be up in LA and those guys up there would be drooling. Instead…,

Pamela poured a few drops of vermouth over the ice in each glass. "What are we having?"

"Teriyaki chicken, grilled with veggies, over rice."

"I brought a chardonnay. Hope you don't mind."

*I'll drink toilet water if I can drink it with you. Let's do it naked.* "Perfect."

Pamela pulled the curtains aside and looked outside. "It's raining."

"Supposed to be with us for a few days."

"I can't drive in the rain."

*Just keeps getting better. We'll get drunk, light a couple of candles and listen to the storm. I'll give her a massage, a few hickeys on her neck, up inside her thighs…,*

"I'm sure I can find a place for you to sleep."

"On the couch?"

"Bed's more comfortable."

"Where would you sleep?" said Pamela, eyes now sparkling.

"Tell you what. I'll…,"

The phone rang. Whoever it was, Jerome was not interested.

"Aren't you going to answer?"

"Nope."

Riiing.

"It could be important."

"I doubt it. I...,"

"It could be your parents, or...,"

"I've been getting a lot of wrong numbers lately."

Riiing.

"Don't you have an answering machine?'

"It broke. I was going to get one today, but I got busy."

"If you don't have an answering machine, you should answer it."

Riiing.

"There is no law that says I have to answer my phone, just like I don't have to answer my door."

"Fine." Pamela returned to fixing the drinks. "It's your conscience."

Riiing.

*Don't want to get on her bad side. Don't want her to think that I'm insensitive. She can find out all of the bad stuff later.*

He picked up the receiver with a sigh. "Hello."

"Oh good. Finally found somebody. This is Pierce, at the Center. We need someone to go over to Building Seven and check for dial tone."

"I don't work in that department anymore. I transferred out a while back. Sorry."

"You used to work there?"

"Yea."

"So, you would know how to check for dial tone?"

"Well..., yea. But I don't work in that...,"

"But you're on the list. Here's the problem. This woman, who lives out in the boondocks, doesn't have dial tone and she's worried that she might get flooded out."

"Dial tone is not going to save her. If she's worried about flooding, she needs to get to higher ground."

"It's a potential lawsuit. We have to dispatch someone."

"Like I said, I don't work in that group anymore."

"No one else is answering their phone."

"You trying to tell me that all of those people, probably thirty of them, are not home on a stormy night?"

"You're the first one I can get hold of. I have to send somebody. Hey, man. It's easy money. Are you close to that office?"

"Yea. It's only a couple of miles. Hang on."

Jerome put his hand over the receiver. "So much for answering the phone. It's the Center. They want me to go over to Building Seven and check for dial tone."

"How long will that take?"

"Half hour."

"Go. I'll stay here and have a drink. See you when you get back."

"You don't mind?"

"No. I'll listen to some music. That all right?"

Jerome smiled. "Perfect."

## Building Seven

*Yes! We have dial tone. Not my problem. Pamela, here I come. They're gonna have to call an outside guy for this. Just need to let Pierce know.*

"Control Center, Pierce here."
"Hey, Pierce. This is Jerome."
"What did you find?"
"Two alarms, cleared them."
"Saw that on my screen. Thanks."
"And I've got dial tone leaving."
"You do?"
"Right. Guess you'll have to get an outside guy."
"Wait. Says here it's going to a concentrator"
"Correct. The other end of that is out in the field."
"Technically, that's still a part of Building Seven. The outside crew has no jurisdiction over it."
"What are you saying?"
"You're going to have to go out there and make sure you have dial tone leaving the concentrator."
"What? That's twenty miles away! It's out in the boondocks!"
"Oh. So you know where it is."
"Of course, I do. But I'm not going. I'm not in this department anymore. My responsibilities are in power. You'll have to call someone else."
"Technically, since you accepted the call-out, you're on the clock for two hours. You've still got an hour and a half to go."
"I've got company waiting for me at home."
"Then you shouldn't have accepted the call-out."
"You didn't give me much choice."
"I can't help that. My job is to get someone out on emergencies. You accepted."

"The concentrator is on a hill," said Jerome, trying to keep his temper in check. "The hut is grounded. That makes it a lightning rod. I'm going to be on my knees out there, in the mud, in a lightning storm. You're going to risk my life by sending me out to check for dial tone so that a woman, who is not in danger if she would only move her lazy ass to higher ground, can have the comfort of knowing that she can make one last call before she is swept away?"

"Yes. And technically, if you don't go, I have to report it."

Technically, he was right. Needs of the company and all that. You can get fired, take it to the union, have it go into some kind of arbitration for months while you try to find some other kind of employment, unless you've got something saved up. Not. Jerome had seen these kinds of cases go both ways.

"All right," said Jerome, coldly. "Against my better judgment. And if I get hurt in any way, I'll make sure that your name comes up in my lawsuit. Put that in your report."

Jerome missed the turn-off the first time by. It'd been a few years since he'd been out here and the brush had grown. They used to keep it clear so that it was easy to spot. But after the hut was vandalized a few times, they put in alarms, better locks, surveillance, and let the brush grow to help hide the turn-off.

It wasn't safe to make a U-turn for another mile, the road being winding and narrow. To be caught half way through the turn in this rain, a sure way to die. Luckily, few other cars were on the road.

All smart people are home, thought Jerome, thinking of Pamela. He'd called, and she'd agreed to stay for a little longer. But she didn't sound too happy about it.

Doubling back, Jerome found the turn-off and drove up the hill. At least they'd managed to keep it graveled. He waited for the rain to subside and then ran to the hut, a small cabinet about four feet high and eight feet wide, inserted the key and opened the doors.

*If lightning's going to get me, at least it'll be instant. I won't know what hit me. I might see a flash and even hear the thunder. But what I'll really be experiencing is my eyes popping out and my ears exploding.*

The hut was bolted down to a large slab of concrete, the only level part of the hill. But years of erosion had brought a layer of mud over the top that no one ever bothered to sweep or shovel away. His last footsteps would be recorded in the mud.

*Damn you, Pierce. Get your lazy ass out of your chair and come out here yourself. Easy to tell someone else what to do.*

He fumbled with the clips of his handset, both being slippery in the rain, and then clipped them onto the terminals, making sure they didn't touch each other and short out.

No dial tone.

Calling in to the Center, Jerome asked for Pierce.

"Not here," said a woman named Cindy. "He left early. Said he had some kind of emergency."

"He sent me out on a no dial tone report."

"Got it, right here in front of me. What did you find?"

"I don't have any dial tone out here. The trouble must be in the concentrator."

"Let me see. I'll pull it up on the screen."

Clicking sounds of her keyboard mixed together

58

with her breathing. Moments passed. It starting raining hard again. Lightning flashed across the sky with a crack of thunder. Jerome twitched involuntarily and huddled against the box.

"I see the problem. It's in software. The switch doesn't know that this line is going to a concentrator. There. That should fix it. Check again."

Much to Jerome's surprise, he had dial tone. "Yea. Yea, I do!"

"Better get out of that rain. I've been on that hill. Aren't you worried about lightning?"

"Yea," said Jerome, feeling his anger building. Cindy was a Goddess as far as he was concerned. "Tell me. Should Pierce have known this?"

"Yea. But that's such a little part of everything else that we do, it's easy to overlook."

"But you found it."

"Only because I've seen this trouble before. Better get out of there while you can."

"Thanks, Cindy. I'll buy you a cup if our paths ever cross."

"Thanks, just doing my job."

Heading home, Jerome saw one tree actually blown over, others looking like they would sometime soon, lots of lightning and heavy, driven rain. Pamela was gone when he arrived. She'd left a note:

Jerome,

Maybe next time. I am drunk and starving.

Call me tomorrow.

Jerome called as soon as he read the note and again two hours later.

No answer.

Sometimes

*It ain't you, Babe.*
*It's got nothin' to do with you.*
*Never. Cause I love how you smile, how you do*
*your hair.*
*I love how we laugh together.*
*It ain't you, Babe. That's true.*

*You gotta believe that.*

*But I've got another, and she's a whore*
*And when I'm with her, my heart's in the wind.*
*I don't wanna go, but..., no way to say no*
*cause she's callin' seven twenty-four.*

*Ain't no excuse for what I do.*
*Don't even know why.*
*I just do.*
*Sometimes, no matter how hard I try*
*to ignore, her call's too strong and...,*
*you gotta understand, I'm tryin'.*

*Inside, there's nothin' here I'm trying to hide*
*but sometimes I've gotta go*
*get away, get along*
*on my own sometimes*
*I can't ignore her call.*
*She's there and she's got what I want*
*so I prostitute myself,*
*and us.*
*And when she says, It's a buck sixty-nine*
*and I don't care*
*about the change*
*cause the colors are red and blue and...,*

60

*any one of these stars*
*will make my day*
*it's not that far away*
*sometimes.*

*I hear all you cars,*
*your brakes and horns*
*and even rain comin' down*
*don't dampen my soul,*
*'cause sometimes*
*I hear music*
*sounds of living*
*cut by the edge*
*spilling out my time*
*just to get this feeling*
*sometimes.*

*She don't like it*
*like I do, sometimes she say*
*I got it all wrong. Oh Baby,*
*you know how I am.*
*Sometimes our souls touch, lying there*
*breathless, falling away, spent.*

*Sometimes I gotta…,*

*What's this?*
*These cars…, I know these cars.*
*What's goin' on inside?*

*Sometimes, life throws a curve.*

## Shutdown

Becky, the night person, midnight to eight, was used to calm, relaxed nights where all she had to do was answer the rare phone call, run routines on the equipment, most of it in software so that all she had to do was start the program, wait a couple of hours and then sign it off after fixing any troubles it had found, mostly nothing, or referring to the day crew the stuff she could not fix, which was most everything. The rest of the time was snooze time.

So, she was not happy when the equipment just started shutting down, sometime after two in the morning, two-sixteen and thirty-four seconds to be exact. No warning. Stuff just started failing, refusing the prompt to reset and go back into service. Everything was going down, down, down and it wasn't long before she knew that the entire office would be off the air, out of service, kaput.

Darin was there by two forty-five. As soon as he entered the room that provided power to Becky's equipment, even before he flipped on the light switch, he knew that something major had gone wrong. He was expecting the steady hum of the transformers, the buzzing of the rectifiers and converters, enough noise that, under normal conditions, one would have to talk loudly for any conversation to occur.

But the room was quiet. And in the middle of all this quiet, the one thing that should have been heard loud and clear was the bell, the annoying bong-bong-bong sound of the major alarm. There should have been red lights glowing everywhere, bells and confusion but, except for the hum of the overhead fluorescent lights, there was hardly a sound.

"Not good," said Becky, following Darin into the room.

"It's like..., everything's turned off," said Darin, now noticing a growing pain in his gut. There was no training for this, no way to know where to start. All of his training had been on working equipment. No one ever said the whole place could just flat-ass shut down.

All of the equipment was still turned on, just not doing anything.

"No rush," said Becky, sarcastically. "No calls are going through, about fifty thousand dollars a minute in lost revenues."

"Don't remind me," Darin replied, knowing that this incident would go far beyond his boss. This would go beyond the district managers, the VP's, all the way to the top. There would be an investigation, the results of which would go to..., what does it matter after that?

Darin couldn't think of anything worse happening and found himself wishing for a major earthquake, a collapsed roof to destroy all of the equipment, anything to divert attention from the scene at hand.

There had been a lot of activity in this room earlier in the day. He had been up here working with the vendors, helping them haul in equipment, making sure everything was going according to plan.

Looking up, he saw that the alarms had been disabled. Someone had stuck a piece of cardboard into the bell that should be clanging and, checking further, he found that someone had jammed a toothpick into the relay that turned on the red lights and rang the bells, sending warnings out to the world. He removed the toothpick. The room remained quiet.

People were starting to arrive now. Becky's boss, looking like he'd jumped straight out of bed and into a pair of jeans and T-shirt, three technicians from another floor, the district manager with pillow hair, Merry Dick Tracy, red-eyed and without her make-up.

Darin turned the AC switch on the rectifier to OFF, and then back to ON. The equipment went clunk, but did not stay on. Everyone was looking to him for guidance, keeping their distance after a few initial questions, letting him think it through. No one else knew what to do. Martin arrived.

"Christ Almighty, Darin! What happened?"

"Don't know. Place was dead on arrival."

"We have AC to this floor?"

"Yea, all three phases. Looks good."

"Control fuses are in?"

"Yea. I don't understand...,"

In the middle of all the commotion, Robby walked in. He stood quietly in the back of the room, preferring the shadowy section of the wall by the long rows of batteries. Then he went to a rectifier away from the crowd, opened the door to the equipment, scratched his head a couple of times, and then reached inside, jammed a stick into a relay, forcing it to stay on, and then turned the equipment back on. It stayed turned on and started humming loudly, going all the way to maximum output, trying to do what twenty rectifiers were supposed to do.

Hearing the sound of working equipment, Darin and Martin joined him, saw what he had done and proceeded onto the next rectifier to do the same. Roberta arrived and joined in. As the place started to come back to life, Martin turned to answer the

64

onslaught of questions.

As the alarms faded, so did the crowd, back to their areas for damage repair. The real questions would come tomorrow. There would be meetings, inquiries, questions, questions and more questions. They, upper management whose bonus pay would be affected, would insure that this sort of thing never happened again.

Two main questions were going to be asked. What caused it? And who blocked the alarms? People get famous for events like this. Your name is in all of the reports. It goes all the way up. At this point, Darin did not know if he would be one of the heroes or the sacrificial goat. He found Robby over in the corner working on an inverter, trying to get the alarm to clear.

"Thanks, Robby. I had no idea what to do."

"Problem is," Robby replied, pushing the ALARM RESET button, watching the red light blink off, delay, and then blink back on, "we don't know why it happened."

"So, the next time is, whenever.?

"Exactly." Robby laughed, an evil kind of laugh. "Kinda scary, ain't it?"

Darin noticed then that Robby was not making eye contact like he normally would, and that his eyes were glazed. "How did you find out? The Center call you?"

"Naw." Robby pushed the button again.. "I was goin' home and saw all the cars out front. So I decided to come in and see for myself."

"Lucky for me. I owe you."

Robby smiled his big, wide smile, looking at his feet, "Well..., you're teachin' me, too. So, we're even."

Turning to go, he pointed to the alarm. "That'll

go out soon as the batteries charge."

"Got it," said Darin . "Thanks, again."

And with no further ado, Robby left the room. Martin came over.

"Is he leaving?"

"I guess. Everything seems to be working fine. There's not much else to do except charge the batteries. I'll stay for that."

"Talked to the Center," said Roberta, joining them. "Alarms test OK now."

"Thanks," said Darin. "The Center call you?"

"No. I was coming home from a movie and saw all the cars out front."

"I owe you. Thanks."

"Good work, you guys," said Martin, patting them both on the back. "I'll call a meeting for tomorrow morning, ten-o'clock, and we'll hash this out. Is it under control now?"

"Yea," said Darin. "At least now we know what to do if it happens again. And we have alarms."

"OK," said Martin, turning to go. "See you guys tomorrow. Roberta, we'll pay you and Robby for a call-out as well. Good job. Thanks again."

Martin left. Roberta lingered.

"Well," said Darin. "That scared the hell out of me."

She laughed. "Glad it was your office and not mine."

"You think you've got it all covered and then you get hit from behind."

"That's the truth."

"That's what I don't like about this job. What movie did you see?"

It was Roberta's hesitation that caught Darin by surprise. You don't know what movie you just saw? The words were out of his mouth before he even had a chance to stop them.

"How're you and Daryl doing these days?"

"We...," Roberta was choosing her words carefully. "We're not together any more."

"Oh. Sorry to hear that. I shouldn't have asked."

Roberta smiled. "It's OK. You didn't know. Nobody else does either, so don't say anything."

"Right. Anything I can do?"

"No." Roberta sighed. "You need any more help?"

"I got it. Thanks. Give me a call if you want to talk."

"Right."

And then Darin found himself standing alone in the noisy, buzzing, humming room.

# Meeting

"OK, you guys. Let's get going," said Martin, setting his papers on the table. "While you're getting your coffee and donuts, pick up a copy of this list on your way back to your seats. It's a list of the latest jobs and whose offices they're in."

"Is this a newer list than the one you handed out last time?" said Darin, setting his coffee down at his usual spot at the far end of the table.

"Yes. Floyd's got six new jobs starting up and they're all over the place. And there's a lot of night coverage coming up, so we're going to be hustling for the next few months."

Carly found her usual spot at the end of the table next to Martin and plopped down. "Did you ever put in any requests for more help?"

"Nope. By the time they're qualified the work will be over. And then we'd have a surplus of people and you guys would be bitching about that."

"We don't bitch," said Tony, taking a plain old-fashioned donut from the pink box. "We point out problems."

"Sounds like bitching to me," said Martin.

"That's because you're in management," said Carly, opening the lid to a bottle of orange juice.

"I've done your job. To hear all of your complaining, you'd think it was hard work. But, I know better. You guys have it easy."

"Nothing ever changed in your time," said Tony. "You had the same old, crappy equipment since forever. You didn't have to test the new stuff, calibrate everything and...,"

"Didn't make the kind of money you guys are making either. With all this overtime, you guys are making more than me."

"Not to mention, higher profiles," said Sergio. "Make a mistake today and you're famous. Back in your day when nothing was going on...,"

"Watch it," said Martin.

Sergio laughed. "OK. In olden times, people didn't worry about losing their phone for a few hours. Today, you'd think the world had come to an end."

"It does," said Martin. "Which is why I called this meeting. Hey, everybody. Let's get seated so we can discuss what happened at Building One last night. It  went down around two A.M. and we don't know why."

Tony seated himself next to Roberta. "Down as in, lost power for a few minutes but customers never knew? Or down as in, off the air?"

"That's it," said Martin. "Off the air for two hours. I'll be writing lots of letters to upper management, so you guys have to tell me what we're doing to find the problem and how we're going to cover our asses until then."

Jerome leaned back in his chair. "We don't know what caused it?"

"Nope," said Darin. "Place was dead on arrival. Everything had shut down."

"You couldn't duplicate the problem?"

"Duplicate it? I was just glad to see it go away."

"Me too," said Martin. "I don't ever want to see that again. But we still have to know what caused it. What are we looking for?"

"No alarms?" said Carly. "Didn't anybody hear or see the alarms? We should have had a few hours of warning."

"What alarms?" said Darin, rolling his pencil across his note pad. "They'd been picked out.

Somebody disabled them."

"Was Spark Electric in the building?" said Carly. "Those guys...,"

"They were, pulling cable up in the racks. But they had everything protected. Kilmore Electric was there, too."

"In live equipment? Tony asked.

"Wiring stuff I powered down. But then we'd test and turn it back up."

"We wouldn't be in this mess if we'd had alarms," said Martin, glancing at Darin. "How long do we have on batteries if we lose power?"

"About four hours."

"Doesn't make sense," said Tony. "If everything shut down at two in the morning, and we had four hours reserve, then the problem occurred some time around ten the night before. Who was there at ten?"

"No vendors in the building at that time," said Darin. "I checked the visitors log."

"Inside job," said Carly, the idea now whetting her appetite. "Who else was in the building?"

"We can't go there," said Martin. "That's for Security. Our job is to figure out why this happened and to cover the place until we do."

"I blocked the alarms in the morning," said Darin, "because I didn't want the Center to keep getting a bunch of bogus stuff while I was testing. But I put everything back to normal and tested with them before I went to lunch."

"What time was that?" Martin asked.

"About one. No one was allowed to do any work when I was gone. We worked until about three-thirty. Alarms tested fine then when I locked up the room."

"So, between three-thirty and ten," said Martin.

"Six and a half hours."

"What time did the vendors sign out," Tony asked. "Maybe somebody came back to finish up."

Darin made a note of it. "I'll call the guard and have him check the log."

"How are we going to split this overtime?" Carly asked. "There's a question."

"Shouldn't be any," said Darin. "We just have to find the trouble."

"What are the odds of that?" Jerome asked. "It's only happened once."

"Could happen again at any time. I should be over there testing right now."

"Overtime is important," said Sergio, getting into the conversation. "You've already got more overtime than the rest of us. We'd like some of that, too."

"Thing is," said Darin. "I know the job and what the vendors have been doing. I know where to look."

"You can have the troubleshooting part of it," said Carly. "Who is going to be sitting in the office twenty-four hours a day until the trouble's found? That's what I'm talking about."

"Collecting overtime for doing *nothing*?" Darin asked, sarcastically.

"Eight hour shifts," said Sergio. "We take turns."

"All of you are right," said Martin, hoping this would not turn into another pissing match. "We should be concentrating on finding the trouble and how to go forward if we don't. Let me make a suggestion. Darin, you go look for the trouble. The rest of us will stay here and finish the meeting. If you haven't found anything by the end of your shift today, we go to the overtime list for night coverage for one night, until you come in tomorrow morning. After that we have to rely on the alarms. Everybody agree to that?"

And for once, the crew agreed.

"Where's Robby?" Carly asked, looking around.

"Don't know," Martin replied. "He sure was a big help last night. Maybe he overslept."

"Did you try calling?" Darin asked, now remembering Robby's odd behavior.

"Calling and paging," said Martin. "No reply. If you see him, tell him to give me a call."

"Right," said Darin, getting up.

# Floating Ground

Sitting on the floor under a fluorescent light, leaning up against the wall, Robby was busy studying a schematic when Darin came into the room. Next to him was a crumpled up white bag which Darin recognized as belonging to the Mexican fast food place north of the building, and a soft drink.

"Hey, Robby. Missed you at the meeting."

Looking up from the prints, Robby smiled. "They never say nothin' anyway."

"Martin wants you to give him a call."

"Yea, suppose I will later. Look at this." Robby pointed to the schematic spread out on the floor. "It can't be a bad piece of equipment that caused the problem cause one of 'em can't do that. It would just turn itself off or burn itself up. We didn't have nothin' like that."

"Right." Darin nodded. "So whatever failed had control over the whole room."

"Riiight." Robby pointed to one part of the schematic. "See this relay here?"

"HV relay? Yea. Controls the whole plant," said Darin, admiring how much Robby had learned.

"So, if it operates everything shuts down?"

"I guess," said Darin, now seeing where Robby was heading, and at the same time feeling nervous with the idea of failing the plant to prove a theory. "What? You going to try it?"

Robby, after taking a sip from his Coke, stood and smiled. "We'll still be on batteries, right. No one will notice anything. You feel lucky today?"

"If that relay operates, the power plant shuts down and...,"

"And we have four hours to bring it back up,"

said Robby. "We already know how to do that."

"Yea, but...,"

This was what Darin didn't like about power, the unexpected and the resulting consequences, being famous for doing something badly.

*If you do this job for twenty years and no one knows your name, you've done an excellent job.*

"You have to know if this part works," said Robby.

"I agree, but..., why do I feel this pending doom?"

"Check this out," said Robby, walking over to the relay in the control panel, motioning for Darin to follow. "That's the relay, right there. Keep your eye on it."

"What are you going to do?"

Robby climbed up a small stepladder and, after insuring that Darin was watching the relay, pounded on the bottom of the cable rack.

Clank. Clank. Bam! Clank! Bam! Bam! Clunk. Clank. Bam! Red lights flashed and bells began to clang.

Darin's jaw dropped. "Jesus!"

Robby was laughing now, giddy with the discovery. "Found this just before you got here. Whole place just dropped dead, said to myself, oh, shit!"

Darin went to the rectifiers, turning them back on.

Robby came back down the ladder. "I called the Center and let 'em know we were testing."

"You could've warned me. Robby...,"

"You wouldn't a done it. Now you know."

"No shit."

"That relay operate?"

"Um, no, come to think of it. Never did."

"Way I see it," said Robby. "You've got a wire that's shorted to ground, right there in the cable rack, maybe the one from the HV relay. Anybody been up there lately?"

"Yea. Spark Electric, yesterday. Man! You scared the hell out of me! Guess I owe you lunch after we fix it."

"I'll take it," said Robby. "And when you come down to my turf to give me a hand, I'll buy."

"Fair enough. How's Tanya doing these days?"

"All right."

"You lucky dog. She's hot."

"Bossy, too," said Robby. "Keeps tryin' to tell me what to do."

## Lunch

Had he been wearing a business suit, the man could have stood in front of the audience and projected the company's earnings for the next quarter or advised the investment firm of the best stocks or mutual funds to buy, all the while presenting the philosophy of the new CEO.

His eyes were lost in thought, seeing some distant vision that the rest of us can only imagine. He was the physics professor contemplating the composition of dark matter, the driven scientist proposing a new dimension, a visionary with a plan for world peace. Had he been successful we would have believed him, this man with that honest looking face.

Sitting at the table, Robby watched his approach, slow, deliberate, checking the ground for spare change, maybe an empty bottle, or perhaps a discarded can. He found a cigarette butt, still long enough for a few more puffs, picked it up, brushed off the grit from the asphalt, blew off the remaining dust and put it in his pocket, the one that wasn't torn.

This was a hole-in-the-wall kind of place. The locals knew about it and occasionally some tourists would stop in, wishing they could have found something a little more upscale with parking. But if you wanted good food and didn't mind who else you sat with, this was the place.

There were only five tables, two with four chairs each, and the other three with benches. Unable to seat the crowd, they'd put two smaller tables outside, each with only two chairs so they wouldn't completely block the walkway for the rest of the businesses that made up the shopping center.

And still the place was crowded, forcing the locals to get to know each other, both a good and a bad thing. Sometimes people ate standing next to the soft drink machine, apologetically blocking the way to the napkins and straws.

The outside tables were interesting, not only because they butted up to the parking lot, but because you could eat contentedly while others, not yet served or, standing in line and waiting to place an order, could gaze longingly as you ate your food. Another dimension to the outside table dining is that you might not always be safe, meaning, eat quickly and watch your back.

There was the guy that stopped by wearing black leather, barely able to stand up in his black boots, more on his ankles than his feet, skin tight leather pants, partially ripped in the crotch, unwashed and sweaty in the hot afternoon sun, gazing drunkenly at the young male executive in a business suit who shifted uncomfortably in his chair.

Or the time that the black dude popped his head in the front door and yelled, "All you white mother fuckers should feel guilty, sittin' here eating while I'm fucking starving. Come on, man! Somebody buy me a meal! You owe me and you know it! I deserve a lunch from one of you rich, white mother fuckers. Who's it gonna be?"

And the place got quiet, all of the Mexicans and Asians, and every other variation of the species, everyone staring quietly at their food.

"I'm going to get a refill," said Robby. "You need one?"

Darin checked his cup, holding it up to the light. "Nah. I'll get one when we leave."

Robby returned with his drink, set it on the table and then headed over to the hollow faced man, handed him a burrito and a few extra dollars. More surprised than anything, the man nodded with a slight smile, and then slowly headed away from the crowd.

"That was kind," said Darin, wiping his hands on a napkin.

"He doesn't get enough to eat."

"You know him?"

"No. But I know what he's going through."

"Why didn't you just give him some money?"

"He won't buy food."

"Just find the nearest bottle?"

"Whatever. He won't even eat all of that, just half and then trade the rest."

"For whatever?"

"Right."

Robby didn't have any training in power and didn't finish high school. But he had good instincts. After learning that Darin knew how to read schematics, Robby invited  him over to one of his buildings to help with a case of trouble.

Together, a good team. Coming across broken equipment, Robby would say what he thought the trouble was and point out the locations of the parts. Darin would point out those parts on the schematic, see what makes it tick and, working together, equipment got fixed.

"They sure put the screws to you," said Robby, between bites.

"How so?"

"Stuck you in the hub. They should have started you out in some smaller offices, help you get used to it."

"Nobody else wanted the place."

"No lie. Anything goes wrong in that building, you make the news."

"Scares the hell out of me sometimes. You ever hear those turbines start?"

"Yea. I used to start 'em. They sound like they're gonna blow up."

"What do they wind up to? About twenty thousand RPM?"

"Don't think it's that high, more like four or five. I hate it when the afterburner's kick in, you know, just when it comes up to speed? Sounds like it's gonna come right out the side."

"I ran out of the room first time that happened. I wanted some concrete between me and it."

"Don't think the wall's gonna stop it," said Robby, grinning. "If that ever happens, just keep runnin' and hope it don't catch up."

## Easy Roller

"Today'll be easy," said Smitty, leading Jerome out through the double doors of the antenna site.

Jerome paused under the tower to look up at the antenna. In spite of all the hard feelings from that day, he was actually proud of the fact that he could always point up at that dish and say that he was part of the team that put it up there.

"Good. I can use an easy day."

Smitty pointed to a reel of wave-guide located beneath the tower, wheels blocked to keep it from rolling. "We're gonna roll it out. Your job is to hold one end of it up here, keep it from sliding down the hill."

Jerome eyed the reel suspiciously. "Don't you have a big bar and a couple of stands so we could just uncoil it in place?"

"I'd need a bigger truck if I had to carry all that stuff and then I couldn't get to half the sites. We do this all the time. I'm going up the tower to set the brackets. I'll be ready 'bout the same time as you and Hal get this unwound."

"Let me go get my gloves out of the truck."

"Won't need them," said Smitty. "All you gotta do is stand here and hold one end while Hal rolls out the other."

"Where's Billy?"

"Had to let him go."

"You fired him?"

"Transfer. Didn't want him hurtin' his self. Got him an inside job but he filed a grievance, so's he may be comin' back."

Jerome didn't like hearing this. The crew worked the whole mountain range up and down the state, couple of days here, a couple of days there, always on the road. And with one guy already missing and the other relieved of his present duties, this crew was now two men short.

And since this was the second time he'd been volunteered, it would soon come to everyone's attention that he had experience in hanging antennas, something he was loath to have on his resume. This could easily become another one of those 'needs of the company' situations.

Coming around the corner of the building, Hal smiled when he saw Jerome and came over to shake his hand. "Didn't expect to see you again. Most times, people only volunteer once."

"I've been volunteered twice," said Jerome. "I've got the back country loop so I guess they figure it's only natural for me to be the one."

"Maybe you ought to consider joining our crew."

Jerome laughed, shaking his head. "No. My parents are getting old," he lied. "I've got to stay close."

"Just hold on to the end of it," said Hal, kicking the blocks out from beneath the reel. He reached down and grabbed one of them as the reel started to roll and stuffed it into his back pocket. "Should only take about fifteen minutes. Just keep this end of it here."

Holding the end of the wave-guide with one hand, Jerome found a place to dig in with his feet and wrapped one arm around part of the antenna's base. Hal looked on doubtfully but didn't offer any advice.

The first few full rotations of the reel had almost no effect at all on Jerome's grip. In fact, he even let go for a few seconds while he readjusted his grip to the antenna tower. Subsequent rotations of the reel, however, with Hal now about twenty feet away, began tugging hard enough that Jerome had to let go of the antenna and keep two hands on the wave-guide.

When the reel was about half empty, it pulled Jerome off of the platform and into the dirt. The reel had momentum, weight, and gravity all working for it.

The outside circumference of the reel, Jerome noticed, stays the same while the inside circumference, the uncoiling wave-guide, gets smaller and smaller. Jerome soon realized that the bigger the difference between the two, the more he was going to slide. Short of Hal picking up the reel and unwinding it in place, a physical impossibility, this operation was only going to get worse.

*How much room does it take to keep a bar and two folding stands in the truck?*

*Why not tie a rope to the wave-guide and attach the other end to the truck's rear bumper?*

*Or..., why not attach the wave-guide to the device that's going to be used to haul it up the tower?*

Sitting, hanging onto the wave-guide and sliding down the hill through the brush, Jerome wondered about many things, until his heel caught a rock, pulled him up to the standing position and then back down, face first, all the way to the end of the ride.

# Routines

"Today," said Martin, opening the maintenance manual for the turbines, "we're going to learn how to clean the impeller."

The crew was gathered in the engine room of Darin's building, facing Martin, who was standing with his back to the control panel of engine number one. The room itself, about sixty feet wide and thirty feet deep, housed two large turbine engines, now turned off but used to generate stand-by power for the building.

"Impeller?" Bart asked.

"On the air intake," said Martin, pointing to the other end of the engine. "It sucks the air in and forces it into the combustion chamber."

"Engine's running fine," said Darin. "Why are we doing this?"

"It's one of our routines."

Darin checked the engine hour meter. "This one's got less than a thousand hours on it."

Martin studied the chart. "These engines are over ten years old. What's it going to hurt to clean them?"

"Nothing," said Darin. "I just hate to fix what ain't broke."

Tony strolled over to the rear of the engine. "I don't see any way to get to the impeller. How are we going to clean it?"

"Says here," said Martin, reading from the book. "Says to spray an approved cleaner into the air intake and...,"

"Wait," said Darin, holding up his hand. "What's an approved cleaner?"

"This stuff right here," said Martin, pointing to

a five-gallon bucket at his side. "Talked to this guy out at the airport."

Robby strolled over to the day tank, set his drink down and then went over to inspect the can. "Did you tell him what we're gonna do?"

"Yea. He said this is what the mechanics use."

Robby smiled his big, wide grin. "You did say, jet engine, right?"

"Yes," said Martin. "I did say that."

"Wait," said Carly, now joining the conversation. "Is that stuff *explosive*?"

"It's approved," said Martin.

Robby and Darin exchanged glances. Even though neither of them said a word, they both knew this was probably going to be the event they had just talked about, keep running, don't let it catch up.

"Doesn't sound too good," said Robby, shaking his head.

"Is the engine supposed to be turned off when we do this?" Bart asked.

"No," Martin replied. "Says to keep the engine running."

Roberta joined Tony over by the combustion chamber. "How hot does it get in there?"

"I think I read something like two thousand de-grees."

"What happens when the cleaning fluid reaches the fuel in the combustion chamber?" Robby asked. "Does the engine run faster? Or does the governor keep a lid on it?"

"Shouldn't do anything like that," said Martin. "Since this is the approved stuff."

"Why are we trusting this guy?" Jerome asked. "Who is he, anyway?"

"He owns the parts shop on the runway. He

waited on me personally."

"Not, auto parts, right?" Robby asked.

"Do jets even land over there?" said Carly. "I've never heard one. He must've thought you meant reciprocating."

"I said, jet."

"If the engine overheats," said Darin, "it'll shut down on over-temp. How do you get it started again with all that fluid in there?"

"We're not pouring it in. It's a fine mist."

"How do we tell when it's clean if we can't see it?" Carly asked, getting her two cents in. This is what she loved about this crew. No mercy for the one in the middle. "If it's already running fine, how is it going to run better?"

"Cooler," Martin replied. "It'll run cooler."

Robby walked back to the day tank. "Think I'll get my drink out of the way, just in case." He put his Coke next to the door leading into the hallway. "Maybe I should put it outside the door."

Using her foot, Carly pushed her purse over to Robby's drink and stood next to it.

"I'll guard your drink, Robby."

"If it was dangerous," Martin replied, with a hint of exasperation. "They'd say so."

"Are they still in business?" Tony asked, going over to look at the can of solvent.

"Because if we blow it up," said Darin, finishing that thought. "*They* are going to have to come fix it. Anybody here knows how to put one of these babies back together? I thought not. Back to you, Martin."

"We'll take turns spraying," said Martin. "Everybody should get a shot at it. Let's get going! Everybody have ear plugs?"

"I'll stay here and watch the engine temp," said Robby, standing at the front of the engine. And then, laughing, he looked over at Carly and said, "Cause if it blows up, it's gonna go out the side."

"I'll be the door opener," said Carly, putting her hand on the knob.

"I'm with you," said Bart, joining her.

Martin pushed the start button and the turbine began its long, slow start, a low hum at first, building to a disconcerting low roar.

Everyone hurried to put in their earplugs.

Just when it seemed like the engine had been winding too long and that it wasn't actually going to start, a secondary burst of fuel was injected into the combustion chamber and, sounding like sustained thunder, the engine screamed up to running speed and leveled off. More than one or two took a step away, edging toward the door.

Since it was Darin's office, it was expected that he be the first to do the routine. After pumping up the pressure for the sprayer, he held the nozzle in front of the air intake and squeezed the trigger once for about a second. The engine didn't seem to care one-way or the other. He squeezed the trigger again, this time for a few seconds with no apparent difference in speed or lower operating temperature.

With the roaring of the engine, talking was not possible. Martin motioned, by squeezing his hand into a fist, for Darin to squeeze the trigger longer for a continuous spray. Darin motioned, as one would to guests at their front door, to come in or, in this case, for Martin to come over and do it himself.

Martin was in management and, by contract, could not touch the equipment unless the crew was not present, as in a strike or in some kind of emergency. Technically, any one of them could file a grievance for Martin having pushed the Start Button.

In other times, they might have done that. To-day, everybody just wanted to go to lunch and get back to their respective jobs so whatever helped that process along, as a crew, they were for it.

Tony took the sprayer and with Martin's prod-ding, squeezed the trigger in longer bursts, moving the nozzle around for even distribution. The en-gine's high-pitched whine sounded lively, spinning a little faster, like having the impeller clean actually meant something.

Carly opened the door to the hallway, Bart at her side and Roberta narrowed her distance to the door. Darin joined Robby at the control panel at the front of the engine.

The first boom was not loud, more like a hic-cup or a burp in the smooth, steady screaming of the engine. Darin had not heard anything like that before and, thinking that it was his imagina-tion, glanced over at Robby whose eyes were wide, and each knew that they had both heard the same thing.

The second boom actually moved a little bit of air through the room. It wasn't just the sound that got your attention. It was the accompanying thud of air hitting your chest. Martin frantically waved for Tony to stop, something that Tony needed not be told as he was already setting the sprayer down and running for the door.

The third explosion was more sustained, boom, boom...., Boom..., BOOM!

Carly was through the door first but didn't stick around to hold it open. On her heels were the rest of the crew and Martin. Hitting the hallway, they went one way or another. It was going to blow.

The urge to turn and run was instinctual. Ev-eryone did, but not everyone could get through the door at the same time. Being last in line, Robby glanced back at the instrument panel and that big, red EMERGENCY SHUTDOWN button loomed larger than life. He raced back into the room, shoved it closed and, without air, the turbine whooshed to a roaring stop.

Regrouping around the slain beast, hot metal creaking against the cooler air, small whiffs of smoke spilling out from under the gaskets, the crew decided it was time to go to lunch.

Later that day, Robby and Darin returned, pushed the start button and put in their ear- plugs as the engine moved through its start sequence. One boom, more like a *whoosh*, exploded inside the chamber, and then two more followed as the engine was winding up.

Feeling the adrenalin, they both laughed nervously, ready to sprint toward the door, yet held captive by the need to push the EMERGENCY SHUTDOWN button. The engine didn't sound right, like it was straining to get air.

Fuel build-up, both of them were thinking.

And then, KA-BOOM! But before either of them could react to the sound, the engine revved up to running speed and sounded normal again.

Later, reading the manual a little more carefully, they discovered that the engine had a Reduced Speed Mode in which the engine routines were supposed to be done.

This was useless knowledge. The routine was discarded, voted out unanimously by the same crew that voted in the requirement that all engines have remote EMERGENCY SHUTDOWN buttons installed on the outside walls of all engine rooms and Darin took possession of a good garden sprayer.

## Going Down

Coming out of the maintenance office in the basement, Norm and Buck headed for the elevator, their intent being to check out the cooling towers on the third floor.

"It's not like your budget has got anything to do with what's required," said Norm. "These parts are necessary for the system to function."

"Can't add more dollars," said Buck. "We're already over budget."

Stepping into the elevator, Norm pushed THREE and CLOSE. Nothing happened. They both stood there for a moment, waiting. Buck finally reached past Norm and pressed THREE.

"I already pushed that."

"Maybe you didn't push it hard enough."

"Yea, I did. This elevator's been acting up lately. I guess it's time for me to call the company and have them come fix it."

"Did you push CLOSE?"

"Yea. I did."

Buck pushed CLOSE anyway. "Maybe you didn't push hard enough."

"I know how hard to push. I push these buttons ten or twenty times a day."

"We're still not going."

"Well," said Norm, with a sigh. "Let's take the stairs."

"It's gotta be bad contacts in one of these buttons."

"Who knows?" said Norm stepping out of the elevator. "I'll call the company when we're done."

Buck pushed button number TWO, and then the CLOSE button. "Maybe we can get to two. That saves us two flights of walking."

"I think you're wasting your time. That elevator's dead. Pull out the Emergency Stop Button and we'll block the doors open."

Buck tapped the ONE button and tapped CLOSE several more times. The door started to close. Buck held it open and motioned for Norm, who was already heading for the stairs.

"Come on. Get in."

"What am I, nuts?"

"It's working now."

"No, it isn't. The door is trying to close, that's all. You're only going to go to the first floor since you already pushed that button. And then you're going to have the same problem."

"I think the button's fixed now, whatever it was."

"You don't even know if it is a button. Could be a loose connection in the signal cable, a bad circuit pack, a faulty relay, a blown fuse...,"

"Naw. It's the simple things."

"Is that so?"

"These buttons get pushed hundreds of times a day. I'll bet...,"

"Riiight," said Norm. "You stand here and figure it out. I'll walk up to the third floor at a normal pace. Ten bucks says, I beat you."

"You're on," said Buck, letting the door close.

The elevator stopped on the first floor and the door opened. Buck pushed CLOSE repeatedly as Norm calmly walked by, smiling, heading for the stairs leading up to the second floor. The elevator door closed.

Bernie, a long distance operator for the last twenty years, had learned long ago that breaks are fifteen minutes. Not fifteen minutes and thirty seconds. Not even fifteen minutes and five seconds.

Your time began when you got up and ended when you sat down and put the headset back on.

She stood outside the second floor elevator door and anxiously pushed the button, unlit cigarette in one hand, lighter in the other. She'd been trying to quit, chewed the gum, tried the patch, forced herself to roll her own, anything to help break the habit.

Today, however, had been especially trying. Due to the storm, traffic coming into downtown was a bitch and, as a result, parking was nearly impossible. Arriving late, she'd been written up and docked pay.

Joe, her husband, didn't come home again last night. And, going out to the chicken coop to get some eggs for breakfast, she discovered that the coyotes had somehow figured out how to open the latch.

Today was a lousy day. Once in a while it's OK to slip. It's OK to give in to your desires and relieve a little pressure. It's OK to want that burning sensation of a deep drag, letting it *all* come in and, just for a moment, giving in.

It's not a menthol kind of day, either, or for social smoking, not even something to do with your hands while the drink goes down, certainly not a filtered cigarette kind of day.

*No. Joe's gone, chickens are gone and the drive home is going to suck. It's a Camel day and a Jack Daniels night.*

The elevator door opened. Bernie and Buck exchanged glances as she stepped in.

"Up, or down?' she asked.

"Just up to the third floor," said Buck. "And then you can have it."

This seemed to satisfy Bernie. Riding the elevator up to three and then down to ground was better than descending a flight of stairs to get out of the building.

Norm walked by, nodded and smiled at the two of them and then waved as he started up the next flight of stairs. Buck pushed THREE and CLOSE, several times and, when nothing happened, pounded on the CLOSE button. The elevator door calmly closed and they headed up.

Bernie studied Buck, who was staring at the elevator door. "What's the matter with the elevator?"

"Nothing."

"You were pounding on that button."

"Bad button," said Buck, not making eye contact.

"Is it dangerous?"

"No. The door doesn't close sometimes."

"That doesn't sound good."

"If it doesn't close, the elevator won't go. That's all."

"You mean, wherever the door doesn't close, you're stuck?"

"Exactly."

The elevator reached the third floor and the door opened. Norm was there, leaning against the wall, smiling.

"Ten bucks."

"I'll buy you lunch," said Buck, getting out.

Bernie pressed ONE and CLOSE. Nothing happened.

"Good luck," said Buck, leaving.

"Wait. What do I have to do?"

"Press the floor you want and then the CLOSE button," said Buck, acting as if Bernie had never pressed an elevator button before.

Bernie pressed ONE and CLOSE, again.

"That's it," said Buck. "It might take a few times."

Bernie pushed ONE and CLOSE several times, harder with each attempt and, as Norm and Buck headed down the hallway, began pounding furiously on the CLOSE button. The elevator door calmly closed and headed up.

"Hmm," said Buck, hearing her muffled shouts. "Might've pressed FOUR, as well."

Norm opened the door leading to the cooling towers.

"It will do all of the ups before it starts to come back down. She didn't look very happy. If I were you, Buck, I don't think I'd let her see you when you leave."

## Benthic

Both Robby and Floyd put their food down on the shady side of the table beneath the umbrella overlooking the courtyard, Floyd sitting so that he could keep an eye on the company car parked about fifty feet away.

The thief had thought the briefcase held something valuable, important enough to break a window. Couldn't have sold the contents for a dime, maybe five bucks for the briefcase. Six months of work. That's what it was. All of the contacts, job numbers, budgets, cost overruns, and...,

*Hell. I'd have given him a hundred just to get it back. No questions.*

"What's the matter, Floyd," said Robby, dipping one his fries into a mound of ketchup. "You've got that far away look."

Floyd poured low fat dressing over his salad, wishing it had more flavor, and then opened up a package of saltines, hoping the crackers had enough salt. "I'm just tired, Robby. I'm wanting to pack it all in."

"Aren't you about ready for retirement?'

"Another year. And it looks like they're going to squeeze me until I go."

"How long you worked for the company?"

"Thirty four years, seems like eighty."

Robby laughed. "Well, after thirty-four, one more should be easy."

"I wish. I haven't had a vacation for two years."

"No kidding?"

"Needs of the company and all of that. I'm in management. They can do whatever they want."

"You gotta have time off."

94

"Tell them. I've forgotten what time off is."

Robby took the top off of his hamburger and centered the lettuce and tomato, added ketchup and mustard. "Maybe you should go back to craft. I'm guaranteed four weeks vacation a year."

"Can't. Too many penalties against my retirement." Floyd stirred his salad around on the plate, distributing the dressing. "You ever been in a canoe?"

"No. Spent a lot of time in a row boat."

"Early some morning or around sunset, when the water's like glass, paddle out across the water and find out what it does for your soul."

"Sounds pretty good."

"I found a place up in Michigan, right on the lake, has its own dock. I could sell my house here, pay cash for that one and still put a hundred grand in the bank."

"Why don't you do it?"

"Another year until retirement. I need that medical."

"A year's not too long."

"Tell that to Darla. I keep telling her it's almost over."

"What's she say to that?"

"Says, I'm right. It's almost over. And I don't like that answer. She's always been a free spirit. She was the one on the other end of that canoe."

"Does she want to go to Michigan?"

"Says all of her friends are here. But she hasn't seen the place yet. As soon as I can, I'm going to take her. I want to launch our canoe from that dock."

"Fishing any good?"

"I hear it's good for bass."

"We used to catch catfish, throw 'em in egg batter and flour and fry 'em up."

"Nothing wrong with some good catfish."

"Bottom fish. Almost don't want to eat 'em," said Robby, laughing. "Because you don't know what they just ate."

"Ain't that the truth. When are you going to retire, Robby?"

"Ten more years. Don't know if I can wait that long."

"Ten years will go by before you know it."

"That's what scares me."

"What would you rather do?"

"Don't know. I need some time to think and I can't do it while I'm still working."

"A dilemma."

"Yea. It's like, do you want to be happy? Or, do you want to have money? Seems like there should be something in the middle. That's what I'm talking about."

"Robby."

"Yea?"

"Do you have a significant other?"

"Yea."

"What does she want to do?"

"She loves me. She'll do whatever I want."

"That's not the question. Bottom line, if you're with the right person everything is going to be OK. You gotta make sure they're with you. And if you don't believe me, imagine your life without them. Think long and hard about that."

"I hear what you're saying. But you know, there's always more to it than that. Thing's get complicated."

"Don't they ever," said Floyd, hating his salad.

A Quick Fix

"No," said Vanessa, setting her drink down. "I will not play doubles with that arrogant bastard."

"I'd do it for you," Roberta argued, pulling the bottle of wine out from the refrigerator. "You even said it'd be good for me to get out and meet new people."

Vanessa held her glass up for a refill. "You go, girl. I'll be tagging along, but not with Ron at my side."

Ron was Todd's best friend. Roberta wanted to see more of Todd. It had been a week since they'd met at the courts where her and Vanessa were playing. Breaking from their own game in the adjacent court, Todd and Ron offered to play doubles.

Vanessa's partner, Ron, tried to put the make on her almost as soon as they were on the same side of the net. They weren't crude or overt comments, just irksome. Stuff like:

Can't keep my eye on the ball. My partner's distracting me.

What's the score? She's making me lose my concentration.

Vanessa hated the man from the start. After the game there was considerable pressure for the four of them to get together again.

"Todd's all right," Vanessa confessed, later in the day. "But if I have to spend another five minutes with Ron, I'll cut his balls off."

Roberta laughed. If Vanessa thought you were a pink polka-dotted grizzly duck, that's what she called you, no matter how many other pretenses you put up.

She'd already nick-named Ron, Big Dick, or BD

for short, not that she thought he had one, she could care less, but that he was one. When Ron discovered her name for him, he took it as a compliment. That's how stupid he was.

Roberta wasn't really in to tennis and had doubts about how much sense it made to run around on concrete in the hot sun, or anytime for that matter, and try to hit a ball over a net that seemed to grow an inch taller every time she swung. To compensate, she'd hit a little higher only to see the ball go long, or wide or, worse, over the fence. What is that? Twenty feet? How much more out of control can you get?

Learning the game seemed hopeless until Todd came along. He was a decent player, unmarried, and more than willing to help her improve her game.

"Hold the racket like this," he'd say. "Your grip won't slip when you hit the ball."

That seemed to help. The racket, not slipping in her grip, allowed her to progress to the next problem, the ball going to the wrong place.

"Watch the ball hit the strings," said Ron. "If the ball hits the racket in the same place every time, you're much better off. Consistency is the name of the game."

That bit of advice got her hitting better right away.

"See you back here on Thursday?"

"Sure. Same time?"


"In about an hour," thought Roberta, coming out of the women's room, heading for the exit.

*Today, just be the two of us. Studying to be an architect, loves art. Wants to show me his sculpture designs. Daryl can take a flying…,*

"Roberta!"

Turning, Roberta spotted Mel, one of the technicians who worked in the building. He waved.

"Hey, Mel. How's it going?"

"OK. You got a minute?"

Actually, she did not. With a little luck she could get back to her reporting office, park the truck, send out a few e-mails and get off a little early.

"I guess. What's up?"

"I'm trying to replace a fan," he said. "I need someone with small hands."

Mel was one of those overweight individuals that always had a soft drink in his hand. From the time he arrived for work in the morning until the time he went home at night, a thirty-two ounce container of something or other, with a straw.

Perhaps it was due to his oversized stomach that he never seemed to be able to tuck all of his shirt in, or leave it completely out. How a person could not notice that about themselves was a mystery to Roberta, who originally chalked it up to laziness. But then she discovered that he bicycled twenty-five miles a day to and from work, even in the rain. His bike was also set up with a cup holder and a long flexible tube.

It must be, she finally concluded, a lack of caring about personal appearance, a low self-esteem. But then she discovered that Mel was a sought after technician who often found troubles that confounded most other employees.

The thing about Mel then, was that he just didn't care one way or the other about his appearance, didn't smell particularly good, due to that long daily ride, smelling more like pickles, onion and stale French fries, was unpleasant to look at, but was in demand for his abilities. If for no other reason, that one alone made him popular. Don't get on Mel's bad side. You might need his help one day.

Roberta sighed. "Except my tools are out in the truck."

Mel picked himself off of the floor and went over to his tools, all contained in a small canvas bag up against the wall, and pulled out a screwdriver. "I've got mine right here."

"Let's make it quick," said Roberta. "I've got to be somewhere."

"Thanks. I appreciate it."

Positioning herself on the floor in front of the gray metal cabinet, Roberta peered into the maze of circuit packs, relays and wires. "Power's off, right?"

"Right," said Mel, coming back with a screwdriver. "It's the fan on the right. There's six screws holding it to the housing."

"I see it. Wiring is already disconnected?"

"Yea. I can't see the...,"

The phone rang.

"Uh. Sorry. I have to get that."

"Bring a flashlight."

"It's in my desk. I'll be right back."

Roberta sat there for the next five minutes staring at the defective fan. Finally, she got up, went over to Mel's desk and stood in his line of sight. Mel looked up apologetically and mouthed the word, sorry.

"Flashlight," Roberta said, taking the screwdriver from Mel.

He opened a drawer, handed her the flashlight and silently mouthed the word, thanks.

Sitting down, shining the light onto the fan, she realized that Mel had grabbed a standard screwdriver. A Phillips was needed.

"I'll get it," said Mel, walking up and seeing her

dilemma.

He returned with a Phillips and handed it to Roberta. But when she tried to unscrew the screw...,

"Tip's too big," she said, handing the screwdriver back to Mel.

"Oops," said Mel. "That's what I get for not wearing my glasses."

Heading back to his tool bag, about twenty feet away, Mel stopped to study a piece of equipment that was making a funny sounding buzzing noise.

"Hey, Mel," said Roberta. "Let's finish up here first."

"Right," said Mel, continuing on to his tools. "Sorry."

"Bring the tools over here," said Roberta, noticing his abnormally slow speed.

Watching him, Roberta decided that Mel was good at troubleshooting because he was never in a hurry. The ceiling could be tumbling down around him and Mel would be trying to figure out why dust was suddenly gathering on his keyboard. Eventually, Mel noticed everything. He returned with a smaller tipped Phillips.

Roberta turned on the flashlight, reached inside the cabinet and began loosening the screws. One thing she did like was fixing things. The challenge of seeing something come back to life was not only rewarding, but it took her mind off all of her other problems...,

"Oops," said Roberta. "Dropped the screw. Have you got a magnet?"

"You dropped the screw?" Mel asked, leaning over her shoulder, looking in.

"Sorry. Have you got a magnet?"

"Can you see it?"

"No. It went behind that coil over there in the

corner."

"You're sure?"

"Yea. I saw it. My screwdrivers are magnetic. It would have held onto the screw."

"You're sure you can't see it?"

"Positive."

"You should always put something beneath."

"Right. But like I said, my screwdrivers are mag...,"

"Let me look."

"It's all yours," said Roberta, getting up.

"I have a hard time getting in there," said Mel, becoming a slow avalanche to the floor. "My hands are so big that...,"

"Did you say that you had a magnet?" Roberta asked. "Or should I go out to my truck and get one?"

"There should be one in my bag."

"OK. I'll bring your tools over here, too."

"No, don't do that."

"Why not? Put them where you need them."

"I don't want them to get dirty."

"What?"

"I always keep my tools away from my work. They stay cleaner that way."

"Mel. Look at this place. It's immaculate. Why walk twenty feet every time you need something?"

"It gives me time to think. And I need the exercise."

"All right," said Roberta, heading for the bag. "I'll get a magnet and leave the tools. It's your case of trouble. But if you ever work with me, watch out. I throw stuff everywhere."

"You know, you're right," said Mel, leaning into the equipment. "I should have magnetic screwdrivers. None of this would have happened. We could've almost been done by now."

"We could've been done yesterday, Mel, if you'd put your tools by your work."

"I can't see the screw either. You say it's behind a coil?"

"The big one in the back," said Roberta, handing the magnet to Mel. "I saw it fall. Do you want me to get it?"

"Naw. There it is. Got it! Hand me that cloth there, will you?"

"What cloth?"

Mel backed out of the cabinet and carefully set the screw on the floor. "It's right..., oh. It's over by the bag."

"Seems like I'm getting your exercise," said Roberta, walking over to the wall. "Anything else you need while I'm here?"

"That should do it. Thanks, Roberta. Some people just complain, you know? I don't listen to them because they don't know what they're doing anyway. Not you. You just jump right in and you don't complain. You're good help."

Roberta returned with the cloth, a twill jean square, and handed it to Mel. It didn't seem like much, what he had just said, but the words struck a cord.

*Yes. I am good help. I'm good at a lot of things. Time to get on with doing them.*

*I've been wanting to paint the living room a different color. Daryl had lousy taste. Come to think of it, he was pretty bad at a lot of stuff. I'm lucky he's gone. I might have been stuck with that guy!*

*Good-bye, Daryl. Wish you the best. Hope you don't catch anything too significant. Close one door and ten more open.*

"Thanks, Mel."

Easy money

Ten minutes to midnight and with a slight let-up in the rain, Darin, sitting in the driver's seat with window down, slid his card into the reader that opened the gate to the parking lot.

*Always takes a long time. Don't know what else it needs to think about. It's just a yes or a no.*

The call had come in just as he was leaving work for the day. He'd stared at the phone, wondering who would be calling so late, thinking it must be trouble. Normally, he would have let it ring but, technically, he was still on the clock.

"Power maintenance, Darin here."

"How would you like to make some easy money?"

"Hey, Boss. What do I have to do?"

"Your office, tonight at midnight. Floyd's got a vendor coming in to remove a piece of conduit. Probably only take fifteen, twenty minutes."

"Yea I can do it."

"Thanks, Darin."

Darin had his pick of the lot for parking. He drove to the north end and pulled into the spot closest to the gate. Before getting out, he surveyed the area.

*Clear left, clear right, don't see anything weird in my rear-view mirror. Looks like I'm the only living thing in this parking lot. Good. Time to go.*

Darin locked his car, went to the gate and slipped quietly through the opening. Stepping around the puddles on the sidewalk, he walked briskly toward the building, heading for the stop-light at the corner.

A sudden splatter of rain hitting the bushes between Darin and the parking lot fence caused him to look up into the leaves of the Eucalyptus trees towering above. Glancing up, Darin confirmed that everything appeared normal.

*Must've been a breeze. Odd how that happens just when I'm walking by. I hope it was a breeze.*

From above, a swish of leaves, branches being pushed aside and of a spray of drops spilling down into the bushes below. Looking up, Darin spotted a man climbing down. He waved, "Nice night, isn't it?" acting as if climbing trees in the rain was normal.

"One can only hope," said Darin, not slowing, hoping that the man stayed up in the tree even though he was deftly climbing down.

"How's it going?"

"Not well," said Darin, continuing on, not wanting to make eye contact.

He hit the ground with a thud. "Have you got a minute?"

"Actually, no. There are major problems in that building and there is a team of people inside waiting for me."

"Oh." The man appeared baffled by that answer. "So..., you work there? I have a question...,"

"Sorry," said Darin, over his shoulder, crossing against the light and jaywalking. "This is an emergency."

He did not look back until he reached the alcove holding the card reader. The man was standing on the corner in front of the trees, watching to see if he went in. Darin slid his card through the reader and was relieved to hear the lock click.

Charles, the night guard, was laughing. "Who's your friend?"

"What?"

"That guy outta the trees. Been watching him for the last hour."

"You call the cops?"

"Naw."

"Why not"

"He's not hurting anybody. What'd he want?"

"Asked how it was going, scared the shit out of me. Who expects a guy to come down out of the trees at midnight?"

"Around here? You're lucky he wasn't swinging naked."

"Never a dull moment. Did Floyd's guy come in?"

"Yea," said Charles, checking the sign-in sheet. "Some guy named Omar, and a guy named Buck, works for the company."

"He's the engineer's assistant. Why is he here?"

"Didn't say. They're waiting for you downstairs."

"Thanks, Charles." Darin turned to go, then turned back. "Hey. If he started to assault me, what's your obligation?"

"If you're on the sidewalk, you're on public property. I got no jurisdiction there."

"So, if I'm assaulted, I have to make it to company property before you join in?"

"Right."

"If I can't make it that far, you would call the cops though, right?"

"Oh, yeah. I'd do that."

"How about if it got violent?"

"Depends. If he's got a gun, you asking me to take a bullet for you?"

"I'd do it for you."

Charles laughed. "No, you wouldn't. Tell you what. I'll make sure I get pictures. You know, so we can identify the killer, or rapist, whichever."

"Thanks a lot. That doesn't do me any good."

"A comforting thought, your last breath, knowing that this guy's gonna be caught one day. Got that camera up on...,"

"Yea, I know," said Darin, heading for the stairs. "Above the loading dock."

"Riiight."

Buck was standing on the top of a four-foot ladder in the middle of the room, looking up at the conduit to be removed.

"Doesn't look safe," said Darin. "I've got a six foot ladder in my office."

"I'm Omar," said a man coming over to shake Darin's hand, "I was told not to start until you got here."

"And there's the reason why," said Darin, glancing in Buck's direction. He shook Omar's hand. "I'm Darin."

The conduit to be removed from the ceiling was fitted with a ninety-degree sweep that hugged the bottom of the ceiling, continuing on for another two feet. The piece could swing from side to side, but would not come out.

"It's broken on the other end," said Omar, pointing to the conduit. "They want to replace the whole thing."

"Probably has a locknut on it," said Darin.

Omar headed for his tool bag. "I'll get my channel locks."

Grabbing hold of the conduit with both hands, Buck put his weight into it, causing the conduit to bend from a ninety to something more like a forty-five degree angle.

"Ah! Almost."

"Don't break it," Omar yelled. "I've got to get a wrench on it."

"I'll get the other ladder," said Darin, heading for his office.

When he returned, Buck was gone.

"Went out for a smoke," said Omar, looking re-lieved. "And then he's going to hold the other end of this thing. Says he knows where it is."

"How are you going to know when he's there?"

"Says he'll bang the pipe."

Omar set up the ladder and, while he was ad-justing his channel-locks to fit the locknut, the conduit suddenly swung around and hit him in the back of the head. Turning, he caught the pipe with his hand. But then it swung around the op-posite way, taking Omar with it. Darin ran over to help steady the ladder, which was rocking itself out of position. Omar descended, bushy eyebrows and wild curly hair accentuating the jerky movements of his body.

"What is he doing up there?'

Darin started laughing. "The guy is dangerous!"

They pulled the ladder out of the way and watched as the conduit swung side to side.

Omar sighed. "How do I get upstairs?"

"Promise you won't kill him?"

"No."

"Then, I'll go. When it stops swinging, he's ei-ther worn himself out or I'm in the room. If you can keep it from turning, I'll take the locknut off up-stairs so that you can just pull it down."

Omar nodded in agreement.

"Do you have to work with him all the time?"

"My company assigned me to work with your company. Buck is the go-between."

Shaking his head, Darin headed for the door. "Sad, isn't it?"

The 1969 Volkswagen Bug had an engineering flaw. The car got around easily enough, weaving in and out of traffic with plenty of zip, got good mileage and it had the sixteen hundred cc engine for more power.

The problem with more power, Carly learned one hot day coming back from Yellowstone National Park, was that when they went to the larger engine they didn't consider moving the oil cooler's location, the result being that while cylinders one, two and four were heating up to about two hundred degrees, number three was running at over three hundred.

Why none of the engineers at Volkswagen questioned it, or if they did, why they didn't act on the possibility of a breakdown due to extra heat was a mystery to Carly. Surely extra horsepower meant extra heat. What you don't want is for the unsuspecting driver, thinking that she is safe and is going to get wherever she wants to go, to experience a total engine breakdown.

That's where she'd met Earl, hitchhiking to town, looking for a tow truck to get her broken bug to a mechanic. Engine blew up, just like that, coming out of a curve, hugging the corner like it always did and then BAM, sounded like a crankcase full of marbles.

"Sucked a valve," said Hank, Earl's cousin, a mechanic. "Damn thing got so hot it lost it's in-teg-gri-ty." That's how he said it, proud that he knew the word. Five hundred bucks to fix it, half of what she'd paid for the whole car.

But, back then she never had any money anyway. She stayed with Earl in his trailer while waiting for the parts to come in, fucking him for room and board and then fucking Hank for the repairs when his wife went to Bingo at church. Fucked both of them at the same time when they got drunk that night and then snuck out at three in the morning.

She thought that would be the end of it but Earl had written down her address from the registration and followed her back home, showed up on her doorstep one night looking for a place to stay and didn't leave for three months.

Earl got jobs fast but lost them faster. Caught stealing beef while unloading the truck at the local grocery store. Caught siphoning gas out of a customer's car at the mechanic shop. Caught with his hand in the tiller at the local donut shop. The best thing you could say about Earl was that he knew more ways to screw up than anybody.

And then it really started to go downhill. He spent days in her apartment, hanging out, drinking, smoking whatever he could get his hands on, always in a surly mood.

The only way to get rid of him, Carly reasoned, was by force. She started an affair with her professor at college, a black belt. Earl didn't like it but there wasn't much he could do. Earl faded back into the countryside. Carly changed addresses, phone numbers and dropped the class. Sex was easy then.

Free spirited Carly went everywhere with her Volkswagen bug, spreading love, taking notes, wanting to write a book someday. But the valve thing was not good. When was it going to happen again? How many more days or weeks or months did she have, and under what circumstances would it fail? Checking the paper to see what bugs were going for, just in case she wanted to sell, she noticed that almost all of the ads said, new engine.

*So, I'm not the only one with the problem.*

No longer trusting the free spirited feeling of the Volkswagen Bug, especially after seeing on TV, another flaw, how a rear end crash of any 1969 or earlier model of Volkswagen Bug, anything over 30 MPH, could propel both the driver and front seat passenger out through the rear window and sever their spines.

That, and Volkswagen's reluctance to address these problems, led Carly to sell her beloved bug.

Step up to a Volkswagen bus, the 1974 model with the eighteen-hundred cc engine, redesigned oil cooler location, twin carbs, and plenty of horsepower without fear of sucking a valve.

Instead of relying on people like Hank, Carly took an auto repair class and learned how engines ran, how to tune them and which tools and parts to carry when heading out for places unknown. Freedom comes in many forms.

It was a good bus, Grand Tetons with Steve, Vancouver with Mark, and then Mario in San Francisco on the way back to San Diego because Mark wanted to stay in Vancouver for a while.

Those were the good old days. The bus saw a lot of action before being traded in for a Vanagon with low mileage, in which she now paused as she input the code to the gate, waited for it to open, and then pulled into the parking lot.

*OK. It's been a late night. Dinner with Alec, a night at the Improv, after dinner aperitif at his place. So, what? I should've gotten some sleep, but I didn't. Vendors know what they're doing anyway. Besides, it's all laid out in the MOP.*

Method of Procedure, a document signed by

111

all interested parties that spells out the exact sequence of operations and procedures to be implemented by the crew, or crews, doing the work.

Work was supposed to start at one AM. Both Hal and Jimmie, having the code to the gate leading into the parking lot, were already there waiting at the rear of the building with their equipment unloaded and staged next to the back door.

Tonight's work was supposed to be a simple operation, just install a couple of breakers into two existing bays, side by side, nothing to bolt to the floor, nothing to drill, all holes factory pre-drilled and matched to the new panels.

"Where's the MOP?" Carly asked.

"Got it right here," said Hal, pulling it out from one of the boxes that contained the new equipment.

Carly took the MOP from Hal. "Easy step number one. Remove blank panel covers."

The first panel came off easily. Four of the six screws on the second panel came right off. Of the other two, one had stripped threads and wouldn't go in or out, and the other had a mangled head, so the screwdriver had nothing to grab.

"And this is supposed to be the easy part," said Hal, half-hour later. "Jimmy, go around back and push on this one." He pointed to the screw with the stripped threads. "Use the butt of a screwdriver to push while I try to back it out."

"Right," said Jimmy, heading for the toolbox.

"And watch out for the buss."

"Right."

Jimmy was a level two. That meant that Jimmy basically knew how to find the building, operate the codes that got him into the parking lot and then wait to be told what to do next. Entering the buildings together, Hal, a level four and qualified to work on most anything, always pointed out to Jimmy what not to touch, the first thing always being the buss. No one had to be told about the rows of huge batteries. They were ominous enough all by themselves.

Jimmy retrieved a screwdriver that had a concave head at the end of the plastic handle, just the tool for the job, Jimmy was thinking. It won't slip off the end of the screw.

"Watch out for the bus," said Hal, peering in through the opening."

"Right."

"Don't touch anything except the screw."

"Right."

"You know which one?"

"Right."

"OK. Push," said Hal, turning the screw counter clockwise. "Harder. There we go. I can feel it start to grab. Okaaay, there it is. We got it. Good."

It was now almost two in the morning.

"I'll drill this one out," said Hal, at last.

Carly had gotten herself a chair and positioned it so that she could see over Hal's shoulder. Under the spell of the steady hum of equipment in the room, the lack of sleep, too many drinks, and distant sounds of vendors doing their work, she started to nod out.

"Screw's out," said Hal, putting his drill down. "We're gonna put the first panel in."

"Right," said Carly, bringing herself back to consciousness. Those two cocktails and bottle of wine were taking their toll. She glanced at the MOP. "Easy step number two. After insuring fuses are out, insert panel."

Hal had done this a hundred times. The process almost didn't even require two people. It was just a matter of inserting the panel straight in and getting two screws into the holes on opposite sides. Make sure alignment is good and then tighten everything down. "Ready, Jimmy?"

Jimmy, being on the other side of the bay, peered through the opening, making eye contact with Hal. "Ready."

Carly yawned. "Go for it."

Hal lost sight of Jimmy as the panel was going in so he couldn't see that Jimmy was about to sneeze. And when he did, his body convulsed slightly, just enough for the fuse housing to touch ground and short out to the buss which, with a bright flash of white light and a loud POP, welded itself in place.

Hal tried to pull the breaker back out, put his feet against the bay and pulled with all of his might, but this was already a done deal. Having a direct path to ground, the many rows of batteries began to discharge, and in the ensuing seconds the entire bay started to pop, crackle and burn, filling the room with smoke.

Bells started clanging everywhere, fire alarms went off, and the Center suddenly had pages of reports pouring in. Smoke filled the room. By then, Carly was wide-awake.

"My fault," said Jimmy, glancing at everyone around the table. "I had to sneeze, no warning. What can I say?"

"I've had those," said Sergio. "Usually happens when I open a jar of ground pepper."

"Me, too," said Jerome. "When I get around cats. Bam!"

"All right," said Martin. "Corporate's breathing down our necks. We need to get back with some answers."

"Next time," said Hal. "I'll be on the other side of the bay making sure it doesn't touch."

"It was an accident," said Carly. "How can you hold anybody responsible for that?"

"They're holding me responsible," said Martin. "And I wasn't even there. But my signature is on that MOP. Hal's suggestion is good. Put the in-charge in the most sensitive position. That's what they're paid for."

"All future MOP's," said Sergio, nodding in agreement.

"No sneezing," said Carly. "Addendum to Step Two."

"We've done the one thing we never wanted to do," said Martin, hoping to make a point. "And that's get famous. We've got the fuel spill in Twelve on our record..."

"Which led to state-wide testing," Sergio added. "A good thing."

"Power Room Six shutdown."

"Which we now know can be a problem in all offices," said Robby. "We're testing all of them and we know how to fix it."

"And now we've burned up Twenty-Three," said Martin. "We are definitely on their radar."

"Been a bad year," said Tony.

"A lot going on," said Darin. "Everybody's got jobs going on in their buildings."

"Amen," said Carly, sipping on her double espresso coffee.

"Always thought you'd be a hot date, Carly," said Darin. "But, I had no idea."

Carly leaned back in her chair. "Fuck you."

"By the way," said Martin. "I just wanted to thank you guys for your response last night. You were great, the way you swarmed in to help. And we got the office back up in record time."

"That's because no one's ever done this before," said Darin . "We just set the standard, that's all."

"Unbelievable, how fast that welded," said Tony.

"As soon as I heard the pop, I tried to back it out," said Hal. "I gave it two or three more tugs and then the whole place lit up. I could hardly see the door through the smoke."

"What about you, Carly?" Martin asked. "What did you see?"

"Just like Hal said. Everything was going fine until the sneeze."

"What I don't understand," said Hal, looking at Carly. "When I turned and headed for the door, Carly was still in her chair. I had a straight shot and I was already running. Yet, when I went through the door she was on the other side waiting for me. I don't know when that happened."

"Sleep walking," said Darin. "Or, maybe we should call it sleep running."

"I was wide awake," Carly replied, coolly.

"Guys," said Martin, holding his hands up. "Let's keep on track. I know we all have a lot of new

116

equipment coming into our offices. And we're all getting tired and overworked, but we have to be more careful. Can we all agree to that?"

The call came in at three in the afternoon. Darin leaned back in his chair hoping that whoever this was would take him up to quitting time. "Power Maintenance, Darin."

"Hey, man. Got an engine problem here at 04."

"Hey, Robby. That's a turbine over there, right?"

"Right."

"Control panel? Or, circuit packs?"

"Circuit packs."

"Bummer. You have spares?"

"A few good ones and a few I'm not sure about. Not the whole set."

"What's it sound like when it tries to start?"

"Winds up, goes through the motions, shuts down."

"Times out?"

"Right. The starter winds for about thirty seconds and then turns itself off."

"It has fuel?"

"Yea. Everything looks good."

"Anybody been working on it?"

"Braynard Electric. I was with them all day. They're wiring in that new monitor stuff."

"Not into the circuit packs, I hope."

"No, into the terminal strips. They do good work."

"You tested the engine before they started?"

"Yeah. Started right up. As soon as I shut it down they started working on it. Been tryin' to start it for the last two hours. I knew you were leavin' so, any ideas?"

"Yea. But I need to hear what it's doing. I'll come over. Why don't these troubles ever occur on normal hours? What is it with two in the morning? Or at quitting time? Why not seven in the morning, right after coffee and donuts?"

Robby laughed. "I hear ya, man. See you when you get here."

"OK," said Darin, entering the engine room. "Let me hear it."

Robby pushed the start button. The starter clacked into gear, wound up for about thirty seconds and then shut down.

"Starter sound OK to you?" said Darin, listening to it wind down.

"Sounds OK. Never really thought about it before 'cause the turbine always starts. Everything was working fine until Braynard did the wiring."

"I hate to say it. I think we have to disconnect everything they did."

"Thought you'd say that. I was gonna do that next, but I wanted to hear what you had to say."

An hour later, after pulling all of the new wiring off, they attempted another start.

"Sounds the same," said Darin. "We accomplished nothing."

Robby glanced over at the batteries. "Maybe the batteries are weak. You know, too many starts."

"How many times you tried to start it today?"

"I don't know, ten? Twelve? Batteries are only two years old, though."

"Let's change out the Start Sequence board," Darin suggested.

"No spare. It's on order. I've been waiting two months."

"Gotta keep on Martin or he won't do it. What is it for one of those? Eight hundred bucks?"

"About six," said Robby. "Yea. He acts like it's his

119

own money."

"You've tried exchanging all of the circuit packs with known good ones?"

"Yea, the ones that I have. Each time I changed out a board, I tried another start."

"Sergio. Doesn't he have an engine like this up in Twenty-two?"

"Yea, I think so."

"Circuit pack type?"

Robby walked to the phone on the wall. "Let's find out. I got his number."

"Queue pasa?"

"Sergio, this is Robby."

"Hey, dude. What's up?"

"What kind of engine is in Twenty-two?"

"Turbine, four-fifty KW. Why?"

"Is it a circuit pack or control panel?"

"Circuit pack. Why?"

"Do you have a full set of spares?"

"First tell me why."

"Engine won't start here in Four."

"No way, man. You stay away from my boards."

"All I want to do is...,"

"No way, Jose. Took me a year to get those boards. God damn, Martin...,"

"Problem is," said Robby, "I only have a couple of starts left. Batteries are almost dead. If we had a good set...,"

"Robby, if I had the problem and you had the boards, would you loan them to me, knowing how Martin is?"

Robby laughed. "Yea, man. In a heartbeat."

"You're full of shit, too."

Darin yelled out. "Hey, Sergio! This is Darin. We need a favor."

120

"Who's that? Darin ?"

"Yea, he's workin' with me."

"Let me talk to him," said Darin, taking the receiver. "Dude."

"No, you're not getting them."

"We need a complete set."

"I already told Robby no. Besides, they're in a locked cabinet."

"Where's the key?"

"I've got it."

"Can we drop by?"

"Fuck, man. It took me a year to get those and...,"

"Dude, how was that pizza the other night?"

"What pizza?"

"In the place by your office. You know, a couple blocks up. Was that your wife? She's hot."

There was a long silence on the line, Darin smiling, Sergio silent.

"What's the problem with the engine?"

"It won't start. Braynard Electric was in there today and...,"

"Fuck. They burned up an engine in L.A, man, just like ours."

"I didn't know that."

"All right, man. I'll bring the packs down because I want to make sure I get mine back. I'll be there in about an hour. Do you need a scope?"

"No. I've got one in the truck. Thanks, dude."

"No problemo."

"Hey, Serge...,"

"Yea?"

"How about a large, The Works, pizza on the way? I'll pay you when you get here."

"You fucker. Anything else?"

"Couple of Cokes. Thanks, Serge. We'll check out

the filters and try to eliminate anything else."

"Adios, asshole."

Darin hung up the phone. "He's on his way. And he's bringing dinner."

"Who was he with?"

"Don't know, not his wife, I guess."

They ate right there in the engine room, sitting around the pizza like it was a campfire on the floor, Sergio sitting on an overturned trash can, Robby and Darin on unopened five gallon buckets of oil, talking over the noise of the ventilation fans.

"Did you lift all of their wiring?" Sergio asked, reaching for seconds.

Robby retrieved the pack of red pepper flakes and sprinkled it over his pizza. "Yep."

"And the engine ran before they started?"

"Right."

"No blown fuses?"

"No."

"We've already been through all of this," said Darin. "We trade out these boards for your good spares and then we'll know…,"

Sergio stopped in the middle of a bite. "You're going to do them all at once?"

"Got to. We've only got a couple more starts."

Sergio groaned. "Shit, man. All it takes is one wire to fuck up all of my boards."

"We lifted all of their wiring," said Robby.

"I need to see it," said Sergio. "No matter what you guys say."

"Good," said Darin. "That keeps us all honest."

Robby nodded. "Good pizza, Serge. Thanks for dinner."

Sergio didn't answer. Instead, frowning, he studied the start batteries and glanced up at the charger, humming loudly on the wall. "You checked all the connections?"

"Right," said Robby, sipping from his Coke.

"Air damper's open?"

"We'll check it again. But it doesn't sound like that. It's more like, it's not getting fuel, even though we know it's there. Or maybe it's not getting the signal to inject fuel."

"Starter's OK?"

"It's the one thing that happens," said Robby. "When I push the button, it winds up, spins for a while and then shuts down."

"Times out?"

Both Darin and Robby nodded. "Yea."

"Hmmm," said Serge, wiping his hands on a napkin. "I want to get this over with. Let's get started."

They de-powered the control panel, removed all of the old circuit packs, Sergio insisting that Darin wear a ground-strap as he slid the new ones into place. Robby pushed the start button. The starter kicked in, spun for about thirty seconds and then shut down.

"Never heard anything like that before," said Sergio. "You sure that starter's OK?"

"Engine started just before I let Braynard start wiring," said Robby.

"Maybe there's an air bubble in the fuel line," said Darin. "I can't think of anything else."

"Could be the low pressure fuel pump," said Sergio. "Maybe it's not getting enough push to get it to the high pressure pump."

"I don't think it's a fuel problem anymore," said Robby. "I'm wonderin' if the batteries are too weak, so the signals aren't strong enough."

"It's just an 0 or a 1," said Darin. "I'll go out and get my scope. Let's see if the signal to send fuel is getting through."

"Good idea," said Sergio.

Two hours later...,

"Well," said Robby. "We know lots of thing's that

aren't causing the problem."

The outside door opened. Roberta poked her head inside. "Hey, you guys. I saw your trucks parked outside. You having a party in here?"

"Hey, Roberta," said Robby, with his big smile.

"Just what we need," said Darin. "More help."

Roberta glanced at the boxes of circuit packs, test meters hooked up to this thing or that, tools scattered everywhere, empty pizza box, somebody's drink spilled on the floor.

"You guys been here a while?"

"Since three," said Robby. "Called Darin at four."

"Called me at six-fifteen," said Serge.

Roberta glanced at her watch. It was almost ten. "Racking up the overtime, huh?"

"Engine won't start," said Robby.

"What's it doing?"

"Starter winds up, runs for a while and then shuts down," said Sergio. "We know it's not the boards. I think I'm gonna take them out and go home. I've got a meeting tomorrow morning."

"No way, man," said Darin. "We need to be able to...,"

While the three of them were discussing the next steps, Roberta strolled over to the starter, got down on her hands and knees, removed a small penlight from her purse and peered into the opening, focusing her light on the starter shaft. And then she started laughing.

"What?" said Darin, looking up.

Roberta started to tell them that the starter gear was as smooth as a broomstick, that all of the teeth were missing, but burst into laughter again.

"What the fuck?" said Sergio.

Robby took her light and shined it through a small opening in the starter. Shaking his head, grinning sheepishly and not saying a word, he handed the light to Darin.

"What?" said Darin, standing. "God damn gear is sheared!"

"You're shitting me," said Sergio, now taking the light. "Thought you guys checked this."

"Hoo! Hoo! Hoo!" said Roberta, now laughing out of control. "Me, man! Me fix!" She threw them a kiss on her way out the door. "That was *good*! Thanks, guys!"

"That sucked," said Darin.

"We'll never hear the end of it," said Sergio. "Damn!"

Darin started cleaning up his tools. "What are the odds of the starter gear shearing just before they wired the engine?"

Robby just shook his head, smiling. "I just learned a good lesson."

"Me too," said Sergio. "Next time, I won't even answer my fucking phone."

# Behind the Scenes

It was the accidental meeting at Luigi's that led to the repair of a problem that had been plaguing the entire crew for years. Even more odd was the fact that the person making the repairs did not work for the company, was not hired by the company, not paid for his repair work and, truth be told, was not even authorized to be in the building.

The standby generator did not start on the first attempt. It always started on the second try and, if not more than two weeks passed since the last time it was run, started right up. The problem was not serious enough to warrant a new engine but was an irritant to the person that had to maintain it.

Roberta tried changing out fuel pumps, exchanged fuel control boards, engine control boards, load tested the batteries, checked and double checked all of the connections. Nothing that she did made a difference.

Next, in the parade of repair technicians attempting to fix the problem, was Robby, Darin, and then Sergio. No success. A call for assistance brought tech support people from around the state and experts from the factory. The trouble lingered and no one knew why.

The main difficulty in troubleshooting this kind of problem was that it took at least two weeks in between each attempt at a fix, more like a month if you really want to put the turbine to the test. Try one thing and then wait a month to see if that was it.

Roberta would have never even met this man had it not been for the fact that the strings broke on her racket while playing tennis with Todd. They quit early and decided to go get a pizza and a carafe of wine at Luigi's, where there are only a few tables and the place is always dark.

They seated themselves away from the noisy foursome near the entrance, across the room from the mother with her two out of control kids, sitting across from each other at a small, candle lit table.

The Tomato Plate comes with sliced tomatoes, thinly sliced sweet onion, capers and olives on a bed of lettuce, drizzled with the chef's special Italian dressing and served with hot breads ticks, all for six-ninety five. How can you go wrong? They also ordered a small pizza and a carafe of Chianti.

Another couple entered the room, made the same assessment of the existing occupants and headed for a table close to Roberta and Todd.

"I think I know this guy," said Todd, over the top of his wine glass.

The couple chose a table next to them and it was during the brief eye contact between the two men that caused Kirk to stop in the middle of seating himself.

"Todd? Is that you?"

"I thought it was you," said Todd, standing to shake his hand. "Roberta, I want you to meet Kirk, the guy who helped me get through two semesters of Physics."

"It wasn't easy," said Kirk, smiling, extending his hand to Roberta. "He's not good with numbers."

"Wasn't my strong suit either," said Roberta, shaking his hand. "He's pretty good at tennis, though."

"Has to use his hands," said Kirk. "Numbers leave him tongue-tied." He turned to introduce his date. "This is Lee. We were on our way to a concert at the park when she had the urge for a pizza instead."

"Great minds think alike," said Roberta, who had made the suggestion to Todd.

Waiting for their pizzas, Todd and Kirk caught up on the past and the conversation moved into what everyone was doing now.

"And what do you do?" said Todd, directing his gaze to Lee.

"I'm an artist," she replied. "Painting and sculpting."

"Is that so? What mediums?"

"Oils, acrylics, watercolor, when I paint. I'll use anything when I sculpt."

"Never could use watercolors," said Todd. "I'm too slow and I think too much. Oils are great."

"How long have you been painting?"

"Since I was six. Who's your favorite artist?"

Lee smiled, sipping her wine. "Anyone who has the courage to pick up a brush and pour their soul into it."

It was like a ping-pong match for Kirk and Roberta, watching those two. Finally, Kirk looked over at Roberta.

"And what do you do?"

"Nothing spectacular," said Roberta. "I work on a power crew."

"Doing what?"

And this is how the conversation ensued, Roberta and Kirk talking in between Todd's and Lee's words...,

"Hockney is great," said Lee, nodding in agreement. "I love his different interpretations of water."

"Do you ever work on standby generators?" Kirk asked, pouring more wine into Lee's glass.

"Part of my job," said Roberta. "How about you?"

"There's a special exhibit of his work in L.A. next

week," said Todd. "But I couldn't get tickets."

"That's all I do," said Kirk. "I work on oil platforms, fly all over the world keeping them running...,"

"I have tickets," said Lee. "But Kirk can't go. He's flying out this Sunday, won't be back for two weeks...,"

"Those engines run twenty-four-seven?" Roberta asked, breaking off a piece of her bread stick and dipping it in the Italian dressing on her plate.

"Right. That's my job, keep them running."

"How'd you get tickets?" Todd asked. "They wouldn't even talk to me."

"My dad's on the board of directors."

"I guess you wouldn't know about an engine not starting first time," said Roberta.

"Starts on the second attempt every time?" Kirk asked.

"I've got an extra ticket," said Lee, "if you want to go."

"Right! Runs fine otherwise. How'd you know?"

"I can't pass it up," said Todd. He glanced over at Roberta. "Hmm. I wonder if she'd understand."

"Is that a little two hundred KW turbine?" Kirk asked.

"We could drive up together," said Lee. "Save gas. Kirk's easy going. He'd understand."

"I've tried everything," said Roberta. "Fuel control boards, pumps. Everybody has tried to...,"

Kirk laughed. "I think I know what's wrong with that engine. I'll bet I've spent a thousand hours on that exact problem...,"

"Is that on Wednesday?" Todd asked, checking his schedule. "I could cancel a meeting and..."

"So," said Roberta, pouring wine into both hers and Todd's glasses. "What's the fix?"

"Wednesday only," said Lee. "Noon to ten."

"I can't tell you," said Kirk. "Because if you turn the wrong screw or turn this one too much, you could blow up the whole engine. I have to see it."

"I'm pretty sure he won't mind," said Roberta, nodding at Todd. "If you have a little time and would like to tag along."

"I'd love to. And if I fix it, you agree to go sailing with me?"

"I don't think Todd would go for that. He...,"

"Hey, Todd," said Kirk. "Are you scheming on my girlfriend?"

"What? No, I...,"

"Tell you what," said Kirk. "Lee's right, I can't make the show. You go with her if I can take Roberta sailing."

"What?"

"Lee gets seasick. And I'm entered in a race. My normal sailing partner is out of town. I need a partner."

Roberta set her wine down. "I don't know how to sail."

"I'll teach you. If you were that persistent in finding that trouble, I'm sure you'd do great. You get seasick?"

"Not that I know of."

Kirk held up his glass. "How about it, guys?"

After a long pause and several questioning glances around the two tables, they clinked glasses.

The next morning, Roberta met Kirk at Building Seventeen. As soon as Roberta unlocked the door and held it open, allowing daylight inside, Kirk started laughing.

"I know exactly what's wrong with this engine. I'm probably one of only two people on this planet who know how to fix it. You have to compensate for the cold start, but not at the fuel pump. Have you got a small screwdriver?"

And that was the end of that problem.

"So," said Vanessa, turning the chair around so that she could sit in it backwards, setting her coffee on the table. "Todd, now Kirk? You're getting around, girl."

"It's not like that. I said I'd try sailing only if he fixed that engine. That was the real incentive, to get rid of the trouble."

"But, you knew he could fix it."

"I don't know, maybe."

"Is he cute?"

"Kinda. Curly red hair, crooked smile, boyish looks...,"

"Uh oh. You're in love. You never talked that way about Todd."

"Todd and I just met. That was our first date."

"Describe Todd."

"He's more mature..., more refined."

"His looks. Not his mannerisms."

"He's handsome, dark eyes, athletic...,"

"Face it. You don't know what you see in Todd."

"I think I do."

"He was your first date and already you're looking."

"That's not true. I enjoy Todd's company."

"Because it beats staring at the walls."

"I don't see any great loves in your life."

"I'm doing fine and you know it."

"Nothing serious."

"Because I don't want serious. I'm happy to play around."

"So, why can't I do the same thing? It's not like I'm dating Kirk."

Vanessa laughed. "OK. You're right. I guess I'm

being overly protective of my friend. You go, girl. My money's on Kirk."

"You haven't even met him."

"Call it, women's intuition."

Standing on the deck just above the cockpit, Kirk took Roberta's hand and helped her onboard.

"Careful. This is a round bottom boat. It'll lean to whatever side the weight is on."

Roberta laughed. "You're off to a bad start."

"Oh," Kirk smiled. "Sorry. That's not what I meant. We're both on the same side, so the boat is going to lean this way."

"Is that dangerous? We both shouldn't be on the same side?"

"No, not at all. I'm just warning you so that you don't lose your balance."

"What keeps it from tipping over?"

"The keel," said Kirk, pointing to the deck. There's about a thousand pounds beneath us. It wants very much to stay down there."

"Seems like we should sink."

"This is a very stable boat. Her name is Stir Crazy, by the way. Welcome aboard."

Roberta found the boat small but tidy. Stepping down three steps through the companionway into the cabin, she discovered two bunks, one on either side of the steps, a small kitchenette, a forward bunk, something that would be queen sized except for near the bow, where the bed narrowed, a tiny chart room, and a bathroom that seconded as a shower.

"How long have you had this?"

"About five years. This is my get-away."

"You're gone two weeks out of every month. I'd think you'd just want to stay home when you get into town."

"This is home as much as anywhere." Kirk opened the fridge, removed a beer from the door, popped off the cap and offered it to Roberta. "Lee likes her solitude, same as me. We both need space. Stir Crazy does that for me."

"So, it works out? You being gone all the time?"

"Probably wouldn't last any other way."

"Funny you should say that. My last relationship, we were together all the time."

"Not good. Where's the mystery? But, we're not here for that. You need to learn the rudimentary points of sailing and the race starts pretty soon."

"Great. Pressure's on."

"No pressure. I always lose."

"Then, why bother?"

Kirk smiled. "Wait until you feel the spray hitting your face, just you and the ocean and the wind."

Motoring away from the dock and out into the harbor, Kirk killed the engine, raised the mainsail and pulled the boom in. It began to fill with the wind.

"Port's left," he said, coiling the rope out of the way. "Starboard's right. Easy way to remember is that both port and left have four letters."

"Why does it matter?"

"Rules of the road. Sailboats, under sail, have right of way over motor boats since they don't have as much control over where they can go."

"Makes sense."

Sailboats going upwind have right of way over sailboats going downwind. And sailboats going upwind with the wind coming over the starboard side have right of way over sailboats going upwind with the wind coming over the port side."

"Way too complicated."

"You have to have the rules. Otherwise we'd all kill each other out here."

"And you call this relaxing?"

"I said, exhilarating."

"Do I need to drink another beer?"

Kirk laughed. "Sure. Grab me one, too, when you go." He pointed to a flag flying above a local hotel. "See that? See how that flag is standing out from the pole? We're going to have good winds today."

"Is that good or bad?"

"Good, I think. Most of the other boats are fin keel boats so...,"

"What does that mean?"

"They have a smaller keel, better maneuverability, less weight, so they can accelerate faster out of a tack. In light winds, that's a disadvantage for me because the keel on this boat is much longer and heavier. But in heavier weather, my boat is sturdier. With today's winds, they're probably going to go to a smaller foresail, a one-ten, most likely."

"None of that made sense."

"The sail that really drives your boat is the foresail, called a jib. The area between the forestay, that wire coming down from the top of the mast and attaching to the bow, and the mast, that triangle, is considered to be hundred percent. Today, they'll run a one-ten, a hundred and ten percent sail. But since Stir Crazy is a heavier boat, we're going to stick with a one-fifty. It'll be a little squirrelly but...,"

"Squirrelly?" Roberta took another swig from her bottle. "What does that mean?"

"We'll have a lot of wind hitting a lot of sail. That makes the boat lively."

"Kirk, I...,"

"Don't worry," said Kirk, raising the Genoa. It flapped wildly until he pulled in on the sheet. "You're going to love it."

As the wind caught the foresail, Stir Crazy began to heel to one side and accelerate through the water.

"These are called sheets," said Kirk, wrapping the rope around the winch, pulling it in and tying off at the cleat. "They're attached to the closest end of the foresail. And this is going to be your job, to pull these sheets in when we come about."

"Come about..., what?"

"Move the bow through the eye of the wind. That's called coming about. We can't sail straight into the wind but we can come close to it on either side of the eye. Going through the eye of the wind is called, coming about."

"OK. Why do we have to do that?"

Kirk pointed to the north side of the harbor, dead ahead. "To change directions, we have to come about, put the bow through the eye of the wind. You need to untie this sheet and hold it tight until I say to let go. When you do, go over to this side, wrap this sheet around this winch, clockwise from the top, pull it in as fast as you can and tie it off on this cleat."

"What's the hurry?"

"The faster you make the change, the less speed we lose. It's also good to set the sail and tie it off in its new position before it fills with wind. Otherwise, you fight it."

"Aye, aye, captain. What happens if I fail?"

"We crash into the rocks."

"What?"

Kirk laughed. "Just kidding."

About twenty yards from the shoreline, Kirk said, "Ready to come about."

"Aye, captain." said Roberta, untying the sheet from the cleat. The full force of the wind in the sail pulled Roberta over to the edge of the cockpit. Kirk reached out and grabbed her.

The bow moved through the eye of the wind while the sails flapped furiously. Kirk tapped Roberta on the shoulder and made her aware of the boom, indicating that she had to duck, as it snapped into place on the other side of the cockpit. Stir Crazy heeled in the opposite direction as Roberta wrapped the sheet around the winch, pulled it in and tied it off at the cleat. Sails set, they headed back across the harbor.

Kirk smiled. "Good job. We're on a starboard tack now. We have right of way over everybody except a boat in tow or any vessel over three hundred feet long."

"Both of those make sense," said Roberta, looking at an approaching sailboat. "What if someone doesn't give it?"

"Like that red boat coming at us?"

"Exactly."

"We always miss. Everybody's only doing five or six knots so there's plenty of time to adjust. Sometimes there might be a little yelling."

"Really?"

"People have to learn. You get yelled at enough, you start to figure it out. Personally, I think everyone should take the Coast Guard class on Rules of the Road before they're allowed to pilot a boat."

"He's not changing direction."

"We'll push it a little bit, see if he's just bluffing..., or ignorant."

The red boat did not change course. At the last

second, Kirk turned the wheel so that they came in behind the offending boat, missing by inches.

"Yell at him," said Kirk. "Say, starboard tack!"

"Starboard Tack!" Roberta yelled, indignantly.

There were two men and one woman on board that boat. Hearing Roberta, one of the men picked up a water balloon and threw it at her. She ducked. It exploded on the opposite side of the cockpit.

"Did you see that?" Roberta yelled, pointing. "He threw a water balloon!"

"The nerve," said Kirk, turning the wheel with a slightly crooked smile. "Ready to come about."

"What are we going to do?"

"Teach them a lesson."

"What? How?"

Stir Crazy was brought about and engaged in the pursuit of the red boat named, Bad Dog, painted across the transom. Crossing the bay, they slowly inched closer.

"We've got their wind side," said Kirk. "When we pass them, we'll steal it. They'll stall and then we can let them have it."

"Have what? What are we going to throw, beer bottles?"

Kirk opened a cover in one of the seats of the cockpit, exposing a large quantity of water balloons. "Grab some ammo."

"My God, Kirk."

"You have to come prepared for everything."

Stir Crazy caught Bad Dog, stole their wind, and as the boat stalled Roberta and Kirk launched several water balloons at the other crew, soaking the girl and the man steering the boat. Their counter-attack was just as brutal. Roberta took one in the chest and one in the back of the head. Kirk, ducking one balloon, got hit by two others before the two boats were out of range.

"Get ready to come about," said Kirk.

"What? We're going to do it again?"

"I don't think we taught them a lesson yet. Do me a favor, will you? In behind the balloons, you'll find a hose with a nozzle. Uncoil it."

Stir Crazy came about and bore down on Bad Dog. When they were close, Kirk flipped a switch next to the wheel."

"My God!" said Roberta. "It's like a garden hose!"

"Don't point it at me! Point it at them. Teach them a lesson!"

Roberta soaked the other crew while they fought back gallantly, throwing a barrage of balloons that almost equaled the hose and pump.

And then there was a second boat on the other side of Stir Crazy, two couples this time, heaving balloons, all four of them.

"Retreat!" Kirk yelled. "We're outnumbered!"

And so went the afternoon, boat after boat, tacking, challenging, yelling and heaving balloons, racing out to Buoy Seven and back. Hitting the open sea, Stir Crazy took the lead.

Standing in the cockpit, looking over the cabin, watching the bow break through the swells and feeling the spray on her face, Roberta realized how confined her life had been over the last few months.

"Ease up on the Genoa a bit," said Kirk, aiming for the buoy.

"What does that mean?"

"Boat's working too hard. The wind's getting pinched between the two sails and it causes a lot of drag on the rudder. So if you let the Genoa have a little more breathing room, about a foot more rope, and if I do the same for the mainsail, Stir Crazy will stand up a bit and the rudder pressure will go away. It won't feel like it, but we'll be going faster. Watch the knot meter."

They made their adjustments and, watching the knot meter, Roberta noted that their speed increased almost one knot, from about five and a half to almost six and a half.

"Doesn't seem like much," said Kirk, taking a sip from his beer. "But every little thing makes a difference. When we come around that buoy, you'll notice that I don't steer directly for the port. That's because we have the swells driving us off course. Instead, we'll use them to our advantage. Now, how would you do that?"

Stir Crazy never relinquished the lead. Back at the dock, after showers and a change of clothes, Roberta and Kirk stopped by a popular hangout for drinks and appetizers. Inside, the crews of several other participating boats were already there.

"Kirk, you rat!" said Charles, captain of Bad Dog. "You finally won!"

"It's the help," said Kirk, putting his hand on Roberta's shoulder. "Roberta, meet Charles, most ruthless balloon heaver on the bay. And this is his wife, Jenny. Can you believe this is Roberta's first time?"

"You got a lot of spunk, girl," said Jenny. "We didn't think you'd come back and battle it out."

"I didn't have any choice," said Roberta, looking up at Kirk. "He was steering."

And so went the evening. After lots of drinks, good food and lively conversation, Roberta and Kirk returned to the boat to gather her stuff.

Roberta stepped from the dock onto Stir Crazy. "It's nice out here at night, all of the lights."

Kirk followed her onboard, leaned toward the companionway and unlocked the door. "It's another

141

world…, magical."

"It must be hard for you to go hop on a jet to somewhere after being here for two weeks."

"It makes me want to cry. But this isn't possible without that. You gotta make sacrifices for what you want."

Kirk removed the three boards that comprised the cabin door, reached inside, turned on the cabin lights and motioned for her to enter.

Standing in the cockpit, out under the stars, looking down into the softly lit cabin and feeling the gentle roll of Stir Crazy in the glassy water, Roberta realized two things.

For the first time in months, she had no feelings of depression, none. In fact, just the opposite, of exhilaration, joy, and freedom.

The other was that she didn't want to leave.

"*Robby. I'm serious. Tonight you'd better be home on time. The Reverend said he wants to talk with you but you're always busy at work. Tonight, be here on time. Please. Do it for me if you won't do it for yourself.*"

Robby wiped his hands on the rag next to his toolbox and then used it to clean his wrench before putting it back, a habit he'd picked up from Darin.

"Got myself a good set of tools," Darin had said. "If I've got cheap, crappy tools, that's how I feel about myself when I'm doing the work. And because they're expensive, I have to take care of them, which means I'm always wiping them down. But that helps me think about what I'm going to do next. Ask the right question, and the answer's not far away. You just have to know what question."

*OK, Robby. You think you're so smart? Fix it. You know how to read prints now. You have all the tools. What's the right question? Engine starts fine, runs fine until it tries to power the building. And then it dies and leaves me standing here in the dark. Engine says it's ready. It sends a signal...,*

*Just like Tanya. Sending signals, always mad about somethin'. What's that all about? So what's the problem if I get home late? Baby, you know I love you. I don't mess around with anyone else. Give it a rest. You never used to be like this. Couldn't wait to move in. Remember? Now all you talk about is moving out. I know she loves me, says so all the time.*

Robby opened the schematic for the Control Panel looking for something, some kind of signal that said that the engine was ready to take over. There were many signal wires coming from the engine. He followed the lines across the page.

*Knows how to cook, makes good money. Best sex I ever had.*

*Everything tests OK but it just doesn't work. I'm out of ideas and don't know what to do next.*

*Just like us, huh, Tanya? I know one thing that'd help, quit trying to change me. I am who I am. Quit trying to take control.*

*Ha! Give it to this engine instead.*

*That's what it needs, control. Hmm, control voltage. Where's that come from? Twenty-four volt source, it says. But, I already know that's good. That's what starts the engine.*

*Wonder if Jose scored. This'll be my last time. I told her…, no more. Yea, Robby, like you mean it. You always say it. You're a fool thinking you can beat it but still make the call.*

*Gotta get control. Ah! Figured it out. Control batteries are different than the start batteries. Where are they? That's the right question. Find them and you've found the trouble. It's a whole different path.*

*I'll get this fixed and take off early. Nobody will ever know.*

## Shear Bolts

Darin answered the phone on Sunday afternoon, right in the middle of the football game. According to the Center there was some kind of problem in Building One, a power failure and, according to the reports, all of the engines started but many of the alarms would not reset. Could he go check?

Darin hurried through the basement hallway over to the west side and, coming through the last security door, walked into complete darkness. He clicked on his flashlight and ventured forward.

*I can hear the engines running so the building should have power. Yet, apparently not. What the hell?*

A second beam of light, reflecting wildly off of the wall to his left, indicated that someone else was in the building, coming down the long hallway perpendicular to this one, and that they were running. Skidding around the corner, Norm appeared.

"Hey, Darin," he said, cheerfully. "Another quiet day, huh?"

"What the hell is going on?"

"I was hoping you could tell me. None of my stuff has power, so the ball's back in your court."

Darin turned and headed for the stairs. "Let's see what's happening with the generators."

One engine was running and one was not.

"That's not supposed to happen," Darin yelled over the high pitched whine of the engine. They retreated to the relative quiet of the hallway and closed the steel door. "Both of the engines are supposed to start at the same time, synchronize, and then share the power load. One, all by itself, can't handle it."

145

"And...,?"

"Not sure. Let's go downstairs and check the transfer panel."

Darin studied the meter on the transfer panel. "We've got commercial power available. Might as well transfer everything back."

"Good," said Norm. "I'll go get the air handlers back on-line and that'll take me out of the picture. Page me if you need me."

The building slowly came back to life, rows of fluorescent lights blinked back on, fan belts screeched loudly as they started to bring the big fans up to speed. Darin returned to the engine room, shut down the one running engine and started to investigate. The hallway door opened and Merry Dick Tracy stepped inside.

"Hi, Darin," she said, talking over the drone of the ventilation fans . "You're missing the game."

"Hi Mary. So are you. What are you doing here?"

"I asked the Center to call me whenever there's a major problem."

"Yea, well, I've got one here."

"I thought I heard the engines running when I was in the parking lot."

"Yea, one was. I just shut it down. Something's not right."

Merry smiled knowingly. "Oh. Well, I won't bother you then. I just wanted to remind you that there is no spill kit in this room."

"Right. When the fuel delivery came in last week, he had a problem with the shut-off on his truck so I had to use it."

"Oh." Merry opened her notebook and clicked her pencil lead down a notch. "What company was that?"

"Merry, I'll give you details later."

"Fuel spills should be reported."

"It was contained. I don't have to report that."

"Yes. But you did use your spill kit and now you don't have one in case you have trouble in here today."

"Right, but...,"

"Did you order a new kit?"

"Merry, if I have a fuel spill in here on top of everything else, I'll just throw myself in it and light a match."

Merry laughed, wondering how she would report that. "Good, Darin. That's good. Talk to you later." And with that, she left.

Two hours later, still baffled by what had caused the day's events, Darin crawled out from beneath the generator long enough to wipe his hands and go answer the phone.

"What?"

"What kind of greeting is that?"

"Hey, Martin. I was down beneath the engine and didn't want to get up. What's up?"

"That's why I'm calling. The Center called me, said you had responded to the alarms and cleared them but that you hadn't clocked out with them yet. No answer at your house, so I'm just making sure you're OK."

"Yea, still kicking. Who won the game?"

"We lost by three, field goal in overtime."

"Damn. I owe Sergio ten."

"What's wrong with the engines?"

"Not sure yet. One of them shut down on overtemp. The other starts and runs but doesn't look like it's developing any voltage. I was just testing the diodes when you called."

"Do you want me to send help?"

"No. It's a personal thing now."

"I just got off the phone with Robby. Said he could stop by."

"He's really getting good at shooting trouble, found that control voltage trouble without any help."

"You two work well together. That's why I'm offering his help."

"If I haven't fixed this by the end of the day, I'll give him a call. We'll work on it tomorrow."

"Fair enough. You know we're taking a chance not bringing in a spare engine. What if there's another power failure?"

"I guess we'll punt. By the time we bring in a spare engine and get it all hooked up, it'll be tomorrow anyway, at great expense."

"OK. I'll call around though and make sure one is available on short notice."

"Thanks, Martin. I'll check in with you later."

Robby dropped by the following morning.

"What's it doing?"

"No voltage," said Darin, crawling out from beneath the control panel. "Engine starts, runs fine, but it doesn't develop any voltage."

"You changed out all of the boards?"

"Yea. Swapped them with the good engine. That's not it. I thought maybe one of these diodes might have shorted out."

Robby looked at the schematic for a minute, studying the marks Darin had made to record which ones he'd tested.

"I don't know about all of that," he said, smiling. "But I do remember to look for the easy stuff, ever since that starter trouble."

"Like..., what? What else could it be?"

"Maybe...," Robby had that gleam in his eye like

when he was about to show Darin the trouble that shut down his power plant. "If one engine shut down on over temp, then it was already powering the building the building when this one tried to join in. If the engines aren't in sync, what happens?"

Darin put his meter down and wiped his hands on a rag. "I see what you're saying. If they were out of sync when the breakers closed, one of them would take a big hit."

"Right."

"You think the generator and engine have *separated*?"

"Maybe."

Darin walked along the engine, looking for where they were connected. He stopped next to two large flywheels, each about four feet in diameter, made of one inch thick steel. "You have any idea how major of a problem that would be?"

Robby laughed. "So. What else you got going on right now?"

Darin retrieved his flashlight and shined the light into the seam. "God, I hope this isn't it. What made you think of it?"

"Before they put you in this building, I used to come in and check things out once in a while, just so I'd know what's going on in case of an emergency. I was going through that locker over there and saw a box of stainless steel bolts. Thing is, they were hollow. And ever since, I've been wondering why."

"Good question. Why would anyone want a hollow bolt? It's like you're getting ripped off."

"I'll bet they cost a lot of money. I'd bet they break at just the right time, before the engine gets ripped off of the floor if the breaker between these two engines closes at the wrong time."

149

"Sacrificial bolts?"

"Maybe."

"Can't see shit inside here. They're too close."

"Got a piece of chalk?"

"For what?"

"If we draw a line across the part that's generator and the part that's engine and then try to start it...,"

"You're too smart for your own good."

Pushing the start button, the turbine flywheel spun around while the generator part stood still.

"Can't believe it!" said Darin, throwing a dirty rag into the corner. "How are we going to replace them?"

"I think I need a tall cup of coffee and a couple of donuts," said Robby, pleased with his analysis. "If you're buyin', I'll get my tools out of my truck and start pulling them out. Shouldn't take too long, should it?"

# Making the Rounds

Seeing that Darin was carrying coffee and donuts, Willy hurried around the desk to give him a hand.

"Hey, dude," he said, holding the door open. "Any of that for me?"

"Screw you," said Darin. "After what you did with Speedos, I'm done buying you donuts."

Laughing, Willy headed back to his chair. "You gotta admit, it was funny."

"Next time," said Darin, handing Willy two glazed old-fashioned donuts, "I'll hold the door closed and you can plead for your life outside."

"Already paid my dues. I worked last week-end."

"Preaching to the choir," said Darin. "I'm on-call twenty-four-seven. I feel no pity."

Willy broke one of the donuts in half and stuffed it in his mouth. "It was Gay Pride Day."

"That parade came by here?"

"What planet you live on, man? Yea, it does! Every year, right down this street. Every year I have to watch the whole thing."

"So..., what? You're in here, behind locked doors."

"Yea, but I gotta make my rounds every hour. You know, walk around the building."

"Oh." Darin removed the lid from his coffee and blew off the steam. "So..., you should fit right in."

"My ass! I was goin' up the east side of the building. You know that old entrance over there, the one nobody ever uses? There was two dudes in there, gettin' it on."

"You're shitting me."

"I ain't lyin'. They was doin' it."

"Doing..., what?"

Willy stuffed the other half of the donut in his mouth. "You know, what they do."

"Like..., what?"

"Aww, man. I'm not even talkin' about it. I told them they had to leave."

"Did they?"

"No. Can you believe it? Said they was on public property and I had no right to tell 'em what to do."

"That's bold," said Darin, biting into a maple crueler, "especially with your pants down."

"No shit. I told them that the entrance is company property and that they had to get out on the sidewalk."

"Did they?"

"No. They were arguin' with me while they was doin' it!"

"Why didn't you break it up?" said Darin, smiling. "That's your job, isn't it?"

"Last thing I want is to get in the middle of two horny dudes. I pointed to the camera and told 'em when I get back to my station, if I still see 'em, I'm callin' the cops. They was gone by the time I got back here."

"Lucky for you."

"Lucky for them," said Willy, wiping his hands on a napkin.

"If it was two women, what would you have done?"

"Well..., that's different," said Willy, biting into the next donut. "I might watch."

"You wouldn't try to break it up?"

"Hell, no. Can't tell what they're thinkin'. Might cut my balls off!"

"That's how I felt about Speedos, you asshole."

Willy laughed. "We should get hazardous duty

pay, workin' around here."

"No shit," said Darin.

Tacos Amongst Friends

"All done?" Darin asked, setting the coffee and donuts down.

Robby opened the lid on his coffee and took a cautious sip. "When the bolts sheared, they mushroomed at the break. They don't come out."

Darin bit into a chocolate cake donut and strolled over to the flywheel. "How much you think these things weigh?"

Robby laughed. "More than you and I can handle. I'd guess they're a thousand pounds apiece. What is that, four-foot diameter, inch thick steel? Gotta be at least five hundred pounds."

"You're right. If we have to take it apart we'd better call in the pros. How many bolts are there altogether?"

"Sixteen, same number of hollow bolts we had in the cabinet, so I'm guessing that's what they're for."

"If they're mushroomed in between the flywheels, there's not enough space to get to them. Can hardly get a piece of paper in there."

"I was just gonna get a bigger wrench."

"Maybe we could spray in some WD40 first. That might help it break. Even so, how are we going to get the other side out?"

"Haven't got that far, yet."

Two hours later, they had the bolts out. Floyd entered the room, steel door swinging shut behind him, looking like it's going to slam and then slowing at the last second. "How you guys doing?"

"Slow, but not so sure," said Darin, looking up. "What's up?"

Floyd joined them by the flywheels and examined their progress. "Tough job, huh?"

"Nothin' else going on," said Robby, grinning. "Might as well get free donuts."

Floyd glanced at his watch. "You guys ready for a break?"

Darin wiped his hands with a towel. "I guess it is time for lunch. Robby?"

He nodded. "How about that hole-in-the-wall?"

"If we hurry," said Darin. "Otherwise it gets too crowded."

Tuesdays – Grilled fish tacos, smothered in tarter sauce, fresh shredded cabbage, rice, beans, hot carrots and soft drink, all for under five bucks. Raphael, the owner who normally took everyone's order and passed them back to the kitchen, was on the phone, taking a long order,

Liani, the cook, recognized Darin and gave him a smile. He smiled back, admiring her tan skin, white teeth and easy going style, wondering how they'd do on a date. But the thing was, he'd never seen the bottom half of her.

Standing behind the stainless steel counter top, she was always there, ready to take your order, definitely a good cook, wore no wedding ring, was friendly, good looking, seemed like she would go out, but Darin wanted to see her bottom half first.

He always sat, when he could find a place to sit, facing her from one of the six small tables, hopeful-ly with a view of the doorway so that he could catch a glimpse of her walking by. That would be terrible, to have a date fizzle with the woman who cooks all of your favorite lunches.

"What're you having?" Floyd asked, looking up at the menu, seemingly baffled by all of the various combos. This was a menu that should be studied while you ate. Something could be gleaned from this menu each time you sat down. But, for new-comers, this menu had no mercy.

"Tuesday Special," said Darin. "Fish tacos."

Floyd glanced over at Robby. "How about you?"

"I might get that carne asada burrito special. You ever have that, Darin?"

"Yea, excellent. But you can't pass up these fish tacos. They're grilled and she knows just how to cook them just right."

"That's it. Fish tacos for me," said Floyd.

Robby nodded. "OK. Me, too."

Raphael, still talking on the phone, looked over at Darin apologetically and rolled his eyes. Darin motioned to Liani that they wanted three Tues-day specials, which she began to prepare. Darin reached over the counter to grab a bowl of chips and salsa while Floyd put a twenty down. Robby snagged the only remaining table.

"Thanks, Floyd," said Darin, reaching for a chip. "But you know you don't have to buy us lunch to pick our brains."

"Yea," said Robby, grinning. "There's not that much to pick!"

"I'd dispute that. You two, this whole crew actu-ally, has done a tremendous job keeping this old equipment going. There's so much work coming down. You have no idea. They're predicting incred-ible growth in this area and this company's not ready."

"Sounds like I better retire," said Robby. "Don't wanna give my whole life to this company."

"You wish you could," said Darin. "Ten more years, right?"

"A little more, actually."

"Well, I'm out of here in one," said Floyd. "And it's about time."

"You mentioned that cabin on a lake in Michigan?" said Robby, sipping on his Coke. "Did you talk to your wife about it?"

"A little. Don't want to get hopes up and then have the company screw me over again. But in a year, it's over. This dude's retired, with medical. We're gonna go on a long cruise to anywhere."

"Must be nice," said Darin, getting up to retrieve their orders. "You guys need anything else?"

Six hours later, Darin and Robby finished up with their repairs, about the same time that Floyd was walking through his front door.

Floyd

Normally Darla would have dinner on the stove
or in the oven, or something in a crock-pot that
had been stewing all day, waiting for Floyd when he
came through the front door.

She would be watching the evening news out in
the studio, or maybe sewing in her room. Hearing
him come into the kitchen from the garage door,
Darla would take a minute to come greet him, ask
how his day was and give him a hug.

But tonight, the house was dark. Feeling along
the wall, Floyd found the light switch and turned
on the kitchen lights. A note was on the table.

Hi Dear,
Just wanted to remind you. I have choir practice
tonight and won't be home till late.

There's lasagna in the fridge and I've made you a
salad.

Love and kisses,
Darla

Skipping the dinner idea, Floyd found a glass in
the cupboard, filled it with ice and poured scotch
over that. Carrying drink and briefcase, he headed
for his office upstairs.

Around ten, Floyd pushed the stacks of papers
off to the side of his desk, leaned back in his chair,
and massaged his temples. Simple jobs mostly. But
each had somehow grown arms and legs. You always expect some problems, but some of these...,

Building Twelve had the misfortune of having
the return line to the main fuel tank blocked, not
a big deal had Sergio been there to stop the pump.
New statewide mandate, have everyone test their

fuel return lines, make sure the lines are open and insure that the room drains are blocked. All of the engine rooms must have dams built into all of the doorways. Insure that all entrances into the engine rooms have a light switch next to the door. "How much will that cost?" they ask.

*You tell me. Some techs will get all the testing done in one day. Others will take two months.*

"How many man-hours to inspect, test and report back?"

*Your guess is as good as mine. Ask the techs.*

"How come it's taking so long for the estimate?"

*I'll give you the numbers when they inspect and test. Otherwise, it's a crapshoot.*

Gotta hire electricians for the lights, concrete people to do the dams, someone to seal the floors. There is no one company that does it all.

Floyd groaned as he picked himself up out of his chair and headed downstairs for the refrigerator. He retrieved a handful of ice from the tray and poured himself another scotch.

*Seems like these choir practices are lasting longer and there's more of them. What is that all about? Are they practicing for some kind of play? I'll have to ask about that when she gets home.*

Floyd plopped back into his chair, took a large gulp of scotch, felt it burn the back of his throat and stared at the pile of paperwork.

*OK. The crew wants to have Emergency Shutdown buttons installed on the outside walls of the doors to each of the engine rooms. State's going to mandate it. But Security says we have to have it keyed so that some joe-schmuk can't come along and shut it down while the building's running on standby power. They want a security cover over the emergency button with a lock on it.*

159

*Defeats the purpose. If it's got a lock, how can you operate it in an emergency? You can't have both. Let's see, what company builds something like that? How many do I need?*

By eleven, Floyd was ready for bed but was very concerned that Darla hadn't come home yet. Used to be, choir practice finished at eight or eight-thirty. For the last couple of months though, the time had been getting later, just socializing after practice, Darla had said. But eleven at night was just too darn late, especially for a weeknight.

Floyd brushed his teeth and pulled back the covers on their bed. An envelope flipped out from within the folds of the covers. It didn't look good, and it didn't feel right. Floyd stared at it for a long time before, hands shaking, he picked it up and began to read.

My Darling Floyd,

If this letter is in your hands, then my decision has already been made. I won't have come home to retrieve it.

I would like to say that my times with you have been the happiest times of my life. I will always remember, with great fondness and teary eyes, all of our precious moments together. We've raised two wonderful kids and, after all of our hard work, they are setting out on their own. I am so proud of them and I know you are too.

Watching them settle into their new lives, watching them follow their dreams has made me restless as well. You and I have talked about it many times. We both know the argument all too well.

When the kids were growing, I felt like I had a purpose. I felt like I was needed and I always, and you know this very well, I always rose to the occasion. Nothing ever came before my family. It was you and the kids first, always.

But for the last two years, this time that the company has stolen your soul, I have been aching for us to rekindle the times and feelings that we used to know. We have talked about this many, many times, to no avail.

Where is your guitar at this moment? Can you tell me?

When was the last time you recited me one of your poems?

This is the man I fell in love with. Where is he now?

There was a second page, but Floyd didn't want to read it. Instead, he walked back down to the kitchen and poured himself another scotch. The house would normally be quiet now anyway, this late at night, Darla either reading or sleeping, her body warm and comforting when he finally came to bed.

*Funny how that makes a difference, same house but, with her not here, it's just a building.*

He unfolded the letter, flipped to the second page, and began to read.

I have been faithful all of these years. And I have no reason but to believe that the same is true for you. Our love has been honest and true. This is why it has been so hard to say what I am about to say.

I have met another man. I wasn't looking, not at all. Please understand. I took up choir because the nights at the house were so lonely, you being gone all of the time. It's a wonderful house and I cry at the thought of leaving it. Over the years, we've spent many happy moments making it special, just for us.

But over the last few years when you come to our bed, our bed, you're asleep before your head hits the pillow and I awake to the sounds of you leaving in the morning. What happened to those gentle touches, our quiet joking, even a short massage?

Sitting there alone, night after night, remembering all of our good times and seeing life pass us by, wrinkles growing deeper and my hair more gray, I felt I needed to get out and see what I was missing.

I know we only had a year to go. We have heard this before. And who knows how they'll stop us next time? How many more days are there left of our lives?

I will love you forever,

Darla

Floyd drained his glass, went to the cupboard, got the bottle and brought it back to the table. He poured himself a stiff one, downed it, and then another. Turning the page over, he took a pen from his pocket and wrote:

To Darla,

And it was dark,
shimmering,
the body that held us
suspended
between earth
and stars.
Silently we paddled,
silhouettes gliding

through shadows,
oars dipping into stars
as we searched
for the moon.

Standing, Floyd stormed to the garage door, slammed it open, found his double bladed axe, made a beeline for the canoe sitting upside down on three sawhorses, ripped off the tarp and proceeded to chop it to bits.

And then, exhausted, he collapsed to the floor and, sitting in the middle of all of the pieces, cried like a baby.

Sometime around two, he awoke, staggered back to the door and made his way upstairs to bed.

*How could you, Darla? We were almost there! I thought we were happy. God damn it! It was going to be OK!!! How could that have been happening right under my nose? Work. They have stolen my soul.*

Five minutes later, he was up, groping his way to the medicine cabinet. Three aspirin and one glass of water later, he was back in bed.

*Arm's hurting. What is that all about? Pain's going all the way down to my fingers. Come on, aspirin. Kick in.*

Five minutes later, Floyd was feeling better. The aspirin was slowly dulling the pain. Grateful for the relief, Floyd drifted into his dreams...,

*On the beach, white endless sands, stunning blue-ocean, gentle breeze blowing up through the palms.*

*Floyd pulled the long, black strands of hair away from Darla's face and kissed her full on the mouth. Touching her hips lightly with his fingertips, memorizing the curves, he brought his hands upward to*

163

*cup her breasts. She did not resist...,*

The pain had gotten worse. Floyd opened his eyes and stared at the black ceiling.

*Seems to be in my chest. Isn't that heartburn? Feels like it. Just have to wait a minute. Whew. Better make an appointment tomorrow. Probably shouldn't have had so much to drink.*

He turned onto his side and repositioned the pillow so that his head was even with his neck.

And then the pain was stabbing, nearly exploding in his chest. Floyd rolled onto his back and tried to burp, thinking that this was an air bubble. He tried to breathe deeply but could only manage short gasps.

*Darla? You awake?*

*Darla?*

*You...,*

*I think you...,*

*You better call...,*

*9 - 1...,*

*Breathing hard, running toward the cove, Darla in front, laughing, pulling him along, waves splashing up over their feet, leaving vanishing tracks in fluid sand, they were together, touching, each wanting to know everything about the other, tongues searching, locked together forever...,*

And then there was only light.

## Meeting

Martin waited until everyone was seated, gave them an extra fifteen minutes to chew the fat, stir the cream into their coffee, get out their papers, pens, chew the fat some more, and then gave them an extra five minutes to come to the slow realization that, yes, a meeting was planned for the morning and that it might have something to do with them, and therefore him since he was the one that called the meeting. Eventually, everyone was quiet, looking his way, waiting.

"I have some sad news," said. Martin "We lost one of our own yesterday. Floyd passed away in his sleep."

For the next minute or two the crew was quiet, everyone taking this in, reflecting upon their relationships with him, their conversations, digesting this new knowledge, wondering how it was going to change their lives. For fifteen years he had been their friend and ally, always bending over backward to get them what they needed.

Carly, writing Floyd's name under the date of her crew notes, looked up. "What did he die of?"

"They're doing an autopsy," said Martin. "But we think it was a heart attack."

"Wow," said Tony. "I thought he was in pretty good shape."

"You never know," Martin replied, shaking his head. "When the Big Man calls, you gotta go."

"How's Darla taking it?" Carly asked.

"Don't know. I haven't talked to her. When he didn't show for work or answer his phone, they sent someone over to check at his house. When he didn't answer the door, they called the police."

"Huh," said Darin, shaking his head. "I just had lunch with him. He said he was going to retire in a year. That sucks. Wasn't he working out?"

"Had a membership," said Martin. "Don't know how often he used it. He was pretty swamped with work most of the time."

Grabbing his pen, Darin opened his note pad. "When's the funeral?"

"Don't know. When I find out, You will too."

"Who's taking his place?" Carly asked.

"Buck will be our new engineer."

Darin groaned. "What? That guy's an idiot!"

"He was his assistant," said Martin.

"That doesn't mean he knows anything."

"Give him a chance."

"I've seen him in action. The guy's a walking disaster."

"He knows all of the jobs."

"Maybe," said Darin. "But whether he can do anything...,"

"Jesus," said Carly, studying Darin. "How do you really feel about this?"

"We should give him the benefit of the doubt," said Martin. "At least until he proves otherwise."

Darin scribbled something into his notebook. "Has anyone in Floyd's family been notified?"

"Don't know. When I find out anything, I'll let you all know."

Buck entered the room with a load of papers in one hand, spilling some on his way into the room, and a briefcase in the other. "Sorry I'm late. I was trying to get all of his jobs together." He plopped his mess down onto the table.

"You guys all know Buck, right?" said Martin.

Buck cleared his throat. "I was very sorry to hear about Floyd. He and I were becoming good friends and...,"

Carly knew this was a crock of shit. She and Floyd had been talking about replacing the burnt up power plant in Building Twenty-three. When she asked if he was getting any extra help...,

"Carly," he had said. "The most help they could give me is to get Buck the hell out of my life."

"I thought you guys were buds."

"My ass. He lost the files I'd been keeping on all of the jobs. Deleted them! Stupid bastard."

Carly laughed. "Just think, some day he could be your peer."

"You know what I do? I send him out to the desert sites to report on the jobs. I could just call the tech and know more in five minutes than Buck will know after a day's work."

"And so," said Buck. "I've got sixteen jobs open, so I'll need your help bringing me up to date. Looks like Floyd had some other ones pending...,"

Sitting back in the corner, Merry Dick Tracy was eying the stack of papers in front of Buck. If ever there was a gold mine within reach, this was it. She quietly took notes as Buck moved from one job to another, talking to this tech or that, updating her own files, taking names and numbers.

"Well," said Martin, at last. "Looks like we got a lot accomplished today. Why don't we break for lunch and meet back here at one?"

That seemed acceptable to everyone. There was a low murmur that passed through the crew as lunch arrangements were made, people going to this place or that, with this friend or that, the rustling sounds of everyone heading out.

Merry converged on Buck before he had a chance to stuff the papers back into his briefcase.

"Hi, Buck," she said, extending her hand. "I'm

167

Merry."

He shook her hand, smiling. "Hi, Merry."

"Do you have a minute to answer a couple of questions about some of those jobs?"

"Sure. Which ones?"

The crew knew better than to dally. They headed for the exit like horses escaping the corral, like birds breaking out of their cage, like a herd of zebras escaping the claws of a hungry lion, silently laughing with the knowledge that the spider had just caught the fly.

"Before I forget," said Merry, clicking her mechanical pencil twice for extra lead while smiling at Buck. "What's your e-mail address and cell number? Or, better yet, have you got a business card?"

# Rum Balls

"I brought these," said Carly, setting a plastic container on the table.

Jerome set the two coffees down between them. "Cream? Sugar?

"With these, it tastes better black."

"What are they?"

"Rum balls."

"What, with rum?"

"Well..., duh."

Jerome and Carly seated themselves in one of the two tables in the window of a hole-in-the-wall coffee shop located between the north and south county loops. They were the only two working today, a holiday, and were paid to watch over the power needs of the company throughout the day.

The morning had been dead quiet, no phone calls, no alarms, nothing to do, so they decided to meet here, on the adjoining perimeter of their areas of responsibility and kill a little time. Jerome studied the container between them.

"Did you cook the rum?"

"No. What are you, nuts? You'll cook off all the alcohol."

"So..., if I eat one...,"

"Yes. You will have alcohol on your breath."

"Can they get you drunk?"

"There are twenty of them. Yes. What's your point?"

"If something happens. What if I had to drive out to...,"

"Jesus, Jerome. When did you turn into a wuss?"

Carly opened the container, set the lid off to the side and pulled one out. "Suit yourself."

"I didn't say I wasn't going to have one," said Jerome, reaching for a rum ball. "I just make it a habit not to drink on company time. You can get fired for that."

"We're not drinking. We're having a rum ball for Christ's Sake. Everybody else is home eating great meals, drinking, partying. There's hardly any traffic. We're the only suckers working today. What's it going to hurt to have a fucking rum ball?"

"Whew. How much rum is in this?"

"As much as it can hold."

"Don't light a match around here. These things are dangerous. You always put that much in?"

"This is not rum ball lite. If I'm going to go through the trouble, I'm going to make it worth my while."

"It is good."

"Peanut butter melts into the chocolate when you drink your coffee. And then the rum hits the roof of your mouth. That's the best part."

Jerome leaned back in his chair, eyes closed. "That's really good, better than apple-mayonnaise toast."

"You're kidding, right?"

"Another good one is peanut butter-banana toast."

"I always thought you were weird."

"Look who's talking, ye who burned up building Twenty-three."

"Low punch," said Carly. "I'll make sure you get all the antenna site jobs."

"That job sucks."

Carly took a second rum-ball and set it on a napkin next to her coffee. "It's fun watching you bitch about it. The only one that complains more than you is Darin."

Jerome laughed. "He sure got quiet after Roberta found that starter trouble."

Carly laughed. "First thing they should have looked at."

"Robby just laughs. Serge won't even talk about it."

"Mr. Macho. He doesn't want a female showing him up."

"I'm getting a buzz off of that damn rum ball. You could sell those."

"Riiight. Health Department would shut me down...,"

"Yea, but you'd have the rum industry behind you."

"Have another."

"I don't want the rum but it's really good with coffee. You should make up a batch without rum."

"And what will I call them? Balls?"

"You got a point."

"Doesn't even help to call them chocolate covered balls. Two won't hurt you."

"Ten would. We wouldn't be able to walk out of here."

"Probably because we'd be stuck on the crapper."

Jerome reached for another. "They are good."

"Hey, how'd you make out with Pam?"

'How'd you hear about that?"

"Word gets around."

"How'd you hear?"

"Can't reveal my sources. So..., you ever get any?"

"Still working on it. I would've had it the first night but I got that damn call-out."

"That was no accident, you know."

"What wasn't ?"

"Your getting called out. Pierce knew she was at

your place."

"What? You're shitting me! How could he know?"

"Walls have ears."

"You mean that whole call-out thing was staged? You've gotta be shitting me!"

Carly laughed. "Where do you think she went when she left your place?"

"What? With Pierce? I'll kill the mother!"

"He knew you were hitting on her. He had already met her when she first came down from L. A., met her at the Center when she..., hey!" Carly pointed through the window toward a couple crossing the street. "Check it out! Isn't that Roberta and Sergio?"

"What are they doing together?"

"Don't know," said Carly, getting up with a smile. "But I'm going to get them in here and find out."


"Looking for a sailboat," said Roberta, sitting down at the table, reaching over and taking a rum ball. "Serge said he saw one up here so I came up to look at it."

"Didn't know you knew anything about sailing," said Jerome.

"I know what they look like," said Sergio, reaching for a rum ball. "This one's red and it's got a mast. These have real rum?"

"Don't light a match," said Jerome.

"Wow," said Roberta, eyes wide. "How much you put in here?"

"As much as I could," said Carly.

Sergio reached for a napkin. "I've never seen rum balls that don't stick together. You should call them rum puddles."

Carly reached for another. "That's what makes them so good."

172

"Ought to be served with a shower," said Jerome, licking the goo off of his fingers.

"You guys are on-call today, right?" said Roberta, reaching for a napkin.

"Right," said Jerome. "That's why we're drinking coffee, to stay alert."

"Double espresso," said Carly. "That ought to yank us both ways."

"Makes for creative trouble-shooting," said Sergio. "Hope you guys don't go up in flames."

"Speaking of that," said Jerome. "What's Buck up to these days?"

Carly laughed. "Engineer and flames in the same thought. I like that."

Sergio reached for another rum ball. "Not much confidence in the poor guy, huh?"

"Actually," said Jerome, wiping his hands. "I was thinking of Floyd, who was cremated. And then Buck came to mind."

"I heard he went up to Corporate," said Carly. "Martin was saying that he had some idea he wanted to push."

"Serge, you want a cup?" said Roberta, getting up.

"Why not? The guy's not going to meet us until one."

And so went the morning. An hour later...,

"Might as well finish them off," said Carly. "One more each."

"This should qualify as an open container," said Roberta. "I feel like I've had a martini."

Jerome took one of the remaining four. "I'm going to have to get something to eat. I've got a buzz going."

Sergio took one of the last three. "Check it out. They just put on Santana. That's the make of the boat we're gonna go look at."

"Always loved that song," said Roberta, leaning back in her chair to listen.

"That's a racing boat, isn't it??" Jerome asked.

"Can't believe the sound system in here," said Carly. "I feel like I'm just now hearing it. Did they just turn the music on? Or has it been going all this time?"

"Fuck if I know," said Sergio. "Boat's red and it has a mast, sits on a trailer and that has two wheels, and...,"

"It has a fin keel," said Roberta, with a big, smile. "Turns on a dime, gives you nine cents change." She started laughing. "Is this one of those magical moments, you know, where everything just feels good?"

"Rum ball, heaven," said Carly.

"What kind of rum is that," said Jerome, now finding Roberta's smile contagious. "I'm gonna have to buy a few gallons."

Roberta leaned forward to take one of the last two rum balls. Picking it up...,

"What's this green stuff in here?"

"That's not mold, is it?" Jerome asked leaning forward to study the tiny, green thing.

"Can't be," said Carly, also leaning forward to look. "I just made them last night."

"You know what?" said Sergio, now looking round the room. "I'm stoned. Carly, what else did you put in here?"

"Shit," said Carly. "I brought the wrong batch. These have pot in them. You should never eat more than two. It's going to be a long afternoon for all of us."

"We should stick together," said Roberta. "Power in numbers."

Sergio started thumping the table in tune to the music, eyes closed, rocking his head side to side. He laughed. "Fuck if I'm going sailing. Ain't no waaay, baby."

"I vote for hamburgers," said Jerome. "And fries."

"Sushi."

"Yuk. Don't make me puke."

"Pizza."

"Had it last night."

"Chicken nuggets?"

"What the fuck? That's not even food."

"What do they serve here?"

"It's a coffee shop. They must have sandwiches."

"Yea. We should stay."

"That's good. Cause I can't even move."

"Amen, to that."

"Here, here."

## Meeting

"I've been up at Corporate," said Buck, standing at the long end of the table as he addressed Martin and the crew. "It didn't take us long to realize our basic problem with all of these jobs. They're patchwork. We keep trying to expand to fit the needs but when you look at the long-term growth expectations we'll never be able to keep up. We have to get ahead of the curve with new power rooms, bigger engines, build for the future...,"

"Jesus," Darin was thinking. "Is this the same guy that couldn't remove a piece of conduit without nearly killing his help?"

"Over the next five years," said Buck, nearly knocking his coffee over as he raised his hands for emphasis, "we're going to modernize the entire power system from the ground up. To help us with this the company has hired Mr. Binko here to assist us...,"

Mr. Binko sported a thin moustache and round, wire-rimmed glasses under a ridge of short brown hair that circumvented the back two thirds of his head, looking rather like a fur lined toilet seat. His smile was wide enough so that two gold molars, one on either side of his bottom jaw, glinted in the fluorescent light.

He had remained seated next to Buck during the entire time that the crew had assembled into the room. When he stood to acknowledge his introduction the entire crew was astonished to note that the difference between him sitting and him standing was only about six inches.

Jerome leaned over and whispered to Carly, sitting next to him. "Did he stand up all the way?"

"Not sure," said Carly, stifling a laugh. "I thought maybe the rum balls were still affecting me."

"Mr. Binko has a normal size head," thought Darin, sitting next to Roberta, across the table from Carly and Jerome. "Sitting, he's about the same height as anybody. But, standing, he's only about two inches taller than Martin, sitting."

Tony was wondering the same thing. But his angle of Mr. Binko standing was awkward so he couldn't actually see if his back was straight when his feet reached the floor. He glanced over at Carly and Jerome and then around the table. Everyone seemed to have something to quietly discuss since Binko stood.

Sergio was working on the name. Must be hard going through life with a name like Binko. Surely everybody called him Bingo or Bonkers or Sinko or Dingo, or...,.

And for the next several minutes the crew hardly heard a word that was spoken, all of them busy calculating the length of Mr. Binko's legs, wondering if they had been severed, whether he was a midget with a normal sized torso, wondering if he had been involved in some kind of accident...,

"And it's going to start with Darin's office," said Buck.

Which brought Darin back into the conversation. "What?"

"Last summer," said Buck. "Do you remember when the city cut off water to your building?"

"Yea. Norm panicked, said the chillers lose about three hundred gallons of water an hour to evaporation. We had to call in the fire trucks for water."

"Right," said Buck, pleased that Darin had inadvertently backed up Mr. Binko's plan to convert some of Darin's underground fuel tanks to water tanks. "Which is why...,"

What Carly was starting to hear was overtime, lots of it. If Buck had somehow pushed through the idea to build for the future they were going to need qualified people to watch this stuff going in, testing it and maintaining it. There were going to be job opportunities galore. This is the kind of stuff that builds portfolios, offers an occasional cruise, a new Porsche...,

"You're going to what?" said Darin. "Those turbines burn ninety gallons an hour and I've got three of them on that side of the building. You can't take away the fuel tanks!"

"I'm not going to," Buck replied, calmly. "I'm going to take away the engines and then convert the fuel tanks to water tanks."

"What are we going to do for emergency power?" said Darin, now getting red in the face. "You can't just remove back-up systems!"

"I'm taking out all of the turbines," said Buck. "Every building. They burn too much fuel. And look at all of the trouble we're having with them. Building Seventeen hasn't been reliable since...,"

"Fixed," said Roberta.

Martin leaned forward in his chair, elbows on the table. "When did that happen?"

"Met this guy who worked on turbines," said Roberta. "Turned out it was a...,"

Buck didn't care. That was not the point as far as he was concerned. Turbines still burned too much fuel and, damn it, they were going to be replaced. "OK. Building Four. Look how much overtime we put into that engine."

"Fixed," said Darin. "Sheared starter shaft."

Carly loved going after Darin in particular, always thinking that he was above it all. "And who fixed it, Darin? Say it, woman, w-o-m-a-n."

"Too bad you don't qualify," said Darin.

"All right," said Martin. "Let's keep on track. Buck, Darin's got a point. We need power from somewhere."

"I want to install three big engines on the other side of the building."

Darin did not like change in general, hated it when he suspected that it wasn't well thought out. "Great! How will you get power back over to the other side of the building? It's gonna cost a fortune in copper and...,"

"We're going to install a 12kv system, " said Mr. Binko.

That stopped Darin. "What?"

Mr. Binko slid his chair away from the table, preparing to stand.

Good, the entire crew was thinking. Now the question will be resolved. How tall is Mr. Binki or Bingi, whatever his name. What was he, five foot? Shorter? To everyone's astonishment, as he stood he just kept going up.

What was he, six-seven or six-eight?

Carly started laughing, holding her stomach. Jerome groaned as he leaned back in his chair.

Sergio realized that no one ever called this guy names. They pronounced it Binko with a Mister in front.

Mr. Binko smiled broadly at Carly's laugh. "I like to do that. It helps break the ice. What we're proposing is to convert the voltage from four-eighty volts up to twelve thousand, ship it across the building and then convert back to four-eighty. Cost of copper is minimal."

"No shit," said Darin, realizing that there was some method to Buck's madness. "What else are

179

you guys going to do?"

"Wait," said Carly, looking around the room and then over at Martin. "Where's Robby? This is important. He should be here."

Time Away

Sitting at his desk, Robby stared at the calendar in front of him. Here it was only Tuesday and already this week and all of next week were taken.

*Gotta meet with the engineers tomorrow and ID all of the breakers and get them tagged.*

*Gotta come in tomorrow night and hook up the temporary engine and test.*

*Gotta come in Thursday morning and make sure everything's been disconnected from the old engine so that it can be removed.*

*I like that old engine. We always laugh about Roberta fixing it. Hate to see it go.*

*Gotta meet with Environmental starting Friday morning and do ground testing before we dig up the tank. Everything's going double wall.*

*Man, that's a lot of work. And in every building.*

*Friday night, Building Three to replace the Controller. That's an all night job.*

*I'll be dead Saturday. Tanya's going to a company dinner Saturday night and wants me to tag along. Nobody goes to company stuff on the weekend. What's with that? I know she's trying to get ahead but we gotta keep our lives, too.*

*She's gonna drag me to church on Sunday.*

*Gotta go to work Sunday night at midnight for the battery change-out. That'll take all night. Appointments with vendors Monday afternoon. Next week's worse and the calendar's already filling up for next month.*

*Buck's just getting started. This'll go on for another year.*

Robby leaned back in his chair and put his feet up on the desk.

181

*Where's my time? I need my time...,*

Robby took a deep breath, exhaled, and closed his eyes...,

*Hot already, sun just now coming up behind the cottonwoods.*

*"Fifty bucks," says Old Man Thomas, weed hanging from between his teeth, bouncing up when he said bucks. "Probably the easiest fifty you'll ever make."*

*Robby studied the ground. The last rain was more than a month ago and the weeds had had plenty of time to get their roots going. "This is a big lot and the ground's dry. It's gonna take a while."*

*Thomas kicked the ground with the toe of his boot and watched the dirt fly away. "It's a little hard on top. But it's loamy further down. What do you say? Fifty bucks, you break it up?"*

*The lot was about fifty feet wide and about twice as long. Robby figured that if he could get the shovel deep enough, turning the soil wouldn't be that hard because he could probably dig up a square foot with every thrust into the dirt. Then the job would be worth fifty bucks.*

*But if a pick was required, that would be at least two swings per square foot plus the shovel at least one time to turn it, twice as hard. And for that much work he should be paid at least seventy-five, more like a hundred.*

*"Tell you what," said Robby. "I'll work five hours, that's ten bucks an hour. I should be able to get most of it done by then."*

*Old man Thomas bit off the chewed end of his weed, spit it out, and put the rest back in his mouth. "How do I know you're not doggin' it so you can get more money to finish?"*

182

"What are you planting?"

"Corn."

"You're too late. Corn's supposed to be knee high by July. It's already June. You're wasting you're money."

"I'm not plantin' corn, jest sayin' I am."

"Why do that?"

"You're awfully nosey for being the digger. You want the job, or not?"

"It don't make sense. You're payin' me fifty dollars to dig up a field that's not getting planted with corn. I gotta ask myself, why?"

"Well, that's a good question, ain't it? Fair 'nuff. The government'll give me a hundred to not plant corn. I want to have the field dug up in case they come check."

"You're payin' me, who does all the work, fifty bucks while you do nothin' and get a hundred?"

"I own the land. If it weren't for me you'd have nothin' to dig. Never heard nobody tryin' so hard to get out of work. You don't need the money?"

"I do. But I want fair pay. Cause if it takes me all day, or maybe even part of tomorrow to dig all of this up, fifty bucks ain't worth it. I'd rather go fishin'."

"You're a whole lot smarter than I thought you were. You understand that sometimes the Good Lord puts obstacles in your path to happiness and that you should be compensated for your extra troubles. The Good Lord gave you a mighty big brain. Tell you what, I'll give you twenty-five bucks and I'll throw in Missy, my favorite mule."

"What would I do with a mule?"

"You could ride her home after all your hard work. It's better than walkin'. How far back to your place? Two miles?"

"About."

"And the mule's worth two hundred. You could turn a profit."

"How much it cost to feed her?"

"Nothin'. That's the beauty of a mule. Just let her graze wherever you got too many weeds growin'. That's more work you don't have to do. She's a gift that just keeps on givin'."

"How about I dig up the whole field no matter how long it takes and you give me fifty and the mule?"

"That don't sound fair. You'd be gettin' two hundred-fifty bucks for about five hours work while I'm only getting' a hundred and losin' a mule."

"You're gettin' a hundred for doin' nothin'."

"But it's my land. Tell you what. I'll meet you half way. I'll give you thirty-seven-fifty and Missy. Fair enough?"

Robby didn't really like the deal but the day was warming up quickly and getting started earlier was better. He held out his hand. "Deal."

Twelve hours later, he was done and done in. As suspected, the ground had been dry and hard to till. Old man Thomas handed him four tens, and the reins to Missy who was suspicious of the whole transaction.

She didn't want Robby out of her sight, turning her head from side to side as he tried to circle her, threatening to kick when he passed behind. She didn't want to be led away and being mounted by him was out of the question.

Who leaves home at this time of the day? Missy knew that, left alone, she could be resting in her stall doing what she knew best, resting. Leave home with a perfect stranger at this late hour? With a boy, no less? Hardly.

"She's a bit temperamental," said Thomas, strok-

184

*ing her forehead. "She don't know you, yet."*

*He disappeared back into his house while Robby tried unsuccessfully to make friends. Thomas returned with some carrots, an apple, and handed them to Robby.*

*"She'll love you to death, now. Kind of dole them out as you head home. Don't give them to her all at once. And give her the apple last."*

*To Robby's surprise, Missy followed. Normally, walking by himself, he could cover the mile and a half, just past two Burma Shave signs, in about twenty minutes. With Missy, after an hour of coaxing, he could see his house in the distance and was down to one carrot and the apple.*

*Missy had had enough of carrots and ignored Robby's bribe. In fact, bed was starting to sound a whole lot better than even the apple. She started looking back toward home.*

*"So be it," thought Robby. "Apple, it is."*

*He let her get the first bite and barely got away with his hand and half the apple. Breaking it in half, he even got her within a hundred yards from home.*

*Apple gone, Missy decided that enough was enough and let Robby know by turning back toward her house and tugging in the opposite direction. When she started kicking and trying to bite, Robby let go. Missy had more strength, more determination and certainly more stamina, now that returning to her stall was in the forefront of her mind.*

*Instead, Robby went home, vowing to take care of the problem in the morning. But early the next morning the phone was already ringing off the hook...,*

Phone ringing, Robby woke up, smiling.

*Simple times. I always felt good back then. Broke, but good.*

The phone rang again.

"Power Maintenance. Robby, here."

"Hey, Robby, This is Sergio. I'm right up the street. You got time for lunch?"

"Seems like I don't have time for nothin' anymore. What are you doin' on my turf?"

"There's an electronics place here on Euclid that carries the parts I need to fix all of those DC lights that have been failing."

"You figured out how to fix them? I know of about five of mine that are broke."

"They blow fuses when they fire up?"

"Yeah. That's it. A bigger fuse works but you're takin' a chance on the whole thing burnin' up."

"That's the same trouble. I'll buy extra and show you what you need to do to get them fixed."

"If I had the time. Buck got you running all over the place, too?"

"I'd kill the mother-fucker if there were no witnesses."

Robby laughed. "Me, too. Problem is, he's got me comin' and goin' so much I don't even have time to go home and get my gun."

"Maybe we can catch him on a midnight shift somewhere."

"He's not workin' nights. He sits at his desk all day and makes phone calls, tellin' everyone to contact us directly. Everybody's got my number now."

"Yeah. My phone hasn't stopped ringing either. OK, amigo. Hasta la vista."

Robby hung up, feeling very much like everything was closing in. There were so many things to do and it was only going to get worse.

*Times like this, I need a little distraction.*

186

Darin was in his office checking e-mail when the phone rang. He answered, thinking it was either Norm wanting to go for breakfast or Martin calling for some inane reason and thinking it was going to be one busy-busy day.

"Power Maintenance, Darin here."

"Darin, is this your truck out here on the east side?"

"Hey, Norm. Yea. I'm saving a spot for one of the vendors. He needs access to that side door. I'll move it into the lot when...,"

"Yea? Well, you should've moved it a little sooner."

"Oh. Is he here?"

"No. Streets closed off. There's been a little accident."

"What? What's going on?"

"Come on out and take a look for your self. This guy's lucky to be alive. Your truck didn't make it, though."

"What? Norm, what the hell?"

"Come on up to the front entrance. I'll explain when you get here. Police want to talk to you anyway."

"What? Damn it, Norm!"

"Meet you at the front door."

Willy and Norm were laughing when Darin burst through the double doors leading up from the basement.

"Took the whole thing!" said Willy, wiping the tears from his eyes. "Hook, line, and sinkah!"

"Watched you come down the hall," said Norm. "Willy's got that camera there by the elevator...,"

"Yea," said Willy. "Merry'll write you up for speeding in the hallway."

"Fuck both of you. So, my truck's all right?"

"Didn't lie about that," said Norm, now opening the door for Darin and motioning for him to go through. "You might have a crack in your windshield."

"What?"

Willy stopped him. "Look here, on the monitor. I'm gonna go back to the main attraction." He selected a camera view that showed Darin's truck parked along the curb and a man leaning down in front of it, doing something to the sidewalk.

"Watch this guy here," said Norm. "He's got a cutting torch and he's going to open up the top of the fuel tank.

"That's dumb," said Darin. "We're talking vapors."

"They were supposed to fill the tank with dry ice. That's a nine thousand gallon tank."

"Did they put any ice in?"

"About a hundred pounds."

"Comin' up," said Willy, pointing to the monitor.

"Right....., there," said Norm. "Look at that! The piece just misses him! Another inch and he loses his head!"

"Holy shit!" said Darin. "That's one inch thick steel!"

"Went up almost as high as the building," said Norm. "What is that, sixty feet?"

"Is he OK?"

Willy laughed. "I think he went home to change his underwear."

"Here's the good part," said Norm. "That's your truck in the background, right?"

"Right. Looks like it anyway."

"Here it comes! Bam! There goes your windshield!"

Norm and Willy burst into laughter.

"Whoosh!" Willy howled, nearly doubled up, holding onto his desk. "Fuckin' thing is *gone!*"

"What are the odds?" said Norm, wiping tears from his eyes.

Darin headed for the door. "What the hell!"

"Tried to warn you about today," said Norm, waving to Willy on his way out. "Sent you an e-mail. But you were in a meeting with the engine movers."

"Well..., yea. If someone's going to remove one of my four-ton engines and roll it through the basement, I'd like to know what they're going to do with it. There's too much going on all at once. I can't be watching everything! Fucking Buck is gonna get someone killed!"

"In his defense," said Norm. "The guy didn't follow the MOP. There was supposed to be ten times that amount of dry ice in there. And he was supposed to have a thermometer inside so he could keep an eye on the internal temp."

"Guy's lucky," said Darin, finally calming down. "You never know when your time's up."

As the Crow Flies

Jerome pulled into the parking lot at eight AM.
He was supposed to meet a representative from the
battery manufacturer so they could discuss an on-
going problem, corroded battery terminals.

Cleaning the terminals was one of the last
things anyone on the crew wanted to do. First, it
was dangerous. Second, after cleaning the terminals, no one ever walked away without battery acid
on their clothes, which would take a washing or
two to show that, yes a growing, unstoppable hole
has arrived and it will be with you until the cloth-
ing is discarded. Third, it was time consuming and
unrewarding. There was no best-looking-battery-
string category.

The problem persisted to the point that it started to become a reliability issue around the various buildings within the county and the crew was
spending more and more of their time attempting to
correct the problem.

Tests were done, decisions were made and still
the batteries continued to corrode. Then it was
noted that none of the old batteries had this problem, only the new ones. Suddenly, everyone had
a scapegoat. The new batteries must be made of
inferior quality. The battery manufacturer agreed to
send a rep out to look at the problem...,

Jerome found him sitting on a small stool alongside the row of batteries, his thick body form looking more like a sitting turtle without its shell. He
wore a red paisley bandanna tied over his long,
straggly hair. When he stood, Jerome guessed
he was six-four and about two hundred and fifty
pounds. He wiped his huge hands with a red rag

190

from his pocket and extended his hand.

"You must be Jerome."

"And you're...," Jerome checked his documents, "Stu, right?"

"That's what they call me to my face. I been called worse but not for long."

Stu sat back down and returned to unbolting the strap from the terminal. "Need to keep going. Got a plane outta here at three."

"You know you're not supposed to open up that battery string unless I'm here?"

"Yea, well, like I said, plane leaves at three."

"How'd you get in the building?"

"Followed the delivery guy in."

"Nobody questioned who you were and what you're doing here?"

"Yea. I just showed 'em my ID card and said I was supposed to meet you in the power room. They brought me here. Look, Pumpkin, I flew in at six-thirty and I'm flying out at three. I gotta get this done, so if you don't mind...,"

"I thought we were just going to discuss what's causing the problem."

Stu looked at Jerome as if he were about the dumbest thing on the planet.

"Well, let me think. I wonder if it could be acid creeping up the post?"

"I know that," said Jerome, starting to get irritated. "Question is, why? Are the seals bad on these new batteries?"

"Seals are better on the new ones."

"But they're the only ones with the corrosion problem. The old ones...,"

"Hey, Pumpkin. The old ones have No-Ox. That means, no oxide. It works. You guys keep using this crappy oil...,"

191

"Your company makes that oil. It's especially for batteries."

"Yea. We made it. We tried it. And we discovered it don't work. When the oil dries out the felt pads act like a sponge. Where's the nearest moisture, huh?"

"I thought the plastic covers were to keep the pads from drying out."

"Like I said. It don't work. You guys are supposed to keep the pads full of oil too but nobody does that either. We told your company ten years ago that this stuff is crap. And yet here I am, out on the west coast cleaning your batteries. And I gotta ask why?"

Nothing like getting the real skinny, thought Jerome. Talk to the people that do the work and they'll tell you what's really going on.

"Hey, Stu. You want some coffee?"

"Thanks, Pumpkin. I'd like a cup."

Jerome started to leave and then stopped, turning. "Why are you calling me Pumpkin?"

Stu laughed. "If I'm gonna fly all the way out here from Georgia to clean your batteries, I'm entitled to give you a little shit. Cream, no sugar. Thanks, Jerome."

Returning with the coffee, Jerome asked Stu if he'd been watching the playoffs.

"No," said Stu, cleaning his hands. "Don't have time to sit around and watch games."

"So..., what do you do with your spare time?"

"That's personal," said Stu, taking a large gulp from his coffee and returning to the batteries.

Jerome watched him work for the next few minutes, noting that the man was quite adept with his hands and that he had this whole operation under control. His information about the oil would be conveyed to the crew, who would now insist that all new batteries come with the No-Ox. The days of corroded battery terminals were gone. Hooray!

Still, since Jerome was assigned to meet with this guy and since he didn't seem to want any help or to talk, Jerome retrieved his book from his truck, sat next to his coffee and began to read. "You ever read any Castaneda?"

Stu glanced up, saw which book Jerome was reading, nodded, and returned to his work. "All of 'em."

"What do you think of this business about crows?"

Stu shrugged, but didn't bother to answer.

"Spent some time in Japan," said Jerome. "Teaching English. The lessons were supposed to be half hour of instruction and a half hour of conversation. One of the students asked what book I was reading and just when I was talking about Carlos Castaneda and crows, one of the birds landed in the windowsill behind me and started cawing. You should've seen the student's eyes. They thought I was some kind of witch doctor."

Stu nodded knowingly. "Maybe you got some power there, Pumpkin."

"Another time, I was standing at a busy intersection waiting for the light to change when this huge crow fell at my feet, deader than a doornail. Stopped traffic, everybody staring at me and the crow. There were some power lines above me, thought that might be what killed it.

"Right after that one of my best friends died. A month later, another friend was killed in a car accident. I started wondering if that crow was trying to tell me something and wondering if bad news comes in threes. And then my mother died. It all happened in a couple of months."

During the telling of this story, Stu had stopped working and listened to Jerome carefully. Finally, he stood, went to his tools and retrieved a cigarette and lighter.

"Hey, Pumpkin. Follow me outside and I'll tell you a story."

"I bought some land in upstate Georgia, got a lake on it. Me and my old lady worked our asses off to get enough money. We ride up there every chance we get, building a house."

"Ride?"

"Bikers, about twenty of us. We go up to party and they help me do the work. Going up there tonight, soon as I get back. About a year ago, we were all getting ready to ride back to Atlanta when this crow lands on my handlebars. And it don't move and I'm thinking, what the fuck? I coulda chased it off but because of Castaneda I'm thinking it's trying to warn me about somethin'. Normally I lead. But that day, Cleve, my best friend, says he'll lead going back and I can catch up when I'm done talking to the fuckin' bird. I took a lot a shit for it when they were leavin' and everybody had a good laugh."

Jerome nodded knowingly.

"Damn bird wouldn't leave for another five minutes. As soon as it did, I rode like a mother-fucker to catch up. Only took me a few minutes. Everybody was pulled over not even five miles down the road. Cleve had hit a slick spot in a curve and went down an embankment, sixty feet. Killed him."

"Jesus."

"Shoulda been me. So when you talk about crows there, Pumpkin, you got my attention."

"I'd sure like a chance to talk to Castaneda."

"Me too. You ever get down to Georgia, look me up."

"Right," said Jerome, laughing at the idea of hanging around with a bunch of bikers. "And what would I do?"

"Bury you underground for two days. That's something you won't forget."

"You did that?"

"Yea. And Castaneda's right. A lot of strange shit goes through your mind down there. But after a while you just feel calm."

"Probably because you know you're trapped. It's hopeless, futile."

"Hey, Pumpkin. It's that already. If you follow Don Juan's advice, you'll never do things that you don't wanna do because you could die doin' them. And then you're just not gonna enter that next world in the proper state of mind, are you? That's why I find it so strange that I'm out here cleanin' your batteries, until now. So maybe this conversation was meant to take place."

Roberta's kitchen counter was where most of the conversations took place. Barstools on either side, and with the refrigerator only a few steps away, it was only natural for Roberta and Vanessa to spend their time there, Vanessa pretty much keeping the glasses full while Roberta kept the appetizers going.

"OK," said Roberta, setting out some crackers and cheese. "This is goat cheese with sun dried tomatoes and garlic."

Frowning, Vanessa refilled their glasses. "Don't you have a date tonight?"

"There's a method to my madness. I have a slight problem."

Vanessa finished filling their glasses, put the bottle down and rubbed her hands together. "I knew it."

"What? You don't know anything."

"You liked sailing with Kirk. And you want to do it again. But you don't know how to make it happen because of Todd."

"It's terrible that they're friends. Either way, it doesn't work."

"Well, at least you have two choices. That's a good start."

"Yea. But I like them both. Todd took me to George's by the Cove...,"

"That's that place out in La Jolla, right?"

"Right. We sat out on the patio most of the afternoon drinking wine and eating hors d'oeuvres, watching the ocean, slowly getting drunk."

"Sounds romantic."

"But, way out on the horizon there were two

sailboats. I don't know if they were racing or if each was doing its' own thing, but they were going in the same direction. And then I noticed where the eye of the wind was and understood why they were doing what they were doing. That's a whole new dimension I've never known before. I kept wondering what it would be like to be out there on one of them, at sunset...,"

"With Kirk, right?"

"I totally enjoyed that afternoon with Todd. We get along, talk easy and I had fun getting drunk with him. But then there's the thrill of sailing with Kirk. I really had fun that day."

"So..., with either of them, anything happen?."

"Nope."

"Why not?"

"Because I want to make sure he's the right one. How do I choose? I can't have them both."

"Why not?"

"You have no shame, do you?"

"I'd bet Todd banged what's her name? Lee?"

"No. Come on. They just went to an art show."

"And wine tasting, meet with the artists, go to the party afterwards. And you think they didn't do it?"

"I have more faith in men than that."

"Let me ask you this. Did you want to linger a while, stay on the boat with Kirk, have another glass of wine?"

"It was a nice night. Yea..., I did."

"But you didn't stay."

"Right."

"Roberta. Roberta. Roberta. What am I going to do with you?"

"They're friends. They talk!"

"Think about it. I hate to be the party pooper,

but what if Todd and Kirk are both having sex with Lee and here you are, Miss Goody, Goody, Two Shoes with your apron and bouquet of flowers. How do you think that's going to play out?"

Roberta laughed. "Well, at least I won't catch what they've got."

"I'd press Kirk for more information about his relationship with Lee. You could be on the brink of something beautiful, all of you secretly lovers with the others. Think of the intrigue."

"And the scandal."

"Being faithful to Daryl, how did that help?"

"Point taken." said Roberta, spreading cheese on a cracker. "Another question. Who is Kirk's sailing partner? He never said."

"If it's a guy, he'll pick you, at least every other time. If it's a girl, then you've got another three-way on your hands."

"It's amazing how you think. Does everything always have to come down to sex? What ever happened to friendship and trust?"

"We never had it in the first place. Part of the Big Lie so they can take advantage of us more easily."

"Speaking of lies, Daryl's stopping by to pick up the rest of his stuff."

"When?"

"This morning. He just hasn't gotten here yet."

"It's almost four. What time's your date?"

"Six. If Daryl doesn't get here soon, he's just going to have to wait until another time."

"I never schedule anything with two different men on the same day. Time means nothing to them. Their chances of overlapping go way up."

"I never even thought about it. That would not be cool for Daryl to be here when Todd arrives."

"Why not? Daryl's the fool. He left you."

198

"He's also got a temper. I don't like stressful situations."

"He's got no claim on anything. He's the one that left. You want me to hang here with you until he leaves?"

"Could you? I'll put another bottle in the fridge."

"How can I refuse? Besides, I wouldn't miss this. I never did like him."

"He liked you."

"That's because I have tits. Get real, lady. As Tom Waites said, "The crack of dawn better be careful around me." Daryl was like that."

"You're saying my taste in men sucks?"

"No. I'm saying it's not realistic. Todd is cool, has money, intelligence, good looks. Kirk is technical, which you like, fun loving, and that appeals to you, romance of the sea, and all that shit. Daryl is the fickle village idiot. They all have their roles. You just have to learn to see them as they are."

"Coming from you, the expert, right?"

"I measure people by how much they contribute. If I always walk away from someone feeling good, I keep them around. Too many bad feelings and they're out of my life unless they're hopeless, like you. Then, I just donate my time."

Roberta laughed. "So now I'm a charity case?"

"Look at how far you've come in the last month. I must be doing something right."

Two glasses of wine later, a knock on the door.

"Daryl the dip!" said Vanessa, clinking Roberta's glass.

"Shhh," said Roberta, stifling a laugh. "He'll hear you."

Daryl entered with a smile. "Hey! Looks like a party."

He tried to give Roberta a hug but she shook his hand instead and led it toward his stuff in the hallway. Walking past Vanessa, Daryl waved.

"Vanessa. How are you doing? Haven't seen you in a while."

"Life is good," said Vanessa, holding up her glass, silently toasting his absence. "How is life up north?"

"A little wild and crazy sometimes. Work is more stressful. How about you?"

"Same-o. Same-o."

"You two just hanging out tonight? Anybody want to go out for Mexican?"

"Got plans," said Roberta, nudging him toward the boxes in the hallway.

Daryl seemed hesitant about going to get them and acted more like he wanted to stay and hang out with old friends, have a few beers and party. Picking up those boxes and hauling them out to his car, clearing out all remnants of his past life here, which he had actually enjoyed very much, was something he was loathe to do, especially after discovering that his new roommate dated around.

More than once, she did not come home all night and when Daryl questioned her about it, thinking that the two of them were now 'together', she was nonchalant about the reasons, saying that she stayed with a friend. Further questioning did not result in more answers, rather the opposite.

"You don't like how I live, Daryl? Move out. You've got cheap rent and an occasional lover. Do not question how I live. That's my business. Got it?"

Daryl soon realized the relationship was not going to work, not for the long term. And the idea of getting back with Roberta, if for no other reason other than to piss off his new lover/roommate by not coming home for a few days was very appealing.

"Vanessa? How about you? I'm buying."

Vanessa shook her head. "Daryl, get a clue. This train has left the station and you aren't on it."

"It's just fish tacos. I'm not asking you to go to bed with me."

"Well that's good. Because that would never happen anyway. You can't just pop in and expect everything to be the same. It's changed. You need to get your stuff, get back to your new life and let Roberta get on with hers."

Daryl took that in, feeling his temper building, realizing that he was the cause. As he stood there wondering what to say next, what to do, Roberta returned to the kitchen counter, found her wine glass and took another sip, hoping it didn't get ugly.

This was vintage Vanessa and Daryl knew she was being nice, holding back what she really wanted to say. He had seen her on the attack before when one of her boyfriends was flirting with one of her girlfriends. A couple more words and it would all come out in a rush, like a hundred knives thrown all at once, each cutting a little deeper than the last, whittling down to the soul.

He smiled, heading for boxes. "You're right. I need to get back, got things to do."

The phone rang. Roberta picked up.

"Hi, Roberta. Kirk here. They're having a potluck here at the marina next Saturday. Everyone's asking if you're coming. Are you in?"

"I don't know. I have to think about it. How soon do you have to know?"

"Whenever. My specialty is BBQ'd chicken wings, spicy hot."

"It sounds like fun. I'd love to, but...,"

"I know where you're coming from. Our situation is awkward, isn't it?"

"I really haven't had much chance to consider it."

"Lee doesn't fit in with this crowd, thinks they're too rowdy. So, she won't mind. What would Todd think?"

"I have no idea. I guess I could bring it up tonight?"

"Whatever you feel good with. The invite stands."

"Thanks, Kirk. I'll let you know."

"OK. By the way, in case you haven't seen it, look outside. The sunset is beautiful. A few of us are sitting out on the dock having a beer. Steve, you met him. He brews his own and it's really good. I'll see if I can save you one. Enjoy."

"Thanks. Bye."

"That phone just never stops ringing," said Vanessa, gleefully.

Daryl picked up the first load of boxes and headed out the door. When the front door closed behind him, Vanessa looked at Roberta questionably.

"Well?"

"That was Kirk. He invited me to a dock party."

"Just keeps getting better and better. I think I'm going to start a diary."

"What? About me?"

"Us. Maybe I'll write a screenplay. What should we call it?"

The phone rang. Vanessa sipped her wine. Daryl came back into the room. Roberta reached for the phone.

"Hello?"

"Hi Roberta. Todd here. I got off work early and I'm right around the corner. Mind if I stop by? I've got a nice bottle of wine and some appetizers. We'll wing it from there."

"Definitely a screenplay," said Vanessa, seeing the alarmed look on Roberta's face.

## Checking Out

Darin did not like the phone ringing as he was coming through the door. That could only mean one thing, bad news, a death, an accident or some kind of emergency. He put his lunch in the tiny refrigerator behind his desk, set his papers down and answered the phone.

"Power Maintenance, Darin."

"Darin, this is Martin."

"This can only be bad news."

"Robby's gone."

"What? What do you mean, gone?"

"His truck is parked here by my office. He left his ID card, keys and a note, says he quits."

"This is a joke, right?"

"I wish. I've tried calling his house but no one answers."

"I can't believe it. He would have said something. There's no reason for him to quit."

"There is..., and he can't kick it."

There was a long pause in the conversation. "What is it?"

"Crack."

Another long pause.

"What do you want me to do?"

"He considers you a good friend. He won't talk to me. If I give you his address will you drop by, just to make sure he's OK? That's all I want to know."

"I can do that."

"And if you talk to him, tell him his job is still here. I'll hold off for as long as I can."

"Right."

"And, since I am sticking my neck out, this is between you and me only."

"Got it."

"Thanks, Darin."

Darin glanced at his watch. "It's not even six yet. Should I go over there now?"

"If he's in trouble, sooner is better. Don't you think?"

"Should we call the police?"

"Would you want the police storming your place when you're high? All he's done so far is quit."

"You got a point. OK. What's his address? I'll head out right now."

There were three two-story buildings that formed a U-shaped complex with walkways in between. Darin followed the sidewalk around to the back of the middle building, looking for 27B.

Suddenly there was a man, a very large man, standing in his way. Darin nodded and tried to go around. The man blocked him, holding out his arm.

"Turn around, fuck-head. You're in the wrong neighborhood."

"I'm looking for a friend."

"You got no friends here. Turn your white ass around while you still can and go back where you came from."

"I'm looking for Robby."

"Ain't no Robby lives here."

Hearing a twig snap behind him, Darin glanced over his shoulder and noticed that two more men had come in behind him.

*What the hell, Martin! What kind of position did you put me in? I get killed checking up on a fellow employee! This should've been a company rep or the police. Now, what?*

"He lives in 27B," said Darin, thinking that either way he was going to get beat up so he might as well ask the question. "He's a friend of mine and I want to make sure he's OK. I've got no other business here."

The man studied him for a minute and then nodded, stepping aside. "27B's over there. We'll tag along. You better know somebody inside."

The three men followed Darin up to the apartment but stopped a short distance away from the door. Heart pounding, Darin rang the doorbell. No one answered. He waited a minute and then rang it again.

*Martin! You better have given me the right address!*

To his relief, Tanya finally came to the door, not that he knew her or that she knew him. He had seen her picture. She opened it a crack, chain lock still in place and studied Darin.

"Tanya. I'm looking for Robby."

"He's not here."

"I just need to know if he's OK."

"Who's asking?"

"I'm Darin. We work together."

"Yeah. He talked about you. He's still not here."

"Do you know if he's all right?"

"Darin, I'm telling you because you're his friend. I don't care about that man no more. He didn't come home last night or the night before. He just spends all his time and money on that shit! When he's straight, he's the best man walking on this earth. But he can't stay straight and I can't deal with it no more. I'm done!"

"I know he really loves you. He's told me he's the luckiest guy in the world."

"Yea, well that's all over. He loves that shit more."

"Can you tell him...,"

"No. I'm leaving, packing my bags right now."

Tanya closed the door. Darin turned to face the men, wondering if he could outrun them, but then decided that it wouldn't matter because even if he could he wouldn't be far enough ahead to get his keys out, unlock the door, get the engine started and drive away before they ruined both him and his car. Instead, he shrugged.

"Well, I tried. I hope he's OK."

The man motioned for him to head back the way he'd come. Without another word, Darin started for his car. The three of them fell in behind. He resisted the urge to turn around or to even glance over his shoulder for fear that that action alone would be enough to provoke them.

Darin didn't want to convey fear by walking too fast or to convey false bravado by walking too slow. He set his pace carefully, wondering when he would be stabbed in the back, when he was going to be thrown to the ground and beaten, or if they were going to kill him after they found out what he was driving, or force him into the car, force him to drive to some remote location, kill him there and then take his wallet and keys.

There was one section of the complex that was out of view of most everything, right where the sidewalk ran between two rows of hedges. Seeing that he had to go through them, Darin's heart sank.

*This is what they were waiting for. No witnesses in here.*

But, to his surprise and with his heart pounding, he came out of the other side unscathed. As he reached for his keys, the man, the first one he'd encountered, approached. The other two stayed behind.

"I know Robby," he said. "You must be some friend to come in here and check on him. If I see him, I'll tell him you were askin'. Now get your white ass out of here."

Days passed and then weeks with no word of Robby. Darin watched the evening news, read the local section of the paper to see if he'd been arrested, checked the obits. Martin had to process the paperwork. Robby no longer worked for the company. A request was put in for a replacement.

Bart was put in Robby's loop, given Robby's tools and truck and everyone on the crew was on-call to help him. He hadn't been to all of the schools yet and was a long way from being qualified.

Buck's modernization project went into full swing in all of the buildings. Everyone was working days and nights and weekends and on-call in-between. There were meetings everywhere and all of the time. Work crews were arriving from around the state.

Time off was a luxury that no one had. Months passed by quickly. No one had time to notice...,

## Checking In

The air appeared orange, no doubts about it. Even the barn, now weathered and gray, needing a coat of red paint ten or fifteen years ago, appeared orange against the dusty, green leaves of the cottonwood trees. And even they glimmered with hints of coral and salmon tones as a timid breeze passed through.

The hayloft door was open, looked like it hadn't been closed for years and even from his car Robby could see that the loft was empty. There seemed to be some kind of light coming from inside and, looking a little closer, he realized that the light was due to a hole in the roof, allowing a shaft of orange light inside.

Twenty years ago, the loft would've been full of hay. And there would've been two or three horses in the stables, sows lying in the mud on the shade side of the barn next to the water tank. This late in the day, the cows would've been coming back from pasture and the chicken coup, now empty, gate half off of its' hinge, would've been full of Rhode Island Reds clucking contentedly inside.

Driving slowly into the barnyard, taking it all in, Robby could see that the cottonwoods had aged, peaking years ago but now crowding the south side of the house, providing orange tinted shade from the sun but little relief from the late afternoon heat.

The wooden steps to the farmhouse sank under his weight, creaking down into place with his weight, moving away from the heads of the loosened, rusty nails and then popping back up after he had passed by.

No one answered his knock. The front door was

open and there was no sound coming from the other side of the screen door, nothing to indicate that anyone was home or even that anyone lived there at all. Hesitating, wondering if he should enter, Robby knocked again. "Anybody home?"

And then a holler from a back room, not a strong voice, more strained, like it was an effort to produce that much sound.

"I said, come in!"

The door opened with a creak, just like in the movies. The screen was torn away from the bottom left corner. Mice, rats more like, had discovered the opening and, judging by the trail of droppings along the wall, had been using it to their advantage for quite some time.

This was a long room, maybe thirty feet to the other end and not quite wide enough, feeling too narrow possibly due to its' fifteen foot width, but also because of the piles of books, magazines, baskets of clothes and endless boxes of stuff stacked along either side.

"Thomas? That you?"

"Who's that? Come in here, so I can see."

Robby walked toward the sound, moving slowly through the dusty room, noting the torn curtains on the windows, cobwebs in the corners and feeling that the place was more like a barn than a room.

"It's me, Robby. Luella's son."

"Luella? She's been dead for ten years."

Entering the kitchen, Robby found Thomas sitting in a wheel chair with a blanket pulled over his legs, thoroughly stained as if it had been used as both napkin and tray for a long time.

Straightening up in his wheelchair, Thomas leaned forward for a better look, appearing as ornery as ever, his eyes dark and sharp like a hawk's but now sunken behind high cheekbones, his leathery skin, heavy with years of too much sun, sagging down into his unshaved jaw.

"Robby?"

"That's me."

"I heard you died."

Robby smiled. "Not yet. Felt like I should've a few times."

"I heard you were a drug addict."

"It's not quite like that."

"You didn't come to your mother's funeral."

"I didn't find out until...,"

"No excuses. You shoulda stayed in touch. Then, you'd of known."

"Life got complicated."

"You still a drug addict?"

"No, I...,"

"You must be. Look how skinny you are. Still doin' the shit, aren't you?"

"Thomas, you're not lookin' so good yourself."

"My mind is clear."

"I couldn't help noticing, coming in, how different the place looks."

"Yea? Well, I don't get around much anymore."

"Barn looks like it could use a coat of paint."

"Why? Got no animals to put in it. Damn thing's gonna fall down one day anyway. And then I'll get the insurance from it. Bout time, after all the money I've paid those crooks all these years."

"Hey, Thomas, how about I take you into town and buy you dinner?"

"I'm not riding with no drug addict."

Robby laughed. "I come all the way from California without so much as a scratch. And you won't go five miles with me into town for a free dinner?"

"Nope. Why you want to buy me dinner anyway?"

"Mind if I sit down?"

Thomas studied Robby for a minute and then nodded to a chair loaded with old Popular Mechanics magazines. "If you can find a place to put those."

Robby picked up the stack and searched for an empty place. Nobody ever came to visit this guy. The top magazine was four years old and had probably been sitting there for the last two. He placed the magazines on top of a stack of old newspapers out in the living room.

"I'm a technician," said Robby, sitting down. "I fix things."

"So, you're not a drug addict?"

"I didn't say that. I'm good at what I do. And what I want to do is clean up my life. Best way I know is to find some things to fix cause that's what keeps my mind occupied."

"So, it's still got ya, huh?"

"Difference is, I don't want it."

Thomas was quiet for a minute, rubbing his wrinkled hands together, working the words through his mind. He motioned to a coffee pot on the stove. "You can heat that up, if you want. Still fresh. I made it just this morning."

Robby grinned, reaching for the knob to turn it on. That would be like Thomas and like most folks from these parts. Fresh is anything in the last two days. "I'd forgotten how good the air smells here, sweet."

"That's cause we don't have a million cars polluting it. Gettin' worse though. Used to be I never heard but one or two cars a day out there on the highway. Now I hear 'em all day and half the night. Too many people nowadays if you ask me."

"Yea. It is getting crowded. In California, sometimes you can't even find a place to park."

Shaking his head, Thomas glanced toward the coffee pot. "Can't imagine anywhere being that crowded. We're gonna ruin the whole damn planet. Better turn that off before it starts to perk."

"I just turned it on."

"Yea. But you turned it on too hard and the bottom's too hot. It's gonna perk."

Robby, reaching for the knob, "How about if I just turn it down?"

"No. Turn it off..., now."

"This must be some coffee. Let me rinse your cup and...,"

"Cup's fine."

"You sure? Looks pretty deadly in there."

"Cup's fine. Just get yourself one and let's get on with it."

Robby began the long, fruitless search for a clean cup. "Get on with what?"

"Whatever it is, you want."

Robby laughed. "I don't want anything except maybe a clean cup. But I don't think you have any of those."

"Probably have to wash one."

"Where's the soap?"

"Soap? Just use that rag there."

The rag looked like one of the rags Robby would toss after working on an engine or wiping down the batteries. He was pretty sure it would not help anything become cleaner. He found the cleanest cup he could, vigorously rubbed it with his hands under a stream of water, dried the outside off on his shirt and poured himself a cup.

"Cremora's on the counter," said Thomas, "behind that bottle of ketchup."

The ketchup, Robby had already noticed, was empty and looked like it had been sitting there for a

while, as indicated by the dried coffee stains surrounding the bottom, probably from when Thomas
had attempted to clean dishes from his wheelchair
some days before.

"What's keepin' you stuck in your wheelchair?"

"Hurts to stand. Got arthritis in my joints."

"You taking any medication?"

"What's it to you?"

"Just curious. You know me. How do you get to
town?"

"I don't."

"You got any relatives or friends that stop by to
see if you're OK?"

"Not your business."

"OK. How do you get your food?"

That brought a slight smile to Thomas' face.
"You know, you're just as nosey now as ever! You
haven't changed a bit!"

Robby laughed. "Neither have you, you old cuss!"

Sipping his coffee, Robby winced as the flavor
settled in. "This is terrible."

"You burned it," said Thomas. "You heated it too
fast."

"It's barely warm. You sure this is coffee?"

"You don't like my coffee? You don't have to
drink it."

"It's not..., bad. When was the last time you
washed the pot?"

"You don't wash a coffee pot. That's what gives it
the flavor."

Robby laughed. "I think it's the beans but, ig-
noring that, it doesn't mean you never wash the
pot. It's been washed in the last ten years?"

"Of course, not."

"Hey, Thomas," said Robby, setting his coffee
down. "I have an urge for a hamburger and a malt.

Or maybe a BLT. If I go get it and bring it back, would you eat one?"

"They charge too much for that, nowadays. Used to be, you could get...,"

"I'm buyin'. And I'm flyin'. An old fart like you should jump on somethin' like that."

A second, thin smile from Thomas. "Cheeseburger and a chocolate malt. Don't let them give you a shake, either. Tell 'em you want a malt."

Robby stood. "Fries? Or, onion rings?"

"Never had onion rings. What are they like?"

"How about I get one of each? You can choose the one you want."

"You don't need ketchup. I have some up there on the counter."

"Riiight," said Robby, glancing over at the empty bottle. "I'll be back in a flash."

## Digging In

It was dark by the time Robby returned with dinner. He parked close to the porch and took note of the steps before turning off the headlights. The porch light was not on. Coming through the front door, he felt along the wall until he found a light switch and, clicking it on, discovered that it did not work. Stepping carefully through the piles of boxes, he headed for a dim light emanating from the kitchen, from a small bedside lamp that had been placed on the table.

"Looks like you've got a lot of things to fix around here," said Robby, handing Thomas a cheeseburger. "Almost killed myself coming up the steps, way that board kicks back."

"Been meaning to get to that," said Thomas. "Except I can't find the hammer."

Robby cleared a small space on the table and set out the fries and onion rings. "I'm surprised you can find anything around here. I can hardly find the floor."

Thomas did not respond to that, choosing instead to attack the food. They ate in silence for the next few minutes. Thomas chose the onion rings over the fries and seemed to be in heaven drinking the chocolate malt.

"So," he said, at last, burping after the word. "You come all the way from California, where I'm guessin' you had a payin' job, to come out here and fix things? What are you gonna fix? And how are you gonna get money?"

Robby tore the corner off of a ketchup packet and squeezed the contents over his fries. "Already applied for a job at Harrison's Grocery. He needs someone to stock shelves early morning. And the Chevron just outside town needs someone to work the late shift. Figured I'd apply tomorrow. What am I gonna fix? Me, and a whole slew of other things along the way."

"Where are you stayin'?"

"That's the one thing I haven't figured out yet. I could rent a place in town but that would give me too much idle time. I need to be someplace where everything's broke, a place where I don't have time to think."

Robby's words hung in the air, mingling with the scents of hamburgers, onions, and fries. Thomas, sucking on the straw, searched for the last few molecules of chocolate malt in his cup.

"And I'm thinkin' you want to stay here. Right?"

"Looks like you could use some help. And I'll pay you rent."

Thomas set the cup down, carefully folded the wrapper that had held his hamburger and stuffed it into the bag that had held the onion rings. "Did you know you can live on Spam and white bread?"

"I didn't know that. Seems like you should have some fruit and vegetables, too."

"Spam's one of the best foods you can buy. And it keeps good, too. You don't even have to refrigerate it if you eat it within a day or two after its been opened."

"You might be taking your chances there."

Thomas shook his head. "Been doin' it for a year."

"Why don't you put it in the refrigerator?"

"Stopped workin' a while back."

"You don't have refrigeration?"

"How do you think we lived before it was invented?"

216

"Life spans were shorter, too. Does the fridge light come on?"

"That stopped workin' before the fridge did. It ran for another year."

"I've got a meter out in my trunk, I...,"

"No sense workin' on it tonight. I've been doin' fine for the last year."

"I noticed your porch light was out."

"Don't need that. Did you come here to agitate me, or what? All these questions. You know how quiet it is around here, without you?"

Robby laughed. "I've got a lot of catching up to do. Tell you what, Thomas. If it's OK with you, I'll spend the night on your property out in my car. And tomorrow morning, after I fix your fridge and that front step, we'll talk again. How's that?"

Thomas nodded. "There's a few things I need to tell you, too." He turned his wheelchair and headed for the back room. "Thanks for dinner."

## Mr. Fix-it

Thomas, still sitting in his wheelchair, using his hand to shield the early morning sun, chose to remain at the top of the steps rather than have Robby help him down. "You don't need no drill. Nail already made the hole. You just need to pound it back down."

"Won't hold," said Robby. "That nail's old and rusted and that hole is worn out. And this isn't a drill."

"Looks like one. But you forgot the cord."

Robby squeezed the trigger a couple of times to show Thomas it didn't need one. "It runs on batteries."

"Well, that's pretty useless. You'll be changing out batteries all the time."

Robby pulled a pack of drill bits from his toolbox, picked a bit, inserted it into the chuck, and squeezed the trigger. It whirred into place and locked. "I can work about a hour continuous before it needs a new battery. And they're rechargeable. The charger just plugs into the wall. Takes about fifteen minutes to recharge."

"So, every hour, you've gotta wait fifteen minutes? What is that? Work, California style?"

"I've got three batteries. One's being used, one's charging and one's a spare."

"You don't need no chuck key for that?"

"Nope."

Robby drilled three quick holes through the top board and down into the board that held the rusty nail. He reversed the drill, released the bit and inserted a screwdriver tip. He retrieved three screws from his shirt pocket, screwed the step back down and then went to the other side to do the same.

"Those aren't gonna rust?"

"No. They're galvanized."

Steps fixed, Robby put his tools back in his tool-box. "Let's go look at that fridge."

He had to move several boxes out of the kitchen so that he could move the fridge away from the wall. The items in the fridge were beyond science projects so Robby found an empty box and threw it all away. He unplugged the fridge, removed an inch of greasy dust off of the floor where the fridge had been and then plugged his meter into the outlet.

"No voltage. Probably a tripped breaker. Where's the breaker box?"

"Don't have no breaker box."

"You've gotta have one. That's how electricity feeds into the house."

"I know all about that. I have a fuse box. I don't have a breaker box."

"Where's the fuse box?"

"Just outside the back door."

The fuse was blown. Robby found a spare inside the cabinet that he used to replace the old. Before plugging the fridge in, he set his meter for ohms and checked the plug to the fridge.

"What're you doin' that for?" said Thomas, watching intently. "The fuse was bad."

"No. The fuse was blown. I'm wonderin' why."

The ohmmeter showed a direct short and, fol-lowing the cord up into the fridge, Robby discov-ered where some rodent had nibbled through the insulation. He held it up for Thomas to see.

"There's your trouble. Rodents. I'll put some tape on it for now but the cord needs to be replaced. I'll fix that screen door so they can't come back."

Within the week, Robby had changed out light

bulbs, fixed dripping faucets, oiled door hinges and hauled most of Thomas' trash to the dump.

He got up at four-thirty, worked at Harrison's Grocery until ten, went back to Thomas' place and worked around the farm until four-thirty, ate a quick supper and then worked at the Chevron until closing, ten at night.

And then came the hard part, having a little time on his hands, time to think about Tanya, his old habits and everything else he'd left behind.

Mr. Cannitt

Carly was at her wit's end.

*The piece of equipment is just crap, that's all. Flip
the on/off switch to ON and all it does is go clunk.*

She called Sergio who, after several attempts to
turn it on, decided that this was a job for Mr. Cannitt. Better to waste his time. He tossed his screwdriver back into the bag. "Damned if I know what's
wrong with it. It just keeps tripping the breaker."

Carly finished wiping her hands on a rag, tossed
it back into her tool kit and retrieved the bottle of
orange juice sitting next to it. "It doesn't even have
a chance to get going."

She walked back over to the breaker cabinet on
the other side of the room, turned the breaker to
the OFF position and hung a red "defective equipment" tag on it. "Well, it's been working for over a
year. It's out of warranty."

Sergio closed the door on the equipment,
latched it, collected all of his tools and joined Carly
near the exit. He laughed. "Sounds like a job for
Super Can't."

Super Can't was one of the technical experts
working for the company who was called upon to
fix equipment when the power crews couldn't do it
themselves. But he did not know how to read electrical diagrams, was not interested in learning, had
no aptitude for this sort of thing and did not know
how to troubleshoot problems.

He earned his name within the first year at the
position. When called upon to fix a piece of broken
equipment, Mr. Cannitt would call the tech responsible for that area, make an appointment to meet
them at the site and make a list of all the techni-

cians that had attempted to fix the trouble and what they had tried, admirable. But then, working with the best tech that he could find to work with him on that day, if the trouble got fixed, he would write up the report with a slight slant.

*After the following list of technicians failed to find the trouble, Mr. Cannitt persevered and, after replacing the defective circuit board, solved the problem. In the accompanying photograph (of Mr. Cannitt performing the operation that fixed the trouble) technician (name) is looking on.*

This did not sit well with the power crew, especially after they learned that Mr. Cannitt could not even read the schematics that he pretended to study while working with them. He relied on the techs for that.

Sometimes, when equipment could not be fixed, Mr. Cannitt would build a case to have the equipment replaced. In these cases, the memo would be written in such a way as to imply that he had been present at every stage of repairs, when in fact he was in his office having coffee and donuts and playing games on his computer, keeping in touch with the progress with a phone call every half hour so that he could make it sound like:

*After discovering that the control board did not solve the problem, we tried the (new name) circuit board with the following results. After exhausting all possibilities, I recommend that the equipment be replaced.*

In this regard the crew loved him and therefore tolerated him, with grumbling. Wasn't it better, after standing around the defective equipment for an hour or so drinking coffee, eating donuts and shooting the shit, to get Mr. Cannitt to replace the defective equipment rather than spend hours troubleshooting? Yes! Better to give Super Can't not enough information to solve the problem and get the newer, better stuff that actually worked.

After learning that Carly would not be available to meet with him concerning the defective equipment and that Sergio had already given up, Super Can't called Darin to see if he could assist in the repairs.

Darin was holding a special grudge against Mr. Cannitt. After he had spent two days troubleshooting a major problem on the third floor of his building, Mr. Cannitt happened by on his way from a meeting and stopped to say hello. During that brief conversation, totally unrelated subjects, Darin finally figured out what the problem was.

Martin saw Cannitt's report and called Darin. "It reads like this," he said.

*Darin, after working for two days without success, solved the problem within minutes after conferring with Mr. Cannitt.*

Knowing this, Darin agreed to meet with Mr. Cannitt at Carly's office.

Entering the power room, Darin noticed that Super Can't was already there and that he had opened up the front door to the equipment. The schematics were laid neatly out on the floor next to the equipment. Seeing Darin, Mr. Cannitt broke into a big smile and came over to shake his hand.

"Ahh, Darin. Good to see you. Thanks for your help today."

"No problem. Looks like you've started without me. What have you tried so far?"

"I was just getting everything ready for when you got here."

"Have you tried turning it on yet?"

"No. I was waiting for you."

"I see that the page is turned to the Control Board section. Is that where you think the trouble is?"

"Maybe. I was going to consult with you."

Darin walked over to the breaker cabinet across the room, removed the red tag and flipped the breaker to the ON position. "Go ahead. Turn it on."

"What's it going to do?"

"Don't know. Carly said the breaker trips as soon as she turns it on."

"Is it going to spark?"

"Don't know until you turn it on."

"Maybe you should do it."

"You're the expert."

"Actually, I'm in management. I'm not authorized to power equipment on and off. You're the craft guy."

"Don't worry. I won't report you."

Standing away from the equipment as far as he could, Mr. Cannitt leaned forward and pressed the ON button. As soon as he did, the breaker tripped with a loud thud. Mr. Cannitt looked relieved.

"What do you think?" said Darin.

"It doesn't even turn on. It must be very broken."

Darin laughed. "Well..., yea. The question is, why?"

Super Can't checked his watch. "How long do you think it will take for us to find the trouble? I have a meeting downtown at ten."

Darin walked over to the schematic and kneeled down to study it. "It's almost nine now. You're not giving us much time."

"How long can it take? If it breaks as soon as we turn it on, the trouble has to be at the beginning. Maybe a bad ON/OFF switch?"

Darin laughed. "Maybe. Also maybe a bad transformer, blown power diodes, bad capacitors, short-ed wiring. Maybe it wasn't wired right in the first place and now it's ready to burn up. You think we'll figure it out in the next thirty minutes?"

"I cannot miss this appointment. It's very important."

"Then why did you schedule this for today? I have other things to do."

"I'll work with you until I have to go. If we haven't found the trouble by then, you can keep working on it as long as you like. Your time will be paid through my budget. I'll stay in touch."

"Riiight."

This was what Darin was hoping for. He started going through the schematic, eliminating this possibility or that, going slowly but mostly noticing how Super Can't was on the phone most of the time and not paying attention unless it was to write down what had already been tried.

At nine twenty-eight, Super Can't excused himself from the problem, apologized for the inconvenience to Darin and promised to return as soon as possible after his meeting if Darin hadn't found the trouble yet.

Prior to Super Can't's departure, all of Darin's focus had been preliminary tests that any knowledgeable tech would see at a glance, mundane things like check to make sure the equipment was grounded. Of course it was. The big green wire was visible to anyone standing near the equipment. Yet Darin took fifteen minutes to confirm that it was working properly. He also gave Mr. Cannitt a screwdriver and told him to make sure all of the equipment covers were properly attached and that the screws were tight, another waste of time. Darin smiled as he watched Mr. Cannitt diligently write it all down.

When he was gone, Darin dug into the problem. He pulled out the section on transformers and found himself flipping between that section and several other pages as the signals traveled through the equipment. After about an hour of testing and two calls from Super Can't, he still had no idea of what the problem was.

Robby would know. Dude would just walk in, ask what the trouble was, glance at a couple of things and go right to the problem. Good instincts.

*Where are you, Robby? You blow your brains out? Somebody else do it for you?*

Darin decided to remove the bottom cover of the equipment and see for himself, as Robby would say, a foolish move because that would mean turning the defective equipment on when his head was inside the cabinet.

Physically, it was not possible to have his head inside and turn the equipment on at the same time. Darin found a broom with a wooden handle, wrapped electrical tape around the handle and the ON/OFF switch, stuck his head inside the cabinet and turned it on.

He was not expecting the huge flash that blew out of the transformer, accompanied with a loud POP. He banged his head on the metal cabinet trying to get out and was grateful that the one smart thing he did was wear his safety glasses.

Being relatively sure that he had just burned off his eyebrows and forward hairline, he walked along the back wall of the office toward the rest rooms, wanting to see himself in a mirror, hoping to make it without anyone noticing him.

When he saw his face in the mirror, he started laughing. Nothing serious had happened.

*That was stupid! Lucky to be alive. But…, what a great story! Only person I'd tell is Robby.*

A clerk in the office approached him as he was returning to the testing area.

"Hi. You're Darin?"

"Right."

"There's a Mr. Cannitt calling for you."

"There is? Please tell him that I'll get back to him as soon as I know something."

"He's pretty insistent."

"Yes. He always is."

Darin walked gleefully back to his tools, put them back into his kit and loaded them into his truck.

*Can't fix the trouble, but I know what it is. And you don't, Mr. Cannitt.*

He decided to stop for lunch on the way back to his office and noted that Mr. Cannitt tried to call three more times on his cell. The phone was ringing off the hook when Darin returned to his office and continued ringing every ten minutes or so while Darin made out a trouble ticket and e-mailed it to Martin, Mr. Cannitt and his boss:

"Concerning the defective equipment in Carly's office, the trouble is bad insulation in the input transformer which shorts out when the equipment is turned on. Since this is both an electrical and a fire hazard. I recommend that this equipment be replaced.

Mr. Cannitt, I hope your downtown meeting went well. Too bad we couldn't have worked together a little longer."

The important meeting was with his financial advisor but that was not what he told his boss who gave Mr. Cannitt a week off without pay and a letter in his personnel file.

## Temptation

Robby knew what it was as soon as he saw it. When he went out to empty the trash bins next to the pumps, getting ready to shut down for the night, he spotted the little plastic bag laying there on the concrete next to the guard post that kept cars from hitting the pump.

There were no customers at the station now. Everybody in town knew that it closed at ten. There was an all-nighter on the other side of town where the two highways intersected, so anybody needing gas went there. Most people, though, were home by eight or nine.

It had been a white older model Ford pick-up that had last used this spot, the one with black primer covering the hood and the driver's front fender, the kind of damage incurred by drivers in trucks who follow too close while driving in the rain.

The driver, in his mid-thirties, had come inside to buy a six-pack of beer, handed Robby a twenty and told him the rest would be for gas on pump four, fourteen dollars and thirty-two cents.

Robby tried to assess every customer that pulled into the station, first noting the make, model and approximate year of car they were driving, and then taking a closer look if they headed for the door instead of using their credit card outside. The camera took their picture when they entered and if they looked suspicious, Robby also inched closer to the forty-five kept out of sight.

The station owner, Wilbur, had been robbed once and had purchased the gun soon after that.

"Don't try to be a hero," he had said. "Give them whatever they want. I have insurance. But if it gets nasty, at least you've got some protection. Shoot right through the counter. Nothing's gonna stop that bullet."

Robby took that to heart. When the guy first pulled in he had noticed that the engine wasn't running on all eight cylinders, more like six, the way it was thumping, and anyone that didn't care about their car enough to keep it running properly was under suspicion as far as Robby was concerned.

But, watching him, he realized the guy wasn't a robber. One, he was alone. Two, the getaway car was a piece of crap. Three, his mannerisms were not aggressive, more like a stoner only wanting to get a little more high.

Robby stooped to pick up the packet. "Poor guy," he thought. "Probably went through his pockets four or five times, searched the truck two or three times and is now very bummed while drinking his beer." He put the packet into his pocket, wondering what he was going to do with it.

The next morning, Mr. Harrison asked if he could deliver an order to Mable Walker on his way home. Robby agreed and, while dropping off the food, noticed that her toilet was running continuously.

"That's costing you money."

"I know. But it'll cost two hundred and fifty dollars to fix it."

"Two-fifty? Who said that?"

"The service man. He said this toilet's too old and needs to be replaced."

"The repair kit is only about twenty bucks," said Robby. "If you buy the parts, I'll put it in for you. How about I do the whole thing for fifty?"

And that was the beginning of Robby's Handyman Service. Mable told Erma, who needed a gate repaired after she backed her car into it, who told Franz, who needed some drywall repair work after he fell asleep while waiting for the bath tub to fill.

Within a month, Robby made a deal with the local hardware store to purchase all products at a thirty percent discount. He hired Ollie, a kid he kept running into in the hardware store, who was building an observatory in his parent's back yard, piece by piece since he was short on cash but big on dreams and full of curiosity.

Trading in his car for a pick-up, Robby earned extra money by hauling stuff to the dump. Mrs. Fergusen needed some cabinets built in her kitchen because her husband had died of a heart attack during the remodel. Bartering, Robby traded his labor for the deceased Mr. Fergusen's table and miter saws.

Thus began Robby's cabinet installation business and, since he now owned a couple of good power tools, major repairs at Old Man Thomas' place, beginning with the chicken coup. Within a week, he had six Rhode Island Reds clucking and pecking contentedly in their new home. People started stopping by for eggs but they had to bring their own cartons.

Even Thomas acted a little more spryly. Robby built a ramp off of the porch so he could leave the house in his wheel chair and soon he was out in the barnyard, following Robby around, making sure everything was done right.

The windmill was one of the bigger problems. Two of the blades had fallen off some years earlier and, unbalanced, it wouldn't rotate. Often, as Robby walked from one side of the yard to the other, he studied the structure, wondering how to make it work. The tower base had some wood rot and the steps going up were unreliable.

"Thomas. I've got an idea."

Thomas had picked up his old habit of carrying a weed in the corner of his mouth as he wheeled himself around the yard. Most of the time he just held it there until it was too limp to hold the weight. Then, he'd bite that part off, spit it out and go to the next section.

"Sour grass," he said, putting the rest of the stem and tiny yellow flowers into his mouth. "It's good for you. Gives you fiber and chlorophyll."

Robby smiled. "Didn't know we needed chlorophyll."

"These scientists. They think they know everything. Sometimes you just gotta trust your instincts. What's your idea?"

"You think Ollie's a good kid, right?"

"Seems all right. Follows instructions. Not as nosey as you. What about him?"

"It's gonna take a couple of us to fix that windmill. The tower's pretty beat up and I figure it's safer to rebuild it with all new wood. Probably cheaper and easier in the long run, too."

"Get to the point."

"Ollie's trying to build an observatory in his folk's back yard and they're giving him a hard time about it. How about you offer him your hayloft for the project if he fixes the roof and helps me with the windmill?"

"What? You want to put a telescope up in the loft?"

"Sounds like a good deal to me. You get your barn fixed, probably painted, too, if he knows he's got a stake in it. And your windmill will get fixed. We can get water back in that tank there. And then we're looking at the possibility of livestock. Gotta take a look at that tractor yet and see what...,"

"What makes you think I want livestock? I'm a dyin' man, Robby."

"So am I," said Robby, thinking of the little packet from the gas station that he had failed to throw away. "That's why we've got to look ahead."

Thomas spent a lot of time these days rubbing his weathered hands together, trying to keep up. He did that now, sitting under the shade of the cottonwood, looking across the barnyard at the failing structures.

Just weeks ago, he figured his life was coming to an end. Everything was closing in, all of those useless possessions, smothering him inside his own house. Clearing it all out, fixing the screens, letting the light and air pass through had been, literally, a breath of fresh air and he felt ten years younger. And now, put a telescope up in the loft?

"Can you put a motor on this wheelchair?"

Robby laughed. "Yea, I can. I've been thinking about it."

"The hallway is ten feet wide," said Buck, walking with Darin through the basement. "And the engines are eight feet wide. They're not going to make two of these corners."

"I could have told you that."

"How did they get here in the first place?"

"Not from the east side?"

"No. They would have had to open up that wall. Company records would have shown that. I went outside and looked, just to make sure. Doesn't look like anything's happened to that wall since it was built."

"Well, look who's here," said Darin. "He's been around longer than us. He'll know. Hey, Martin. How did they get these engines into the building?"

That brought Martin to a stop. "Not the east side?"

"Nope," said Buck. "That wall's never been touched."

Martin patted the wall that they were standing next to. "I remember. Brought them in from the loading dock on the south side. Rolled them right through here."

Both Darin and Buck had the same question. "How'd they get around the corners?"

Martin put his hand on the wall. "This room wasn't here, then."

Darin nodded. "Oh! So it was a straight shot? A whole lot of engineers work in there. You're going to make them move their desks and unplug their computers?"

'No choice," said Buck. "Engines have to come out."

Martin set his briefcase down. "Why don't we just leave the engines where they are?"

"Can't, new water pumps are going in."

"Wait," said Darin. "I thought that's where the new 12KV substation was going."

"It is."

"You're going to put twelve thousand volts in the same room as the water pumps?"

"We're going to build a wall between them."

"My thought," said Darin, shaking his head, "has always been to keep electricity and water as far apart as possible. What does Binko say?"

"He doesn't see a problem with it."

"Just remember," said Martin, picking up his briefcase. "Make a mistake in this building and you're famous overnight. Believe me. I know."

"Got it covered," said Buck, confidently.

Darin and Buck continued on around the corner and headed west toward the doors that provided access to the loading dock.

"We can roll them out over here," said Buck. "Pull them right up on a truck, don't even have to hire a crane."

Approaching from the other direction, Merry Dick Tracy met them at the loading dock doors. She smiled.

"Hi, guys. Heard we had an accident while I was away."

"No big thing," said Buck. "Nobody's hurt."

"But the guy's got religion, now," said Darin, smiling. "After the explosion."

"It wasn't an explosion," said Buck. "The guy wasn't following the MOP."

"Welding a fuel tank that still had a little fuel left inside," said Darin.

Merry pulled out her note pad and pencil. "I remember going to that meeting. There was supposed to be dry ice inside. Did that happen?"

"He forgot about nine-tenths of it," said Darin.

"Who was the company observer?"

"Norm, but he got called off to hash out some details with the company shipping the pumps."

Merry made a note of that.

"Merry. Did you hear about what happened to my truck?"

"No. What?"

"Meteorite," said Darin, holding back a smile.

Merry started to jot that down, and then stopped. "What?"

"When the fuel tank exploded," Buck explained. "A piece hit Darin's windshield."

"About a fifty pound piece," Darin added. "Buck, tell her how high it went."

Merry double clicked her pencil and turned a page in her book. "I'm supposed to meet with Martin," she said, glancing at her watch. "I'm already late. Buck, I think we need to talk. How about if you go with me back to my office?"

"In that case," said Darin, excusing himself, feeling gleeful that someone was going to put the brakes on Buck. "I've got work to do on the other side of the building."

## Restructuring

Thomas became the paid company accountant of Robby's Handyman Services. Together they set up one of the rooms in the house for the office.

"Tax deductible," said Robby. "It's legal. And we gotta take advantage of everything."

"I understand all that," said Thomas, wheeling his chair over to the computer. "What I don't know is what this thing's gonna do."

"That's the company computer. Your job is going to be to enter all of the data into it and...,"

"I don't know about computers."

"Good. That way you'll be doing what I teach, so we'll both be doing the same thing. We'll be using a program called Excel...,"

"What's a program?"

"The computer does different things, depending on which program you're using. It...,"

"How do I turn it on?"

"I'm getting to that. I'm just tryin' to give you a basic understanding so that...,"

"I'm a visual person. Don't talk about nothin' I can't see."

Robby pointed to the on/off button of the monitor. "This turns it on." And then he pointed to the button on the computer. "Push this button next."

"In that order? Why?"

"Well, because...,"

"Never mind. I push these two buttons. This one first?"

"Right. Normally you won't have to do this. The computer goes to sleep to save energy so we'll just leave it on. It wakes up when you move the mouse."

"What?"

Robby laughed. "I know what that sounds like but it's not that complicated."

After the computer booted up, Robby pointed to the Excel logo. "The computer is telling us that it has this program, Excel, installed, and that it's available for us to use."

"What's an X gonna do? Looks pretty much like nothin'."

"I'll show you. We talk to the computer through this thing." Robby moved the mouse across the pad. "It's called a mouse. See that arrow on the screen? That's the other end of this thing. It tells the computer what we want to do."

"How does it do that?"

"Watch." Robby moved the mouse so that the arrow landed on the green X. The square surrounding it lit up. "See that? See how the square lit up when the arrow was on top of the X? The computer is asking us if we want that program to start."

"How did you do that?"

Robby moved out of the way so that Thomas could get in front of the computer.

"Hold the mouse like this and move it around on the pad."

"Where'd it go? Soon as I touched it the arrow disappeared."

"That's because you moved it off screen. You have to get it in the middle of the...,"

"There it goes! Out the other side! Fast little devil! How do you catch it?"

And so went the morning. While Thomas practiced moving the mouse, Robby went out to work with Ollie, who was in the barn.

"What do you think?" said Ollie, seeing him approach. "Let's put in a stairwell here by the door, since that's where I'll normally be coming in."

Robby smiled. "I'm thinkin' you don't like that ladder nailed to the wall?"

"Well, yea. I've got to haul a lot of stuff up there and the ladder's just not going to do it."

"We'll use the loft door. I'll get a pallet from Harrison's and we'll use that pulley. We've gotta check that, too, see what kind of shape it's in."

"How about the stairs idea?"

"Fine with me. We've gotta run it by Thomas, though."

"How's he coming on the computer?"

Robby laughed. "Kind of like teaching a fish how to row a boat."

Ollie smiled. "Yea. My grandpa's the same way."

"How are you coming on your design?"

"I'm thinkin' of building a second platform, about four feet up above the loft floor. Then I can cut out all that dead wood. If he'd of fixed that leak ten years ago...,"

"Can't blame Thomas. He's had a hard time getting around."

"Actually, it's good because it gives me an excuse to build it how I want it."

"Let's go up and take a look. We're gonna have to run a whole lot more electrical out here, too. I'm figuring we can put in a second service panel right there on the north wall. We got our work cut out for us, Ollie."

"Yea. But we're doing good things. Stuff I want to do."

"You like pullin' wire?"

"No idea. Never did it."

"The house needs to be rewired, only two outlets to a room. And then there's that tractor. It's an old John Deere Model A, twenty-nine horsepower. Looks like it's got a six-speed transmission, best I can tell. Battery's shot, so I'll have to replace that first. I already soaked the spark plugs with WD40, hopin' the rust will break loose."

"To replace them, right?"

"That thing's been sitting for at least five years, probably more like ten. I want to replace the spark plugs and, while they're out, squirt some oil in the cylinders before we try to start it. Cause if those rings are rusted in place when we try to start it, we could find ourselves in the tractor engine rebuilding business. And I don't want that."

"Me neither. I've got a telescope to mount. Robby, how do you know all this stuff? I mean..., you seem to know about everything."

Robby laughed. "I've got a busy mind, can't seem to slow it down."

## Midnight Madness

Reaching up under the box springs, Robby felt along the smooth board until he discovered the strip of duct tape stuck to the side. Old Man Thomas was snoring at the other end of the house and Robby knew he wouldn't wake until sometime around four when he stumbled into his wheelchair and headed for the bathroom.

Behind the tape was the small plastic pack that he had found at the station. All of these months he had been good, resisted the temptation to prove to himself that, yes, at last the urge was gone.

*Then, why haven't I thrown it away?*

That was the harder question. The tractor was fixed, running like a charm, the laughingstock of the town because it was so old. Anyone in their right mind would have upgraded to the 4020. But Robby lovingly kept the old A running, much to Thomas' satisfaction, smiling as he watched it chug around the property dragging a tree or plowing a field.

And the barn was painted red with white trim, two coats. A service panel had been installed so Ollie had just about moved in, modifying his observatory during the day and, at night, gazing at the stars.

"Might as well put in a bed," he had said. "Better than driving home at four AM. And since the bed's there, might as well put in a small fridge and hotplate so I can get a quick breakfast before going to work.

*So..., what's the problem if I do it one more time? It's not like I'm going out looking for it.*

He found the sticky edge of the tape and, groping his way toward the bulge in the middle, quietly pulled it away from the board.

The pipe had been easy to make. A three-inch long piece of one-inch diameter doweling with a quarter-inch hole drilled lengthwise to intersect with the bigger, half-inch hole coming in from the top. A little bit of tin foil with a couple of pinholes and it was ready to go. It was only for one use anyway.

*I'll go up to the loft. Ollie's in town tonight and he's put in a good sound system. Nobody'll ever know.*

The screen door didn't squeak anymore. And the steps did not creak. It was easy to get outside without waking Thomas, whose habit was to go to bed at nine, get about two hours sleep and then wake up for an hour of sleep-reading, more dreaming what he'd read than actually comprehending, and then go back to sleep for another few hours before getting up for his four AM toilet visit and glass of water.

*It's one-fifteen now. That gives me a few hours. I'll just tell Harrison I overslept if it comes to that. He can't complain. I haven't been late or missed a day, yet.*

Crossing the barnyard, the barn looked good, the dark red looking more a charcoal-gray color than red in the night, contrasting against the white trim glowing in the moonlight.

The windmill had required a lot more work. Taking it down, Robby discovered that the gears had sheared and that all of the seals were gone. It had been easier to replace the whole thing, at a cost of two thousand dollars including the wood for the tower. But, now it hummed along smoothly, even on light wind days. Thomas had been thrilled.

241

Inside the barn, going up the steps, Robby admired their handiwork. He and Ollie had built the staircase so that if you turned left as you entered from the front door, you would ascend the staircase up to a platform built into the corner. The second half of the staircase went up the adjacent wall.

They had talked about painting the staircase weathered gray-brown so that it would look like everything else, and then decided on a dark gray sealer/stain. Thomas approved.

The roof had been trickier. Much of the wood was rotted out so they had built a second set of rafters alongside the first with the goal of ripping out all of the old stuff next spring when they planned to replace the whole roof.

Ollie had built his platform directly beneath the hole, three feet above the loft floor, four steps going up and with rails around the perimeter. They had installed a sliding roof to cover the hole, with complications, mostly coming in the form of leaks whenever it rained. Knowing that a new roof was to follow, they installed a gutter right below the leaks and modified a vent so that it would accommodate the drainpipe passing through.

Thomas complained that he was not able to see what they were doing up there and would have been more insistent about Robby building some kind of access had the computer not kept him busy several hours of the day.

He had learned how to input data into Excel and even learned how to pick out different jobs after Robby showed him what folder that they were in and spent half a day explaining that they weren't actual folders, but rather virtual folders, which Thomas thought made no sense at all.

Thomas also discovered computer games, Solitaire, Checkers, and Chess. When he wasn't cussing at the computer for not doing what he wanted, he was cussing it for cheating and more than once whirled his wheelchair around and made a hasty, fuming exit out of the room.

Ollie had installed a red photo light up in the loft with the switch mounted at the top of the stairs, a way to get around without hindering the optics of his telescope. Turning that on, Robby walked over to a small table next to the refrigerator and sat down to fill the pipe.

*Good. I can finally be rid of it. And I won't have to think about it any more.*

It seemed odd to be following the same motions that he'd followed so many times back in California, tapping the side of the package to make sure everything fell into the crease, carefully unfolding the packet over a solid, flat surface in case something spilled, wondering about the quality.

And then Robby sat there for a long time, studying the pipe in his left hand, holding the lighter in his right.

Perihelion!

*How could I have forgotten? Tonight is the night!
Hale-Bopp is at its perihelion!*

Turning off of the highway and onto the gravel
road, Ollie resisted the urge to punch it. That
would wake up Old Man Thomas and he might put
the screws to these unscheduled nighttime visits.

*Don't want to piss the old man off. Got a good
thing going here. Gotta keep it quiet.*

It had been almost two years since he had heard
about the comet, C/1995 01.

But he and Robby had been so busy with both
the handyman business and rebuilding the barn
that he had forgotten. Turning off his lights and
slowing the car to a crawl, he pulled into the barnyard and parked next to the barn door.

Hearing music when he entered the barn, Ollie proceeded up the stairs quietly, wondering who
could have possibly invaded his space. The devel-
oper's light was on, casting a dim, red glow over the
area.

Head coming up to floor level of the loft, Ollie spotted someone on his cot over in the corner
next to the stereo. Whoever they were, they were
lying on their back and looking up at the ceiling.
He couldn't tell if the person's eyes were open or
closed.

Ollie removed his shoes, stepped up onto the
loft and approached his bed, walking slowly, quietly
along the wall. He considered grabbing the knife
out of the drawer in the table next to the refrigerator but remembered that it made a scraping noise
when pulled open. He had intended to wax the run-
ners, had even bought the wax but hadn't gotten

244

around to it, yet. Instead, he advanced on the bed.

*It's..., Robby! What's he doing up here?*

He appeared to be asleep. Keeping his distance and staying near the foot of the bed, Ollie touched Robby's shoe and, when nothing happened, tapped the sole with his knuckle. "Robby? You OK?"

*Hanging from the ceiling by a wire, a single incandescent bulb cast a dreary yellow light into the drafty room. Two of the six panes of the only window, located across from the door, were broken and all of the others were cracked. The wooden floor, dried and splintered, allowed a glimpse of the dirt below. The door was locked.*

*Missing the inner wall, two-by-four studs visibly spanned the distance between the footers and headers, covered on the other side with ill-fitting, cracked and weathered boards..., allowing the night to filter in.*

*It was out there somewhere. He could feel its presence, ominous, dark and patient, understanding that it had all the time in the world.*

*Robby knew he'd have to open the door sooner or later and go through and then his time would be up. Standing away from the window, looking out, he saw a calm, quiet night.*

*Deceiving. It's out there. Opening the door will be a very bad thing to do...,*

"Robby. It's me, Ollie."

Robby sat straight up, wild-eyed, staring blankly into the dim red light.

"Are you OK?"

*Red! The air is bleeding! It's..., in here!*

"Robby. You must've been dreaming."

*Words, drifting away, dissolving..., what?*

Ollie stepped closer. "It's me, Ollie. What are you

doing up here?"

"Ollie?" he stammered.

*Get with it Robby!*

"I, uh…, I thought you were staying in town."

"I was. And then I remembered that tonight is the night of the comet, Hale-Bopp. Tonight it's at its perihelion."

"What?"

"Remember? I was telling you about the comet, Hale-Bopp? Tonight's the night! It's as close to the sun as it will ever be in our lifetime."

"Did we talk about that?"

*Up there! Streaking across the sky, ripping up the Universe…,*

"Yeah, we did. Don't you remember? It's the reason I wanted to get this ready in time."

*Tearing a seam, a place to slip through…,*

"We won't see this comet again in our lifetimes, Robby. It won't be back for another twenty-five hundred years!"

And then Ollie was up, heading for the platform, grabbing the pole along the way so that he could slide the rolling section of the roof away.

"You gotta check this out, Robby. Grab my camera, will you? It's on top of the fridge."

It was coming back now, the packet, making the pipe, sneaking out of the house. Robby waited until Ollie's back was turned and then reached down beneath the bed, grabbed the lighter and pipe and stuffed them into his pocket. Carefully, he stood.

"What are we lookin' at?"

"Hale-Bopp. A comet discovered July twenty-third, nineteen-ninety-five, dubbed the Great Comet of nineteen-ninety-seven. Tonight, it's at its' perihelion."

"It's what?"

246

"The closest it gets to the sun in its orbit. For Hale-Bopp, that's a little over dot nine AU's."

"What's an AU?"

"Astronomical Unit. It's based on the distance between the Earth and the Sun. Ninety-three million miles. So, right now, Hale-Bopp is closer to the sun than we are. That means it will be at its brightest. And that's what I want to see."

"How do you know all of this, Ollie?"

Ollie grinned. "I learned from you. Watching how you figured things out, I went home and did the same. And look at this, an observatory! Crude. But one, just the same. Check this out."

Looking through the telescope, Robby saw another world he had not even imagined. Sure, everyone looks up at the stars and wonders. But to open a book and study, to learn how to put things together, to make your life go forward in the direction of your dreams, to build an observatory for crying out loud so that you can get a closer view of the universe?

"Pretty awesome," said Robby, feeling truly awestruck.

"There was a religious group in California called Heaven's Gate, that committed mass suicide in some place called Rancho Santa Fe."

"Committed suicide?" Robby knew Rancho Santa Fe. He had driven through there many times trying to get from Interstate Fifteen to Interstate Five. "This just happened?"

"Where you been, Robby? It's been in all of the papers. They believed that the Earth was about to be done in. The only way to survive was to leave and the comet was a vehicle...,"

Robby didn't really hear the rest of it. His eye was still on the comet and his mind was on the idea of chasing after your dream, bringing in those things that you love and keeping them close, surrounding yourself with them. Tanya, her knowing smile, that gentle touch...,

*What's it been now? A year?*

*I hope I'm not too late.*

Robby turned away from the telescope and, not really listening, watched Ollie go on and on about the stars. And then he put his hand on Ollie's shoulder and smiled.

"Ollie? You're awesome! Don't ever change. Thanks for showing me Hale-Bopp."

And then he headed for the stairs, wanting to get away before Ollie could see the tears forming in his eyes.

"Way I see it," said Buck, pointing to the chart beside him. "It's going to take another year to implement the final part of the system. What I need to know is, where do we start? Who wants to be the one with the test office?"

The crew was gathered around the long table in the conference room. Bart stirred his coffee quietly, not wanting it to be him but, being junior man, not having much say-so in the matter.

Carly looked the crew over, wondering who she could stick it to while Sergio silently made up excuses as to why it couldn't be him. Tony had his excuses already. Everyone thought they had a good enough reason as to why it shouldn't be them.

"Well," said Martin, interrupting the long silence. "You guys make the decisions. Whose office will it be?"

Darin leaned back in his chair. "Why are we even doing this?"

"We want to know," said Buck, with a gleam in his eye, "everything there is to know about each piece of equipment, it's status, capabilities, if it's in trouble and what made it fail."

"We have that already," said Darin. "It's called an alarm. It already goes to the Center and it doesn't cost a million dollars."

"Think of this," said Buck. "All of this knowledge right at your fingertips. With dial-in capabilities you could retire an alarm from your home and get paid for it."

This was a fine selling point. Everyone wanted the ability to get an extra three hours pay for a call-out when they never even had to leave home, a truly great feature.

"We can't test in any of my offices," said Carly, at last, clicking her ballpoint pen several times. "They're all in disaster mode already with all of the new stuff that's going in. I think it should be installed in some power room that's stable, where all of the modernization work has already been done. Isn't that what it's going to be wired to?"

She had an argument. There was absolutely no good reason to install an unknown program with unknown consequences into an unstable environment, unless you're the government. However, her statement did cause a ripple effect through the crew.

In one efficient move, Carly had eliminated herself from the competition and stepped into the role of judge, now helping Martin pick whose office it should be. Everyone else was left to fend for themselves.

"It can't be in my loop," said Tony. "I'm all over the back country. I don't have time to baby-sit one office."

"He's got a point," said Carly, now Queen of the Selection Process.

Martin nodded in agreement. "Yeah. You're right. He's all over the place. If he had a trouble in Cuyamaca but was watching the job in Lakeside, someone else would have to break free. Can't have that."

"I'm working nights for the next two weeks," said Sergio. "The installers would have to work nights to install it and only in the building that I'm in. And then, who's going to cover my loop during the day? And Carly, that would probably fall over to you."

Darin glanced over at Sergio, sitting next to Carly on the other side of the table.

*Man! That was a good move. Didn't think Serge*

250

*had it in him.*

"He's right," said Carly. "I'm already watching his loop during the day and he's covering mine at night. We can't be taking this on right now."

"They can't work nights anyway," said Buck. "That'll put us over budget."

"Days are better anyway," said Carly. "More coverage in case something happens. Serge is out."

Roberta sighed. "Well, I'm on scheduled vacation for the next two weeks. If you want to start Monday in my loop, somebody's gonna have to cover."

"And I'm already covering for Roberta while she's on vacation," said Jerome, now seeing his chance to jump on the bandwagon. "So, I'm already covering two loops."

"It can't be any of my offices," said Bart, shaking his head. "I don't know enough."

Carly nodded. "All of these are pretty good excuses. Who does that leave?"

"Let's take a break," Darin suggested, now seeing the direction this was heading. "That'll give us a chance to refill our coffee and think about it."

"The new equipment is already installed in your loop and you're good with troubleshooting," said Carly. "Who better to oversee the test installation, than you?"

"And you're in the same place all day," said Sergio, grinning. "You only have one building."

"But it's the hub! You don't want to experiment in the hub! Try it out in some rinky-dink office where it won't affect a million people."

Carly knew she had the majority she needed to put the screws to Darin. "All in favor of Darin's office, say aye."

And there was a resounding affirmation and nodding of heads.

"So be it," said Martin, marveling that this crew could sometimes come to an agreement. "Darin, the crew will be at your doorstep Monday morning."

"Now, let's take a break," said Carly, smiling mischievously at Darin. "Gotcha."

"Fuck you, Sergio," said Darin. "I thought we were allies."

Sergio laughed. "Had to pay you back for ruining my reputation."

"Your reputation has always sucked. Which part are we talking about?'

"You, me, and Robby in Building Four."

Carly laughed. "Can't let it go, can you? You macho bastard!"

"They said they checked the starter. I believed them."

Carly turned and headed for the coffee pot. "Give it up! Roberta plucked the feathers off of all three of you. Ha!"

## The Cincher

Robby spotted her coming out of the grocery store. Tanya was dressed just like he remembered, tight fitting jeans, classy, snug fitting top that showed off her tiny waist and well proportioned body. She was wearing the silver necklace that he had given her two years before, the one that formed a V at the end, accentuated with several small lapis stones and matching earrings. He got out of the car and hurried across the parking lot toward her.

"Tanya!"

She turned toward the sound, spotted Robby and stopped in her tracks, looking like she'd just seen a dead man walking, unaware of the car that was waiting for her to finish crossing into the main parking lot. Robby hurried toward her.

"Robby?"

"Tanya! My God! You're looking good."

The car honked. They retreated back to the front of the grocery store.

"I thought you were dead!"

Robby laughed. "Not yet. I'm done with all that. I'm cleaner now than I've ever been."

"Good for you. So, what are you doing these days?"

"Working on a place back in Kansas. Got my own business. You?"

"Working at a new company, same line of work. But now, I'm the manager."

"I always thought you'd make a good manager. You're good with people."

"Not with you, apparently."

"You were right. I was in trouble. You got time for a cup of coffee?"

"No. Actually, I don't."

"Later then? Can I take you out to dinner?"

She shook her head and moved the plastic bag from her left hand to her right and then showed him her ring. "Robby. I'm engaged."

"Oh." Robby didn't know what to say. "I see."

"Did you really think I'd wait?"

"Do you love him?"

"Of course, I do."

"More than me? You can break it off. We're good together, Tanya. You and me, soul mates."

"No, Robby. We're not. We thought we were good together but it just never worked out, did it?"

"Who is this guy?"

She reached up, gently touched Robby's neck and kissed him on his cheek. "It's over between us, Robby. I'm carrying his baby. We're getting married. And I love him more than anything."

She smiled, a kind and gentle smile. "I wish you the best of luck with the rest of your life. Our time together was good, Robby, sometimes. But now it's over."

And then she walked away.

Darin hurried through the short corridor, turned left and headed east, down the long dimly lit basement hallway toward Norm, who was standing at the far end, looking up and pushing a broomstick handle into the ceiling.

"What are you doing?"

"Oh, good," said Norm. "A second opinion."

"About what?"

"Is the can big enough?"

"What?"

"It's almost four, now. If I come in at six tomorrow morning, will the can hold all the water?"

"Why would you even care?"

"If too much water stays on the floor all night, I'll have to call in the waxing crew. They're not scheduled for another month."

"Norm, go home."

"Or, if Merry comes in early, she'll write me up. To her, it's a slip hazard."

A drip fell between them, hitting somewhere in the growing puddle, splattering.

"Where'd that land?" said Norm.

"I didn't see. Why don't you just get a rag, clean up the floor and see where the next drop falls? You'll know exactly where to put the can."

"My office is already locked up."

"It's just down the hall."

"Willy has my keys."

"He has his own set."

"Locked 'em in the cable vault, borrowed mine to go get his."

"I thought they were supposed to be attached to his belt."

255

"Well, they weren't." Norm glanced up, inspecting the leak. "Think the can will spill over before tomorrow morning?"

"When are you coming in?"

"Six."

"It's four now. How long between drips?"

"About a minute. Do me a favor, will you?"

"Norm, I've been in a meeting all day and both you and me have been here since...,"

"One drip. Tell me when it's going to happen so I can watch."

"I can't look up, hurts my neck. I'll watch for one drip and then I'm out of here."

"Drop's forming," said Norm.

"I've still got go lock up my office."

"Do you think the can's big enough?"

"What'd you say? A drop every a minute?"

"About."

"Eight hours until midnight, six more after that. Fourteen hours? Sixty drops times fourteen hours. How many is that?"

"Sixty times ten is six hundred," said Norm. "Even if I don't get in until seven..., oh! There it went!"

"Missed it, damn it."

"Wasn't here this morning. Maybe all of that starting and stopping of the pumps put too much pressure on the pipes."

"What are you saying?"

"The only liquid I know of in this area is from the building cooling system. I dread the thought of having to drain it, if that's what this is."

"This is water, right?"

"Don't know of anything else. I was on my hands and knees smelling it to make sure when Pricella came around the corner, going into Admin. She didn't say anything. I'm sure she thinks I'm nuts."

"She's sure got some nice tits."

"Well, I'll never get to see 'em, not after that. "

"What is this? A one pound can?"

"Two, I think. Check the side."

"Doesn't say. Jesus. How old is this thing? Most of the writing's gone."

"Found it in the other room. I think that's the first can I've seen around here that wasn't full of something, maybe a two-pound can. That means it'll hold two pounds of water, right?"

"How's that drip coming?"

"Not yet. Let me think, if water is eight pounds a gallon, two pounds would be a quart, right?'

"I guess. Jesus. Can't you hurry that thing up?"

"Two pounds of water is probably smaller than two pounds of coffee. It's denser."

"We don't know if this is a two pound coffee can."

"Did they ever come in one and one half pound cans?"

"How the fuck should I know? I just drink it. Why don't you just get a bucket, put up some cones and not worry about it? Merry can't complain about that."

"Those are in the janitor's closet on the other side of the building.

"You're sure this is from the cooling system?"

"Probably."

"Aren't those eight inch plastic pipes?"

"Ten, I think."

"How many gallons in the system?"

"About thirty thousand."

"Norm, if we have that much water above us in pipes made of plastic, leaking and held together with glue, we shouldn't even be standing here. Thirty thousand times eight equals two hundred and twenty-four thousand pounds of water!"

"You're right. I better come in early to deal with it. Here comes the drip."

"Got it," said Darin, placing the can. "I'm outta here."

## It Floods!

Charles was not at his post when Darin came through the door. Normally he was right there, wanting to get off work, wondering where Willy was and why he was late again.

There was a code between around-the-clock guards, each shift relieve the other five minutes early. Sometimes, if lucky, your relief would arrive fifteen minutes early and let you go. That's how it was supposed to work.

But Willy wasn't going to relieve Charles, the night guard, early because Charles wouldn't relieve BJ, the evening guard, early.

"You're fuckin' with me," Willy told Charles one day. "I can't get a break because you don't give him one."

"You relieve him early," said Charles. "See what you get. Lazy-assed bastard doesn't do shit until the last ten minutes. You let him go early and you're stuck with all his paper work and walkin' his rounds. He's just a lazy-assed bastard."

"And I'm the one that suffers," said Willy.

Continuing past the deserted guard station, through the double doors that lead to the stairs, Darin headed for his office in the basement. Descending down the second flight of stairs, he found water lapping up against the bottom step, an inch or two deep for as far down the hallway as he could see.

This was not in the playbook. The lights were still on, reflecting across the endless sea, glimmering under the ventilating ducts. Darin sat down on the steps, chin in hands, elbows on knees, and tried to figure out what he should do next.

Norm came sloshing around the corner, wearing knee high rubber boots.

"Guess what?'" he said, cheerfully. "The coffee can wasn't big enough! I can't even find it. We in heap big trouble kemo-sabe."

"My God, Norm. What happened?"

"Pipe broke. I should've taken the time to get a ladder and check it out."

"The big pipe?"

"Got the call at three this morning. The Center said the chiller was sending a low water alarm."

"No shit. Is this what thirty thousand gallons looks like, laid out flat?"

"It's better now. It was a lot worse when I got here. You know that drain over by your office, the one in the hallway?"

"Can't say as I do."

"Well, take note when you see it. It's an inch above the floor. What kind of drain is higher than the floor?"

"Doesn't sound too smart."

"Didn't work for you especially. The water went through Admin, through the engineer's room and down the two steps leading to your office. You won't like what you see when you get there."

Darin groaned. *This is going to be a shitty day. Got two more crews coming in, night shift tonight, a meeting this afternoon.*

*Fuck you, Buck. Fuck you and your damned modernization project.*

"Sorry to say," said Norm, wading over to give Darin a hand with some of his stuff. "Since your office was the lowest part of the building, it all went through your room."

"My test equipment?"

"Unplugged and drying out."

260

Darin took off his shoes, rolled up his pants and stepped into the water. "You know, also on this floor is the twelve thousand volt transformer. It's only about eighteen inches off of the floor. How high did the water get?'

"Apparently not eighteen inches," said Norm.

"Wonder what would happen if groundwater reached the transformer."

"I wouldn't want to be in the room."

"Even being in the area could get you electrocuted."

"I'll remember that next time this happens."

"If it does, call me at home so I can take a vacation day."

"By the way, all of your prints are gone, the ones in the lowest drawer of your file cabinet."

"Damn."

"Your little refrigerator? Motor burned out."

"Double damn."

"Everything in the bottom drawers of your desk is soaked."

"What a lousy way to start the day."

"Tile's already coming up in your room."

"Haven't you got any good news?"

"Got one crew working on the pipes, they're fixed. We're filling the system now. It seems to be holding. Got a crew vacuuming out the carpet in Admin and the Engineer's offices and..., hey, check this out."

They walked past Darin's office to an old mostly unused elevator on the north end of the building. Norm pried the doors open and pointed up. "Lucky for me, the elevator was already up there on the first floor."

And then he pointed down into the black, murky water, to a light bulb mounted on the wall about two feet underwater, glowing brightly.

"I'd say that's a pretty good light fixture, wouldn't you?"

Darin studied the light, wondering why it didn't blow up, or why water hadn't gotten into the inner workings of the fixture, or why...,

His phone started ringing back in his office.

"And the day begins. Gotta go. I'll get back to you."

"Stay dry," said Norm.


"Power Maintenance, Darin here."

"You still workin' that place?"

"Who's this?"

"Thought you'd have a cush job by now."

"Who's this? Robby?"

"Who else'd be calling this time of the morning? You haven't even changed your start time."

"I thought you were dead! You didn't tell anybody!"

"I had to do it by myself. Couldn't have anyone tryin' to help."

"Almost got my ass killed looking for you. Fucking Martin...,"

Laughter. "Sounds like nothing's changed."

"Everything's changed. You wouldn't believe all of the shit. Remember Buck? Ever since you've been gone...,"

"I left the state. Thought I'd find the simple life and start over. But that stuff's everywhere. It's gotta come from inside, man. Hey, is that little taco shop still open over by your office?"

"Yea, just had lunch there yesterday."

"Oh, so you probably don't want to go there again today?"

"Robby, I'd be happy to buy you lunch. What time?"

"You don't have to buy me nothin'. I got more

262

work than I can handle."

"Doing what?"

"Handyman."

"Robby. You're supposed to be a tech! Have you called Martin?"

"Not yet. Just got into town a couple of days ago. Everything's going OK for you?"

Darin looked around at his office. The water was starting to clear out now. Pretty soon a crew would come in with squeegees and buckets and mops and fans to dry everything out. He'd probably get a new floor out of it. The phone would ring incessantly, and then there were the night shifts, more meetings, more of everything...,

"Great, Robby. Everything's going great. My God, we have a lot to talk about."

## Catching Up

"So here I am," said Darin, setting his burrito down so that he could wipe the juice off his hands before it went down his arms. "Everybody on the day shift is gone and I'm gonna have a nice, quiet night to myself. I go into the break room, make myself a pot of coffee and sit down to read the paper."

Robby, dipping his chip into the salsa, started to smile. When Darin started off like this, it was going to be a long story. They had shared many while troubleshooting together.

"So I get my coffee, unwrap my sandwich and then I hear this banging on the front door. Someone's pounding on it! So I go to open the door and there's this short, bald, guy who wants to come in. I've never seen him before."

"I'm Jim," he says, holding up an ID card. "From B & S Construction. I need to get into your cable vault."

"He was nervous, fidgety and was starting to regard me as an obstacle. He tried to go around, but when I stopped him, he handed me this MOP. When I started to read it, he jumped by me and started running like a madman through the building. I took off after him and we have this crazy conversation, doors flying open and slamming shut, us running through rooms, down hallways. He was fast!"

"You can't come in! This is not a public building! You're not allowed!"

"I've got permission. You don't have time to read the whole fucking thing!"

"What's happening in the cable vault?"

"Water is pouring in."

264

"What?"

"I've drilled a hole in the wall for more cable runs."

"OK. I'm trying to understand. Are we talking trickle? Or, more?"

"This office is sitting on a spring. Water's pouring in!"

"That's not good. But the vault's not ventilated. We have to test for gas first."

"You don't have time."

"It's company policy."

Jim headed down the stairs two at a time. "Fuck that!"

"How come nobody told me anything?"

"He opened the door to a flood of water, already up to the bottom of the steps. There was a four-inch stream of water gushing across the room."

"Holy shit! What the hell? Jesus!"

"Call Building Maintenance!" Jim yelled, trudging through the water. Walking into the stream, he tried to cap the conduit. "Tell 'em to bring their biggest sump pumps!"

"I can't believe this! What's their number?"

"It's on the MOP! You left it back by the door! Don't just stand there!"

"And here I thought I was going to have this nice quiet evening in the office by myself."

Robby laughed. "I kinda miss it. Always somethin' bad happening, huh?"

"Yeah. Lot of good times, too. Are you gonna try and get back on the crew?"

"No." Robby smiled. "I'm done here. I'm workin' on a farm back in Kansas. Got a little handyman business goin'."

"You making good money?"

"Nah. But it's slow and friendly. And that's worth

a hundred grand a year."

"You come back looking for Tanya?"

"Yeah. But she's got a kid comin'. She's happy. I can't blame her. I was messed up."

"You're clean now?"

Robby laughed. "Hell, yeah. I don't even drink. Maybe a beer every now and then."

"You feeling better?"

"Not so many ups and downs. I can relax. And that keeps me happy."

"You dating anybody?"

"Nothing serious."

"Reason I ask," said Darin, looking past Robby with a smile. "This is Liani. She's the one who cooked your fish tacos last time you were here."

Robby laughed. "I remember those!" He stood to shake her hand. "Best I've ever had."

Liani looked down at his plate. "But you're eating a burrito."

"He's been in Kansas," said Darin. "Go easy on him."

Liani nudged Darin to move over, sat down and kissed him on the cheek. Robby had that puzzled look.

"We're dating," Liani explained. "After I found out he could dance, I figured he was OK."

Robby laughed. "He can't dance. I've seen him. He has white man's overbite!"

"Not when he dances with a fish."

"She's trying to be funny," Darin explained. "Since you've been gone, I bought a sailboat. I took her out sailing one day. Turns out, she's a fisherman."

"Fisher woman," Liani corrected. "Sailboats go just the right speed for trolling. So I throw out a line."

Robby found another chip and loaded it up with salsa. "What's that got to do with dancing?"

"She caught a barracuda. I didn't want it flopping around down in the cabin so she left it on the deck, in the cockpit with us. Well..., I'm barefoot. After a while the fish just lays there, so I'm thinking it's dead. And then I accidentally stepped on it. The thing goes berserk. You ever see the teeth on a barracuda? Man! They're like razor blades."

Liani, laughing. "You should've seen him! Too bad I didn't have a camera."

"I can see it," said Robby.

"That thing would take your toe off," said Darin. "You'd be dancing, too."

"I wouldn't be out there in the first place," said Robby. "I get seasick. What made you decide to buy a boat?"

"Remember Roberta?"

"Yeah. How's she doin'? She still on the crew?"

"Still there. Bought a sailboat and took me out sailing one day. We got in this huge water balloon fight with some other boats. What a kick in the ass! Anyway, she got me hooked."

"She was breaking up with her boyfriend when I left. How'd that turn out?"

"He's gone. I think she's dating a couple of guys now."

A boy walked up to their table and put his arm around Liani, who smiled and gave him a hug.

"This is Carlo, my sister's son."

Robby smiled and held out his hand. "Carlo, good name."

Carlo was like Robby in that his smile was contagious. It was a wide, genuine smile that lit up not only his face, but the entire room. After they shook hands, Robby took a quarter out of his pocket.

267

"Carlo, maybe you can help me. This quarter is driving me nuts."

Robby held both hands face up, put the quarter in his right hand and then made both hands into a fist.

"The problem," said Robby, "is that I never know where this quarter's going to be. And it's only this quarter that does it."

Opening his hands, the quarter was in Robby's left hand.

Carlo thought about that for a minute, dark eyes studying Robby and then back to his hands. "Do that again."

Robby closed both hands. "It's not me that's doing it. It's the quarter."

When he opened them again, the quarter was in his right hand. "See? I can't stand it!"

He closed his hands. When he opened them again, the quarter was gone.

"Sometimes that happens," said Robby, sounding disappointed. "Should be around here somewhere. Darin, you got it?"

Darin held both hands open. "Nope."

"Liani?"

"Nope."

"Carlo?"

Carlo checked his hands. "Not me."

"Wait. What's that?" said Robby, reaching for Carlo's ear. "It's right there, in your ear!"

He held the quarter out for everyone to see and then handed it to Carlo. "Here. I don't want it. Like I said, it's driving me nuts."

Carlo examined it for a moment and then carefully put it down on the table between them.

"You don't want it either, huh? Can't say as I blame you. If I give you a dollar to take it, will you do that?"

Carlo looked up at Liani, questionably. She nodded.

"Sounds like a good deal to me."

Carlo took the money, said thanks, and headed back to the kitchen.

Darin finished his burrito and wiped his hands. "That's his mom cooking back there. You're pretty good with that quarter. I didn't know you knew any magic."

"I got a book out of the library."

Carlo's mother was watching Robby over the counter as Carlo explained the trick. She smiled.

"What's her name?" Robby asked.

"Leticia," said Liani. "My little sister."

Leticia came out from the kitchen, introduced herself, thanked Robby and hurried back.

Lunch was over. Darin had to get back to work, Liani had a class to attend and Leticia was swamped in the kitchen. Robby returned to his motel to pack up his stuff for the trip back to Kansas.

And it was during that time that he slowly came to the realization that the farm, by itself, was not going to be enough to satisfy his needs. The long winter months were coming up and there would be days, months of sitting inside, watching the snow, waiting for the ground to thaw so planting could begin, with way too much time on his hands.

*Tanya's gone. Get over it, Robby. You had it coming. Time to move on. No more reasons to stay in this town. It's gonna be a long winter.*

The most immediate problem was that the storm windows, sitting out in the shed behind the house, had been stored improperly. The ones that were laid out flat were most likely broken. The ones leaning heavily to one side were probably warped. Some were cracked. None were marked. It was impossible to tell which ones went to the second story windows up in the attic. It would be trial and error, going up and down the ladder trying to find the ones that fit.

Robby, sitting in the front room with Thomas while playing checkers, figured that tomorrow would be a good day to get that done. The nights had been noticeably cooler and, just yesterday morning he had seen a thin sheet of ice in the water trough. Better to do the work now than when it was freezing.

Hearing the wind against the window, he glanced outside and noticed that the field just west of the barnyard needed to be mowed again. Even with no rain it seemed to produce massive amounts of weeds.

"Thomas. You ever plant anything in that lot?"

A thin smile passed across Thomas' face. "Nope. Made more money doin' nothin'."

"Sure was a lot of work digging it up."

"Good. It made you strong."

"What ever happened to Missy?"

"She just drifted back one day. I kept thinkin' you'd come get her. But, then I found out you'd gone to California."

"You said she was gentle."

Hearing that, Thomas actually chuckled. "No. I

270

said she was my best mule. I didn't have any others so she was the worst, too. Stubborn old bitch, huh?"

"Probably my mom let her go. She hated that animal. Your move, by the way."

"Don't know how a drug addict can be so good at checkers."

"I'm not a drug addict," Robby lied, knowing that he always would be.

"I heard that stuff rots your brain."

"Not like you think. Most times, nobody could tell I was even doin' it. I could still do everything I normally do but was a lot happier doin' it."

"Why'd you start?"

"Bored, I guess."

"But then you got hooked?"

"It makes you feel good. Once you've had it, you want more."

"If you had it now, would you do it?"

"The point is," said Robby, "I don't have it. And I intend to keep it that way."

"Can you find it here in Kansas?"

"It's everywhere. I don't even like talkin' about it. I try to keep it out of my mind, which brings me to my next idea."

"Every time you have an idea it costs me money."

"This is a good idea. I say, let's put up the storm windows that fit and aren't broke...,"

"That makes sense. How else would you do it?"

"And the ones we can't use, let's replace them with dual paned windows."

"What's that?"

"There's an air space in between two panes of glass, in the same window. There's no need for storm windows anymore."

"Who thought of that?"

Robby laughed. "Probably someone who had to put them up and take them down every year."

"So, you want to open up holes in the wall of my house in the middle of winter? To put in new windows?"

"It's not the middle of winter. It's just starting."

"Worse."

"You'll never have to mess with that window again."

"Robby, I probably won't make it through the winter anyway. So, that's not a selling point."

"You're gonna live another twenty years."

"If you were on this side, looking out, you'd disagree."

"You look better now than when I got here."

"Because you're working me to death. Blood hasn't had a chance to settle."

"Look at you. You're computer savvy. You know Excel. You know what computer programs are."

"I know they cheat at solitaire."

"Your farm's gettin' put back together."

"Look what it's costing me? I'm gonna *have* to die. I won't be able to buy food anymore."

"Thomas. I've got a good thing going here. I'm not going to let anything happen to you. If we go down, we go down together. We're a team."

"Some things, you just can't stop." Thomas tapped the table lightly with his fingers, looking for a way to start. "So, before that happens, there's a few things I need to say."

Robby leaned back in his chair. Thomas almost never gave out information about anything freely. When offered, he had learned to shut up and listen.

"Before you were born, there was a fella named Hoffman who owned a farm about two miles down the road toward town...,"

"I know which one you're talking about."

"A bunch of us got together and helped raise his barn. Afterward, he threw a party. There was dancin' and some drinkin' and, to help raise money, women sold lunches to the highest bidder."

"That's where you bid to have lunch with the woman who's selling it?"

"Right. Well, your dad, William, was out of town for the week, so I bought the lunch that your mother was selling, paid twenty bucks, a lot for those days. We sat out back, behind the barn under an old tree that overlooked the valley. There was a full moon that night.

Before I go any further, I want to say that I loved your mother ever since the first time I saw her. For a while I thought I had a chance that maybe we could get married and raise a family.

I thought that might come to pass. But, she was never as enamored with me as I was with her. When William came to town, all of that changed. She fell madly in love with him."

Thomas picked up his coffee cup, fiddled with the handle for a moment, raised it to his lips and then decided not to drink. He set the cup back down and stared out the window, watching the wind blow through the weeds.

"That night, I asked her for a kiss. She refused. I reminded her that I paid more than anybody for a lunch and surely I should get one little kiss. She finally gave in, not because she wanted to, but because she wanted to get back to the dance and away from me.

"I didn't let it stop at one. I kept going even though she resisted. I thought, deep down, she really wanted it and next thing I know we had done it. At first, I was elated. I thought, now she'll love me.

We're gonna get married. I thought I had done the right thing."

Robby waited for Thomas to continue, but when the old man just sat there, looking down at his cup, he finally stood and headed for the kitchen.

"Thomas, you want a refill on your coffee?"

He shook his head. "Go get what you're wantin' and hurry back before I change my mind. I've got more to say. I'm just ashamed to say it."

Robby decided against the refill and seated himself back down.

"I sent her flowers the next day. When I didn't hear anything back, I tried calling, lots of times. I wrote letters. I sent more flowers. I wanted her to know that it was my love that drove me. I never heard a word back. She married William two weeks later.

In town, when our paths crossed, she refused to make eye contact. As far as she was concerned, I did not exist. I couldn't believe that the whole affair was turned around so completely. I was embarrassed by her unwillingness to acknowledge my presence, even in front of other people, people who had known that I had bought her lunch that night. But if there were rumors, I never heard them.

You were born nine months into the marriage. I think people overlooked the fact that it was a little early, about two weeks by my calculations. Nobody suspected a scandal because she never said anything about us."

"Wait. You're saying that you are my father?"

"I'm saying that the possibility is there."

This time it was Robby who stared out the window, elbows on the arms of his chair, hands working. This was a twist he hadn't seen coming. Returning to Kansas was supposed to be a time of

274

healing.

"Don't know what to think about that."

"Can't say as I blame you. It's not like, do you want pancakes for breakfast?"

"That changes my thinking about everything."

"How? Nothin' changes, Robby. You're still who you are."

"Yea. But the ground under me just shifted. Didn't think that would happen in Kansas." Robby stared at his empty cup and then looked back outside, up at the sky. "Clouds are building. You might be right. We might get snow."

"Easy to predict the weather in Kansas," said Thomas, following his gaze. "It's the people that are hard to figure out."

Robby smiled. "Just the opposite in California. Never know what's gonna happen with the weather. People? Expect anything, because it could be just that."

"It's gonna be cold, comin' in from the north."

"I should've put the storm windows up before I left."

"Winter does seem to be comin' in a little early." This time Thomas did take a sip of his coffee. "So, you want to replace those windows with dual-paned? That's the way to go?"

"I say we put in the ones we can. And then take a few of the worst ones and order replacements. Then, we won't have to mess with them anymore. It's still your move."

After Robby had moved in and set up his drip
coffee maker, perked coffee became a thing of
the past. Thomas took one sip of Robby's freshly
ground, freshly brewed coffee and that was the new
standard by which all subsequent coffee was mea-
sured.

"The problem with perking," Robby had said, "is
that each time hot water goes over the grounds, it
leeches acid and that's what gives coffee a bitter
taste. Better to have the water pass by once."

Thomas didn't even argue. Within a week the
old coffee maker was sitting out on the back porch
awaiting a new use. And, taking it a step further,
Thomas never even bothered to get up until he
smelled Robby's coffee brewing.

On this morning, Robby got up, looked outside
to see if they had gotten any more snow, turned
up the thermostat, visited the bathroom and then
headed for the kitchen to make a pot of coffee.

Thomas' room was on the other side of the
kitchen. Customary by this time, Robby cracked
the door open to let the scent of brewing coffee
waft into his room. Then he headed for the fridge
and retrieved bacon and eggs. If the smell of coffee
didn't get Thomas out of bed, then the smell of fry-
ing bacon surely would, even on a cold morning.

But when Thomas failed to appear, even after
the bacon was done, Robby knocked on his door
and peered inside.

"Thomas. Breakfast is ready. Come get it before
it gets cold."

This was Robby's worst fear. As he stepped into
the room he started thinking of all the things they

had not talked about.

"Thomas? Hey, old buddy, I know it's cold but...,"

Thomas was turned onto his left side, in a fetal position, eyes closed. Robby approached slowly and, kneeling beside the bed, discovered that he was not breathing and that he had no pulse.

He studied the old man's face, pushed his gray hair back behind his ears and touched Thomas' cheek with the back of his hand, all the while slowly coming to the realization that this stage of his life was over. School was out.

Robby was not a religious man, believing instead that the universe was far too large and complicated for any one thing to have control. And if it did have control, how come it hadn't eliminated evil? And if there was such things as Heaven and Hell, and if man was the chosen one, he hadn't met very many that qualified for Heaven, in his estimation.

No. As far as Robby was concerned, it was a matter of being true to yourself, doing the best you can and if there was a higher authority, it would recognize his worth without anyone or any thing between him and It.

Watching Hale-Bopp with Ollie that night. Now there was a religious experience. Peer into the belly of the animal, see the enormity of the universe and experience the insignificance of self.

OK. Drugs were used. But that was mind-boggling by any standard.

Taking Thomas' hands and putting them into his, Robby closed his eyes...,

*Lord,*

*I don't know if you're there, or even if you exist. For me, it doesn't matter too much. But for Thomas here, I hope you'll lend an ear.*

*This was a good man, a lonely man who had*

*no place to put his heart. He was good to me. I can vouch for that.*

*If Heaven is a place where there is only love, I can think of no one who would be a better fit. And you can trust me on that one, too.*

*If you heard me, thanks for listening.*

Within the week, Robby was told that he had inherited the farm. He hadn't been quite sure what to expect, seeming as Thomas had never talked about anything like that. The man had no sisters or brothers, a few cousins, but no one who had been in recent contact.

Business was slow in the winter. Nobody was doing any remodel work and, except for emergencies, most repair work was put off until spring. So, as far as Robby was concerned, he was just getting by and not much more than that.

And then he learned that Thomas had taken out a reverse mortgage on the farm. After a day of crunching numbers and talking to loan officials at the bank, it soon became apparent that a hundred thousand dollars was coming due at the end of March.

Thomas' ashes were now in an urn in the living room, sitting on the table where they used to play checkers. Robby still ate dinner there every night and for the first week after Thomas died, set up the checkerboard and placed a hot, steaming cup of coffee on his side of the table.

Working in between the grocery job, the gas station job, and his handyman job, Robby spent time replacing the windows. Thomas had sprung for them as soon as all of the measurements were available. It took about one full day to convert one window. Before long, all of that work had been done.

But that did not stop all of the other leaks in the old house, as Robby discovered when temperatures dropped. Taking one wall at a time, he began cutting holes in the inside walls and filling them with insulation and, at the same time, replacing all of the house wiring. Completing that, Robby replastered the walls and painted. Slowly, the house began to stay warm.

But warm, Robby discovered, did not satisfy. He bought cookbooks and experimented on soups. He learned how to bake bread, make pizza dough and he started planning a spice garden for the spring, always knowing in the back of his mind that all of this was futile. He was going to lose the farm. Winter dragged on.

Ollie was busy with school. Now absolutely positive that he was going to be an astronomer, he was taking night classes as well and now had use of the school's observatory, which was heated, unlike the barn.

They had talked about enclosing part of the loft for just that purpose, a small insulated area, but that was one of those things that slide down the list as other things come up.

Alone in bed, lying on his back, hands behind his head, Robby stared into the darkness.

*What difference does it make what I do? Who cares? Tanya is gone. Thomas is gone. I'm all alone.*

*OK, Thomas. You out there? You watchin' me to see what I'm doin'? You waitin' to see if I crack? I'm doin' OK, old man.*

*Question is, how are you? They treatin' you OK? You find a checkers partner, yet?*

The man's name was Billy. He came in late one night while Robby was closing up. He wanted ten bucks worth of gas, bought a pack of cigarettes and a six-pack of beer. They had gotten to know each other, not as friends, more like frequent customer and the clerk talking about the weather, sports, and one night weeks ago, Robby even had to run out to his truck and hand him his beer before he drove off.

"You know, your truck may not be too hard to fix," said Robby.

"Don't know much about motors."

"If you got a minute to start the engine and pop the hood, I might be able to tell you what the trouble is."

Billy studied Robby for a moment. "Why would you want to do that?"

"I fix things. That's what I do."

Billy popped a beer open and offered one to Robby. "Sure. I'll pop the hood. Engine on or off?"

"On."

It was quite obvious what the trouble was, looking down into the engine at night. The spark plug wires were old and on two different wires they were sparking through the insulation where it was rubbing against the metal.

"Turn it off," said Robby. Anticipating this, he had brought out a roll of electrical tape. He taped the two wires and when Billy started it back up, the motor sounded good, better than it had sounded since the first time Robby heard it.

"You need a new set of spark plug wires," said Robby. "Buy them from here, not tonight, I'm goin' home, and I'll help you put them in."

They became friends and Robby got his connection.

## Por Favour

*OK, Thomas. It's down to you and me. I know you're dead cuz I got your ashes in the other room. Yet, here you are, night after night, lookin' over my shoulder, judging what I do. I can feel it.*

*What do you care? Does it matter if I get stoned? Is your house any worse off? Do you think I shirk my responsibilities when the walls are breathing? What does it matter what else I do if the bills are paid, the farm kept up and I'm paying my taxes? Not to mention the fact that you're dead.*

*Yet, here you are, night after night. So what, if I want to see this picture through a different frame of mind? I've still got control. I'm waitin'..., not slippin'.*

*There's nothin' goin' on in the winter. Not in Kansas. Except us losin' this farm. Why didn't you tell me? We coulda done something. Don't know what. I don't have a hundred grand. What are we gonna do, Thomas?*

*House is lookin' good. And, if you were alive, I know you'd love the stews. Bread's pretty good, too. I miss you, old man. You know you're always welcome to come back. Of course, that'd scare the hell outta me, see you crawlin' out of that urn.*

Robby got up from the couch, put on a new selection of CD's and then headed to the kitchen.

*Hey, Thomas, tell you what. I'll make you a deal. You give me a reason to stop, a good reason, not just something to help pass the time, and I'll quit. I'll turn it around for life. I promise.*

*Come on. If you got connections, make it happen. I'll give you a week. Otherwise...,*

The phone rang. Robby turned the music down, took a sip of his drink and waited for the answering

281

machine to kick in.

*OK. That's unexpected. Thomas, you're messing with me.*

"Hi. You've reached Robby's Handyman Services. We've gone home for the day but please leave a message and we'll get back to you. If this is an emergency, press pound. Thank you."

Beep.

"Robby. This is Darin, calling from San Diego. You there?"

*Now is not a good time for a coherent conversation. Things are a little garbled here in Kansas. California calling, ten at night?*

"Robby. I need to talk with you. When you get this message and when you have a few minutes, give me a call at...,"

Robby hesitated, hand on the receiver...,

*It's not just California. It's Darin! My trouble-shooting buddy. What's the matter with me? Why don't I answer the phone?*

Forcing himself, Robby picked up. "Darin? Man, you're the last person I expected to hear from. What's up?"

"Hey, Robby. How are you doing?"

"OK. I guess. Waitin' for the ground to thaw."

"What's you situation out there?"

"My situation?" Robby laughed. "Wait a minute, man. I'm feelin' like I'm Sergio and you're tryin' to get my circuit packs. I know how your mind works."

"Have I got a deal for you."

"I'll bet. How much it gonna cost?"

"Nothing. You dating anybody?"

"Nothing serious. Tell me what's going on."

"You remember Carlo? The kid you did the magic trick on?"

"Yea. Good kid."

"You remember his mother, Leticia?"

"How can I forget? Wish I had her here to keep me warm."

"You might get your wish. Her husband was killed a couple months ago. Gunned down while walking from his car to the house, bringing home groceries."

"What? You're kidding!"

"Wish I was. They caught the guy. He was the father of another kid that goes to Carlo's school."

"Aw, man, cruel. How's Carlo takin' it?"

"Not so well. He doesn't want to go back to school. Can't say as I blame him. There was talk of sending him off somewhere for a while, but Liani and I both don't think that's such a good thing.

I talked to Martin and he can give me some time off. The Modernization Project is all done in my loop and it seems to be holding. Knock on wood. I'm thinking the four of us come out to Kansas and give you a hand on the farm for a while. Carlo likes you and you can show him that telescope you were talking about. And..., just for you, buddy. You can get to know Leticia, not to mention fine cooking from two great cooks."

"You're bringin' out good food *and* women?"

"What can I say? I'm that kind of guy."

"I learned how to make soup."

"Nothing like a good bowl of soup."

"Darin, there's not much to do in Kansas in the winter. If you don't mind being bored to death, I'd be glad to have visitors. Just to let you know, though, it looks like I'm gonna lose the farm."

"I got your e-mail. Too bad about Thomas. It's always sad to lose a friend."

"He was a good man," said Robby, looking around the room. "I wish I could have known him a little longer."

"You might lose the farm?"

"Yeah. Thomas had a reverse mortgage on it."

"Oh? How much? If you don't mind my asking."

"A hundred G's."

"Ouch. More than I've got. Maybe you can get a loan extension or something. Oh. That reminds me. Martin, remember Martin?"

"How can I forget?"

"I guess he's got something for you. Wouldn't say what. Says it's between you and him. If you call him before I leave, maybe I can bring it out, whatever it is."

"When are you planning on comin' out?"

"I'm going to run it by the girls right now. They're all here at the house. Liani and I are engaged. Since the shooting, Leticia and Carlo have been living here as well."

"Too crowded for you?"

"Are you kidding? I've never eaten so well. In fact, I gotta go. We're having Spanish rice, grilled fish with a spicy mango sauce, handmade tortillas, fresh homegrown tomatoes, guacamole, chips, and margaritas. Life is good! Too bad you're not here, sucker."

Robby laughed. "You're makin' my mouth water."

"You're sure you're OK with this?"

"Carlo doesn't happen to play checkers, does he?"

"Kicks my ass. He's the school champ!"

"I can hardly wait."

"Thanks, Robby. You're a lifesaver. See you soon, if they go for it. I'll call and let you know, one way or the other. Adios, amigo."

Robby put the receiver down and, keeping his hand on it, stood there for a long time.

*Didn't think you could pull if off, Thomas. You old*

284

*fart. Guess I'd better straighten up.*

Robby walked back from the kitchen into the living room. And as he passed by the small dining table next to the window, out of the corner of his eye, thought he saw Thomas sitting there, holding a mug of coffee, cupping it between his wrinkled hands to help keep them warm and, as their eyes met, thought he saw a thin smile spread across the old man's face.

# Dinner Time

Robby gave up his bedroom to Darin and Liani and moved into his office on the other side of the bathroom. He'd bought a futon couch at a garage sale and it seemed to fit his immediate needs. He also bought two new sets of sheets and pillowcases, a set of pots and pans and a new set of dishes.

Leticia moved into Thomas' old room off of the kitchen. Leaving the door open for coffee aromas to filter in was no longer an option. The door stayed shut until Leticia was up and about.

Carlo claimed the narrow storage room at the back of the house that shared the long wall between his and Leticia's room. Not being very wide, all of the furniture was placed in a row along the wall with the bed at the farthest corner from the door, which made it just about impossible to see if he was in there or not. Carlo liked that, his own private little tunnel.

As far as he was concerned, this was about as good as it could get, given the circumstances. Not that Robby was a bad guy, because he wasn't. Carlo just felt like Robby was an imposter, even though he was living in Robby's house.

The image would not go away, his dad face down in the front yard, lying in a pool of blood, groceries scattered everywhere. And then the sounds, sirens, police car radios blasting, crowds gathering, yellow "Do not enter" tape draped across the yard, reporters, TV crews, helicopters.

This room was good because he could spend some alone time and think things through. Not that there was much to think about. Nothing changed. Nor would it ever. The feelings, the memories, they would always be there. The question was, how to live with them.

Carlo did not want to play checkers, was not interested in the telescope, didn't want to feed the chickens or gather their eggs, did not want to slop the pigs or even ride Nellie, an old horse that Robby took in because she was going to be turned into glue, and he didn't particularly like the idea of coming to Kansas, even though it was better than staying where he was, better than going to a school where everyone knew whose dad got shot and whose dad was responsible.

And it was fine that everyone got along, playing cards and games every night, and that they all cooked together, drinking and playing music. All of that was OK. He just didn't want to be a part of that. It soon became apparent to all that Carlo wanted nothing to do with Robby.

They were out of flour. Liani and Leticia had gone to the store to get more. The girls left for town. Carlo remained in his room, reading.

"What do you make of Carlo?" Darin quietly asked, after he'd heard the car drive away.

Robby rubbed his chin, feeling the sharp bristle of his newly grown beard. "He's got a lot to think about, right now."

"Yeah. I thought he might like the place.

"I think he likes the place. I don't think he's ready for another man in his life, especially if he thinks I'm trying to hook up with his mom."

"You haven't been obvious."

"Good. Tryin' to keep it that way."

"Gotta get Carlo back in school."

"Your move."

"I know. I've been avoiding it. You're gonna get my rook, aren't you?"

287

Robby smiled. "Didn't know if you'd seen that."

"You take my rook, I'll get your black bishop. Bishop's are useless without both of them, sucker."

Robby laughed. "Riiight. Losin' your rook is like takin' the cannonball out of the cannon. You got no back-up, now."

"What are you going to do about the farm? You've done all this work. It'd be a shame to lose it."

"Gonna get it reappraised. Should be worth a lot more after all this work. Quit tryin' to change the subject. It's your move."

"I gotta think about it. Want another beer?"

"No. I'm gonna see if Carlo wants a cup of hot chocolate. That part of the house doesn't stay as warm as it does here."

Carlo was not in his room. Coming back through Leticia's room, heading for the kitchen, Robby noticed that the door from her room to the back yard was unlocked. That was not like Leticia at all. He flicked on the back yard lights and opened the door. Nothing. He headed for the kitchen.

"Carlo pass by here while I was gone?"

Darin tossed the bottle opener back into the drawer. "No. Why?"

"He's not in his room. I think he went out the back door."

"Come to think of it, I haven't seen him for a couple of hours."

"Did the girls talk to him before they left?"

"I heard Leticia tell him they'd be right back. Don't know if he answered."

Robby went to the closet and grabbed his jacket. "I'm gonna check the barn. Better give the girls a call and let them know."

Carlo was not in the barn, not up in the loft with the telescope, not in any of the storage sheds, not in the chicken coop, nowhere to be found. Robby hurried back to the house. "Did you call the girls?"

"Yeah. They're heading back now. They're going to keep an eye out along the highway."

"It's supposed to get below zero tonight. And they mentioned a storm."

"The girls said the road was already icy. He doesn't have that good of a jacket. They don't know about below zero degree weather out in California."

"Did you check his room to see if he left a note, or something?"

"Yeah. Nothing I could see."

Robby went back to Carlo's room and sat on his bed.

If I were Carlo, what would I be thinking?

Looking at his night stand, Robby saw that the novel was still there. He picked it up, opened it to the book mark and started reading...,

Toby pulled the lifeboat back to the ship and signaled for Jake to lower the food, not much, a few biscuits chock full of baked weevils and some jerky. As soon as it was secure, Jake lowered himself down the rope and took up the other oar. They pushed away from the big ship and silently headed toward the mouth of the cove, toward the beach, where they could pull the boat up onto the sand.

"What are we lookin' for?" Jake asked, at last.

"There's somethin' special happenin' over there," said Toby, studying the cliffs to find the best way up. "The way we was steered right into that sand bar, almost like it was told to go there."

"You think it's got somethin' to do with that stone? They say it's got some magic to it."

"You ever seen that stone?"

"Not yet. But I keep hearin' about it."

"I ain't seen it, neither. Empty words, far as I can

tell. But the storm blowin' us here, that's something else. This place isn't even on the map."

"What if we get caught?"

"Jake, way I see it. It don't matter if you get caught. Better if you don't. But if you do, make sure what you're doin' is the right thing. That way you won't have no guilt 'bout payin' the price. Know what I mean?"

"Like when you...,"

"He had it comin'. The law wasn't gonna do much. So I had to do it myself."

Robby closed the book. Glancing back at the night stand, he noticed another wider, flatter book, a road map of the United States. Scanning through it, he noticed that Kansas, Colorado, New Mexico, and Arizona were gone. Robby went into Leticia's room and yelled toward the kitchen. "Darin! You'd better look at this."

Darin called the sheriff and Highway Patrol. The girls came home and there was chaos everywhere. In the middle of all that, Robby grabbed his heavy jacket, flashlight, spare batteries, stuffed a down vest into his backpack along with some food and water and headed out the back door.

The ground was icy but, Robby was thinking, there should be enough snow around to get a feel for the direction he'd gone. He had to leave some kind of tracks.

## Ned

*Walkin' down this road tonight? Way out here? In this cold? Nobody comes out here, almost never. What kind of fool is this?*

*All alone. Nobody in their right mind would be out, not tonight, except me. Yet, there he is. Got his self a new jacket, too. And look at them boots. Wonder where he's goin' all alone. Can't be up to any good, just like me.*

Crouching behind the brush, Ned waited until Carlo had passed by, his steps crunching at a fast pace down the road.

*Can't be more'n ten or twelve. All by his self. Better hurry up little boy 'fore somethin' comes along and gits ya. Shoulda stayed home with mommy and daddy...,*

Matching Carlo's cadence, Ned stepped out onto the road behind him and started closing the distance to his target. When Carlo finally did hear extra footsteps, he whirled around. But, it was too late. Ned let Carlo see the long blade of his knife.

"Don't be thinkin' 'bout runnin', pretty boy. Cause I can run faster'n you."

"I don't have any money."

"I'm thinkin' you do. Hand it over. Cause if I find out you're lyin' later, well, that just won't be a pretty sight. Gimme your money..., now."

Carlo reached into his back pocket, retrieved his wallet and started to open it. Ned grabbed the whole thing.

"Fifty dollars? That's all you got? Don't lie to me, boy."

"That's it. Everything. Can I go?"

Ned laughed, more like an evil kind of snarl. "You think fifty dollars is gonna do it? Hand over that jacket."

"But,....,"

Ned waved the knife menacingly. "Now! Unless you want it to be full of holes with you still in it!"

Carlo started to take his belonging out of the pockets, compass, pocketknife, flashlight...,

"Gimme all of it! I'll take your boots, too."

Quietly, and now shivering in cold, Carlo removed his boots.

"Your pockets, turn 'em inside out."

Ned took everything, then removed his stained, smelly and torn Navy P-coat. He handed it to Carlo. "Put it on."

"My boots?"

"Boots? You don't got no boots. You gave 'em to me, remember? Here, take these. They got holes in the bottoms and they're wet clear through but the ice won't cut your feet. Put 'em on. We gotta get."

"You got everything. Let me go."

Ned smiled. "No. Not everything. Put 'em on! We gotta get off this road."

## Small Change

Robby knelt down, removed his glove and picked up the change, a nickel and two pennies. They looked like they'd recently been dropped. There was no snow or ice on them and they weren't all scratched up like they'd been run over by a car.

He carefully put them back down, retrieved a can of spray paint, fluorescent pink, and sprayed a circle around the coins. Next he sprayed an arrow in the direction he was going, further up the road.

Carlo had been heading west, as Robby had suspected. He had picked his route carefully, making sure to stay away from traffic and it looked like this back road was going to meet the highway on the western side of town, a smart move because anyone heading out in that direction would probably be going all the way to the next town, twenty miles.

After going another fifty feet, flashlight scanning the icy surface and skimming over the snow and weeds all the way to the barbed wire fence on the right and into the brush on the opposite side, Robby decided that the tracks did not continue on.

A few cars had traveled by since the last snow, three days ago. And a lot of it had melted, leaving mud and the tracks of some horses, maybe a couple of cows, dogs, all pressed into the soft earth before it froze up again.

Robby reached for the spray can and drew a U-turn on the road with the arrow pointing back toward the coins.

*Don't feel right. Walking down the road, drops some change and disappears.*

Shining his light back the way he'd come, Robby retraced his steps, now realizing how stupid he had been following directly behind the steps he was tracking rather than staying off to one side. He'd messed up the clues with his own big feet.

Reaching the spot where he'd found the money, he discovered another set of footprints in a patch of snow, a shoe with a missing heel, certainly no tread like Carlo's hiking boots. Following the footprints backwards, Robby discovered where they came up from the side of the road from behind the trees.

*Carlo's been abducted?*

He tried calling both his house and Darin's number but reception was non-existent. He painted another arrow pointing to the footsteps, turned off his flashlight and followed their tracks back into the trees.

## Rat Shack

The structure was a little less than a storage shed. It looked like it had been washed away from someone's land in a flood and had been deposited at this spot. The creek was fifty feet away on the other side of a dam of fallen trees, broken branches and scattered debris left from the flood.

The shed was leaning to one side but being held up with an old branch that was jammed into the mud and shoved up against the wall. What used to be a window was boarded up and, as far as Robby could tell, there was no light coming from inside. But there was a sound, a muffled sound of a man's voice, soft against the harsh, cracking sounds of a freezing night.

Robby was torn between moving in quietly, or just rushing the shed, throwing the door open and taking his chances. Time was not on Carlo's side. He hadn't brought any weapons. Abduction was not on his mind when he had left, only that Carlo got back into the warmth of the house before he froze to death. This was not a good night to run away.

Robby retrieved a small pocketknife that he always carried, opened it, and quietly started toward the structure, stepping over an old tire that was jammed into the frozen mud. Silence was not possible. Every step crunched down onto something, weeds cracking, twigs snapping, frozen mud breaking apart as it was smashed into the ice.

Robby reached the side of the shack and was attempting to hear what was happening when the door swung open. A man came out wearing Carlo's jacket and boots. This man was bigger, broader through the middle with long straggly black, matted hair and beard. He headed down toward the creek.

When he was out of sight, and when Robby heard him taking a leak, he hurried inside. Carlo was stripped naked, his wrists tied to the frame of the cot. His mouth was gagged.

"Holy Jesus! Carlo. Shh. Stay quiet!"

Robby cut the first strap away from the frame and was leaning over the bed to do the other when he heard footsteps at the door. As he turned to face the man, he saw the knife coming, a long blade, maybe ten or twelve inches, sharpened by a man who had nothing better to do than rub the blade against the stone.

Robby deflected the thrust away from his chest but felt the blade slice into his upper arm. Spinning sideways, he tried to get hold of Ned's wrist but accidentally grabbed the blade. When Ned pulled the knife back, Robby's hand began gushing blood.

And then the knife was coming down in a slashing motion, sweeping across his jacket, slicing diagonally, cutting through the down. Feathers exploded into the air. Another thrust, a jab straight at Robby's face. He ducked right, reached up with his left hand and grabbed Ned's wrist.

Fighting to get his balance, he pushed Ned back toward the door, both of them struggling for control of the knife. Robby hit him hard with his bloody fist. Falling, breaking free, Ned went down in sole possession of the knife.

Robby tried to kick it out of his hand but Ned brought the blade across horizontally, slicing into Robby's shin. Back on his feet, he attacked with the blade slashing between them.

Robby fell backward, lost his balance when he hit the bed and landed on top of Carlo. Ned plunged the knife down. Robby stopped the thrust but the blade was slicing his good hand, pouring blood down into his face.

During the struggle, Carlo had managed to get hold of Robby's pocketknife and free his other hand. As Ned leaned down for the kill, slowly inching the blade toward Robby's face, Carlo reached up and slashed the blade across Ned's throat, making sure to get the big artery.

Ned looked surprised, mystified at how something came out of the dark and cut him. As the blood drained away from his head, gushing out of the hole and spilling down into the jacket, he looked baffled at how his hands did not obey his commands.

His grip loosened on the handle of the knife and his hands failed to stop his fall to the floor. Kicking wildly, arms flailing, blood gurgling and splattering with every gasp for air, Ned died a quick, convulsing, death.

Robby rolled over onto the floor, surprised at how warm the room had just become, like it was suddenly summer. Carlo was saying something, his lips were moving but the words had no meaning. He laughed.

"English, Carlo. I can't..., understand."

Carlo was speaking English. "Robby! Don't move! Don't even try to move! Gotta stop the blood! Jesus! Holy Jesus! Please, somebody! HELP!"

"Carlo," Robby whispered. "Go. This...," he smiled at his own little joke, "is not a happy place."

Feathers were still in the air, gently floating down, sticking to the blood on the walls, the orange crate being used as a table, the filthy, stinking blankets, the mud on the floor.

Moonlight spilled in through the doorway, a silver shaft against the black walls, displaying Ned's blood-drained and hollow face. Seeing this, seeing that Ned was done, Robby relaxed and closed his eyes.

*Tanya was on top, bare breasted and smiling. He was inside her and the night was theirs. From some distant place a dog howled and there was an argument coming from the apartment upstairs.*

*None of that mattered. Tonight there was only the two of them, together, making love for what seemed an eternity, touching, kissing, living.*

*Thomas was standing in the doorway, weed hanging out of his mouth, moonlight behind him, glowing off of his shoulders.*

*"Thomas? What are you doin' here?"*

*He shook his head, his mouth set hard as he glanced around the room. "Robby, you should never grab the blade."*

*Robby laughed, blood oozing harder as his muscles convulsed. "That wasn't the plan, old man."*

*"Put your arms up, Robby. Get 'em up above your heart. That'll slow the bleeding. I didn't know a drug addict could be so dumb sometimes. Get 'em up!"*

*"Pretty dumb, me grabbing the blade."*

*They were back at the house, sitting at the table playing checkers while Thomas nursed his coffee. There was some kind of commotion coming from the kitchen and, as Robby stood to investigate, out came Darin and Liani with a plate full of fish tacos, grilled just the way you like them, and Floyd groaning at the thought of not being able to over-indulge and Martin calling the meeting to order.*

*Everyone was there, the whole crew, sitting around the big table, holding a meeting, discussing unimportant things, eating fish tacos, with the smell of freshly brewed coffee in the air...,*

## Springtime

"*Hey, Thomas. It's about time to plow up the south field, don't you think?*"

*Thomas set his coffee down, shaking his head. "Nope. More weather comin'. Give it a month."*

"*Old man Smith is already turning his fields up.*"

"*Yea? Well, he's an idiot. Ran over his own car with the tractor.*"

"*Speaking of that, I just gave yours a tune-up.*"

"*Why? We're gonna lose the farm, Robby. Where you gonna keep that tractor?*" *Thomas took another gulp of coffee. "Where are we gonna go?*"

*Robby, sitting across the table from Thomas, turned his gaze from the old man to the unplanted field on the other side of the window, weeds bending with the breeze. Another storm was moving in.*

"*Can't be that bad, old man. We'll find a way. There's gotta be a way.*"

*Out in the dirt, on his hands and knees scooping it up, seeing that the soil was depleted, Robby was wondering how to replenish the nutrients. Shoulda burned all them weeds last fall, scattered the ash. Doesn't do us much good lying around in a big pile.*

*And then he was in the dirt, right there with the ants and worms and gophers and dead leaves and cow manure and bird droppings, right there with all of them, helping to distribute the nutrients, a little here, a little there.*

*Gotta get it right. Gotta make sure crops are gonna grow. What crops? How are we gonna pay for seed? Can't grow nothin' but weeds without seed.*

*When the dirt was right, big, black rolling clouds rolled in from the west, visible for fifty miles over the flat terrain casting a dark, slanted shaft of gray beneath them, soaking the land.*

*Everything waking up, reaching for the light...,*

Robby's eyes blinked open, only for a second, wincing against the light coming in from the window next to his bed. He closed them just as fast, eyes hurting from the brightness. Better to be inside where things are under control.

*What was that about spring? It was raining, everything getting soaked. I'm feeling rain but not hearing it, thinking I'm standing but feeling like I'm lying down....,*

"Robby? You awake?"

*Who is that? I know that voice.*

"Robby. I saw you blink. Wake up."

*Sound's coming from behind...,*

Robby turned his head, finding the whole process exceedingly difficult, and tentatively opened his eyes.

"Robby, keep them open. Stay with me."

Darin, who had been sitting in a chair next to the bed, now stood and tossed the magazine back into the chair.

"Robby. Man, am I glad to see you! It's me, Darin."

Robby studied Darin for a long time, memories slowly coming back as he quietly took in the room.

"Where..., where am I?"

"In the hospital. Take it easy. Relax. Man! It's good to see you with your eyes open."

"Hospital? Wha..., what happened?"

"Of course, you wouldn't remember. Robby? You won't believe what I'm about to say...,"

## Carlo

Hearing the sound of someone sitting in the room, Robby opened his eyes. Carlo got up and joined him at his bed.

"Hey, Robby. How are you doing?"

"Still breathing. So, I guess it's a good day."

Robby hadn't been able to assess completely the wounds that he had. Both hands were heavily bandaged. That much he knew, as was his right arm and torso. And his shin screamed pain beyond belief just thinking about it. Everything else was still a mystery.

"Good to see you, Carlo. How are you doin'?"

"OK."

"I heard we had quite an adventure."

"You saved my life."

"From what I heard, you saved mine. So, I guess we're even."

"I shouldn't have been out there. I..., I wasn't thinking."

Robby laughed, wincing with the pain of it. "Well, welcome to the rest of the human race."

"How are you feeling?"

"Ask me tomorrow."

"It's in all the news."

"Well, they gotta talk about something. This is Kansas, you know?"

"That was a good idea with the paint."

Robby grinned. "I'm not as stupid as I look. I was just trying to make sure I could find my own way back."

"I..., wanted to say thanks."

"You don't have to."

"You can't do any work. I want to stay and help."

"Carlo. Thanks for offering. But you need to be in school. And then you need to go to college. You don't want to wind up like me."

"You're a hero. Wait'll you read the papers."

"I'm a broke hero. Carlo, there's no sense doin' anything on the farm. I'm gonna lose it. I'll sell off the livestock soon as I can walk, get what money I can and walk away. That's life."

"Word got out. People been sending money."

"We'll, that's nice. But it won't be enough."

"Darin says he's got something for you. From Martin? You know someone named Martin?"

Wincing again, Robby laughed. "Ow! Yeah, I know Martin. What's he done this time?"

"Sent a package, special delivery. We had to sign for it. Darin's on his way, bringing it over."

"Carlo. There's somethin' I gotta say. It didn't seem right before, but maybe now's the time. You've been through more than anyone should have to go through for their whole life. And yet here you are, still standing, doing the best you can. I gotta admire that.

What I want to say is, I can't be your dad, not one grain of sand in a thousand miles of beach. Not one. Cause he can't be replaced. Besides, I never had a dad or been a dad, so, I'm pretty clueless. But I imagine that it could be pretty special.

What I can be is your friend, your best friend if you'll allow it. I can be there for you, help you with your homework. Well, a little bit. I'm not good at math. But I've got a friend, Ollie, who is. I can fix your bike, tune up engines, build windmills, and fix just about anything." He paused, thinking of Tanya. "Don't know about a broken heart. I've got one, too. Haven't figured out how to fix that yet."

"Who?"

"She used to be my best friend. Now she's marrying somebody else."

"You still love her?"

"She's on my mind a lot." He laughed, wincing again. "Well, she was. I got a new set a problems, now."

"Why did you break up?"

"Bad habit. Still grabs me sometimes. That's why it's good for you guys to be around. You keep me busy. And if I'm busy, I'm happy. So, in a way, we're all good medicine for each other. There's a lot of healin' goin' on in that house."

Carlo smiled, a smile far too serious for a twelve year old. "I heard you play checkers."

Darin entered the room. "Hey, Robby! About time you started showing a few signs of life. When are you coming off vacation? We got work to do!"

Robby smiled. "Gonna be a while. Right now, I can't even scratch my ass."

"Which is why I brought this over. Figured you wouldn't be coming back to the farm for another few days. It's from Martin. Special Delivery. Should I open it?"

Robby studied the thick bandages on his hands. "Yeah. It's not like I can do anything about it."

Darin ripped open the manila envelope and started reading. "It's a 401K. You've got eighteen thousand dollars here."

"I never signed up for one."

"You must've. They don't just hand this stuff out."

"Martin must've forged my signature. That's why my checks never got any bigger. He said it was because I was missing so much work."

"Sounds like he was looking out for you, illegal as that was. Oh. The bank called. Seems like

303

they're taking a lot of heat for foreclosing on a hero. When you're up to it, they want you to come in and talk."

Robby sighed. "How bad was I cut up? Don't know that I'll ever be able to handle the farm again."

"They've reattached the ligaments in your right hand. Your right shoulder had a pretty bad cut, but the muscles are stitched together. You had a couple of stabs into your ribs but no organs were damaged. And you've got a nasty cut into the bone on your shin. Hurts just to look at it."

"You ought to feel it from this side."

"My heart goes out to you, buddy. That's why I've taken a leave of absence from work. I've got six months. Liani, Leticia, and Carlo here are all staying on for a while. We figure we can keep things going until you're up and about.

"I appreciate it."

"So...," Darin pulled a note pad from his pocket. "I need to make a list of all the things that need to be done."

"A list?"

"You know, how much to feed the chickens. How do you milk a cow?"

Robby started laughing and then groaning, it hurt so much. Tears ran down his cheeks.

"You want me to tell you how to milk a cow, on paper? My God, Darin. Don't make me laugh. It hurts!"

"Where's my pen? Damn. I think I left it out in the car. I'll be right back."

And after Darin had left the room, Carlo cleared his throat. "You never answered my question."

"What question was that?"

"You any good at checkers?"

Robby smiled. "You're looking at the champion

of the Universe."

And this time Carlo's smile did light up the room. "We'll see about that."

# # #

Dave's work revels with the fanciful, ponders the inscrutable and enigmatic, and examines the human character.

To hear audio readings of these works by the author or to learn about the history behind the stories, please visit his web site at:

www.ddriessen.com

I appreciate your comments. I always strive to make each story the best that it can be and I love that you take the time to read them.

This is my passion.

Thank you,

dave

About the Author

Dave Riessen earned his Associate's Degree in Electronics at San Diego City College and then attended San Diego State University where he changed his major to English and focused on creative writing. He has written two other novels:

You Gotta Have Wings - young adult fiction, Nebraska, 1954

Sometime Tomorrow - science fiction, Los Angeles, 2132

Please check out the free downloads from The Bad Fortune Teller series:

Ernie's Great Adventure
Bill's Bricks
Melvin and the Mud Daubers